TALE OF THE PENITENT THIEF

Don Willis

WestBow
PRESS
A DIVISION OF THOMAS NELSON

WestBow Press books may be ordered through booksellers or by contacting:

WestBow Press
A Division of Thomas Nelson
1663 Liberty Drive
Bloomington, IN 47403
www.westbowpress.com
1-(866) 928-1240

ISBN: 978-1-4497-9195-7 (sc)
ISBN: 978-1-4497-9194-0 (hc)
ISBN: 978-1-4497-9196-4 (e)

Library of Congress Control Number: 2013907099

Printed in the United States of America.

WestBow Press rev. date: 04/25/2013

DEDICATION

To my loving wife and muse Julia: Some people come into our lives and they have a tendency to bring out all the best qualities in the people around them. I happen to be married to such a person. Thank you for everything you did to help me bring this story to life.

I also want to give thanks to God for revealing to me this wonderful story that I am now sharing. I have no doubt that his hand was in every bit of what you are about to read. It was a wonderful God-filled journey we have been on to bring this story to you and I hope you all enjoy reading it as much as I did writing it.

CHAPTER 1

Serah awoke to see the sun shining from behind the head of her oldest child, Dismas, as he wiped the sweat from her brow. The little specks of dust circling in the rays of sun around his head made him look like an angel, and for one brief moment, she imagined that this is what heaven must be like. Then the pain in her head began to set in again and quickly reminded her that this was not heaven. In fact, this was probably the furthest thing from it.

She found herself lying in a pile of straw in a stable, and the smell of stale urine from the nearby animals stung her nostrils. Dismas was still wiping the sweat from her brow as she tried to sit up. What a wonderful boy she had. Without him, she was certain that she and his two younger brothers probably would have died already.

Dismas was only eleven, but his face was beginning to show the signs of distress of someone much older. He was always more wise and clever than most children his age—actually, more wise and clever than many of the adults she had known—but now he was beginning to look it as well.

The boy should have had an opportunity to play every day like other children, but instead Dismas spent his days caring for his sick mother and his two younger brothers. Normally, this would have been his father's responsibility, but Dismas' father could barely care for himself, let alone three sons and a sick wife.

Dismas' father, Benjamin, was content to spend most days drinking and spending whatever money he could find in ill-advised business ventures whose only purpose was to finance the next day's drinking. The family hardly ever saw him anymore, and when they did, he turned his eye from them in his shame and acted as if he did not even know them. To them, he was already dead.

Serah was not pleased with the terrible situation she was now in. It would have been bad enough without her boys paying the price, but now their fate weighed heavily on her as well.

Benjamin had not always been this way. She remembered a time when they were deeply in love and he was a wonderful father and a devoted husband. He was not particularly bright, but he was certainly not a simpleton. He had worked hard and provided well for them for many years. He changed when the Romans came to the village during the previous harvest season. That day had left an indelible mark on the lives of many in Bethlehem.

On that dreadful day last harvest season, Benjamin was in the fields tending to his small flock of sheep when he heard the first commotion. He dozed off for a short nap after chasing several sheep out of the hills that morning. The day was beautiful, and he had a magnificent view from his vantage point on the hill.

The first scream barely aroused him from his slumber because he knew the bleating of sheep can play tricks on your mind. The second scream followed by the shouts of men and women alike woke him completely. He immediately sprang to his feet and surveyed the scene playing out on the hillside below him. He could see soldiers on horseback riding through town waving their swords at frightened women and children. He knew he had to get to Serah and his two sons quickly and take them into the hills where the Romans could not find them.

He ran as fast as he could to the town below. He only wished he had not napped so far up the hill. It seemed like it took an eternity to reach the walls of Bethlehem.

He reached the first building and was about to make a run for the courtyard behind his home when he saw two Roman centurions with swords drawn. They were throwing food into baskets to take with them. A frightened family sat cowering on the ground before them as the soldiers hovered menacingly over them. Benjamin had heard tales that the Roman army would occasionally travel into Jewish townships to gather supplies, and he could only assume that this is what they were doing.

Benjamin knew that the Romans' disdain for Jews often meant they would kill or injure citizens and sometimes even violate their women if it pleased them, all without provocation or fear of punishment. Benjamin didn't care if the Romans took food or livestock; he feared only for his family. He had a beautiful wife and two small boys, Dismas and Jotham, who were his world. He could not bear to know that any of them were in danger.

When the two soldiers made their way inside the next home, Benjamin ran as quickly as his sandaled feet would carry him to the opposite side of the courtyard behind his home. He heard his boys crying on the other side of the wall and fear overwhelmed him. Regardless of the consequences, he would not allow them to be harmed.

Benjamin picked up the first weapon he could find, a large rock on the ground. He made his way around the home quickly and cautiously, and he was promptly grabbed from behind by a centurion who has seen Benjamin grab the rock. He struggled to get free, but the man was too strong.

Just then, Benjamin saw a large smiling centurion with a fat belly stride out of his home fastening his belt. He looked to the man holding Benjamin and said, "She was a fierce one, but I've knocked some of the fight out of her."

Benjamin went white with fear, for he was sure he knew what the burly centurion had done. He struggled even harder to free himself but could not break loose from the other centurion's iron grip. The burly centurion stepped up to him, looked him in the eye, and then said, "Was this one yours? Is that why you look like you want to kill me?"

Benjamin spit in his face in anger, for he had no other weapon. Suddenly, he saw a large fist and then no more.

He awoke to the sound of Dismas and Jotham crying, "Father, Father! Wake up, Father!" As he opened his eyes he saw them and knew immediately they were okay. Not so for his beloved Serah. Her once beautiful face was now dark with bruises. Her right eye was swollen shut, and her lip cut and bleeding. Still she cared more for him and his health than for her own.

Suddenly, he recalled what had led to his unconscious state and asked Serah if she had been violated. It wasn't a delicate question; it was blunt and brutal, like the act itself. He didn't care that the boys were listening. Nothing in the world mattered to him at this moment.

She did not answer. He looked her in the eye and held her face in his hands. "Did they violate you?"

Tears streamed from his swollen eyes. She tried to pull away from him, but she could not. She looked away from him. She couldn't bear to see the look in his eyes when she answered his question.

She closed her eyes and the tears flowed. It gave him the answer that he already knew. Benjamin moaned and then wailed as if the angel of death were upon him. He tore at the cloak on his shoulder. He then screamed in rage, cursing all of Rome, and ran into the night. That was the last time his family had seen him sober.

The worst came a couple months later when Serah told her beloved Benjamin that she was with child. She knew that even though the child could have been his, he had it in his mind that it could be the bastard child of the smiling centurion. This thought would never again leave his mind as he drank himself into a stupor night after night after night.

Eventually, he stopped even coming home. The boys who were once his joy would cry themselves to sleep every night wondering why their father did not love them anymore. Jotham had always been the tender one of the two boys. He would soon be five years old, and Dismas was nearly eleven.

Jotham would frequently cry over his father's absence, and it seemed that every time, her beloved Dismas became more the man of the house. He was always such a good and kind boy. He was so clever and funny. He always knew what to say to make Serah smile and how to take Jotham's mind off his worries.

Soon money became a problem because Benjamin no longer cared enough to even give them money to live on. Dismas took up the slack left by his father by trying to work wherever he could. He would muck the stables for small change, and occasionally it would be enough to feed them all. Serah had become very ill as she approached the later stages of the pregnancy, and Dismas felt that she may not survive it. This pained him more than anything.

When his father left, Dismas still had his mother, who loved him dearly and for whom he would have done anything. He knew he still had Jotham, and Jotham would need him too, but his mother's loss would be unbearable.

He often remembered the good times before the soldiers came, when his mother and father would take him to synagogue. As a woman and child, Dismas and his mother were not allowed in the same room with the men, so they would sit in the next room with only a low reed wall between them. He could hear the rabbi's teachings from the Torah and the men's prayer.

As he started to understand more and more of the teachings, he began to have more and more questions every time the family left the synagogue. Dismas' father was good at explaining the rabbi's teachings, but his mother had a special way of illustrating the real message by using stories, examples, and short parables. His fondest memories were of the dinners after the family had gone to the synagogue and hearing his mother's stories about the teachings. Even his father delighted at this because he knew she was a far better teacher than he.

Soon they began to hear word in the town that Augustus had declared that there would be a census of the people in Herod's kingdom and that, according to the Jewish custom people would be required to return to their ancestral home to be counted. That meant that many people from the House of David would be returning to Bethlehem to be counted. Serah told Dismas that they should prepare for this because there would be an opportunity to make some much needed money by allowing boarders to stay in their home during the census. She knew there would be other work that she and Dismas could do for money as well with so many visitors coming. She also knew Dismas was resourceful and that he would find work easily. For her, the goal would be to cook and clean for her guests. She feared she would even struggle with that since she was soon to have her child and she was constantly ill.

Soon after the word had spread round town, Benjamin came home, not to return as the family had dreamed, but to add more insult on to the pile of injuries he had already caused his family.

He announced to them that they had to leave because he had sold their home. A friend of his convinced him that he should sell it so they could start a business together. The home was already sold and they needed to leave now. Serah started to protest with him and he would not even look her in the eye. He simply said "It is done" and then he walked away. She fell in the floor sobbing as Dismas and Jotham gathered by her side to comfort her.

And so it was, Serah and her two sons were cast out of the only real home they had ever known. Serah was under more stress than she could bear and she started feeling pain soon after. She knew this was not a normal pain. She became aware that the child would soon be born and she needed to find a place to lie down and give birth. Dismas ran to the neighbor Edith's home and begged her for help. The old woman called for her only son Jediah to assist Dismas to bring her into their home. Jediah was a large young man with a kind heart and he was a simple shepherd by trade. He was home this day caring for his mother, who had been sick herself. He lifted Serah with ease and brought her to his home to lie down on his mother's bed.

That night, with the help of Edith, Serah gave birth to a baby boy. She named him Aram, after her brother. Her own brother Aram had become very ill at a young age and died, but his short life burned very brightly and many loved him. She felt it was a fitting tribute to a boy that she loved so much as a girl. Aram's birth was very difficult for Serah and she became very ill from loss of blood. Jediah and Edith were able to take care of them for a few days, but Edith was gravely ill herself and Jediah felt that there was no choice but to send Serah and the boys away.

Dismas went to the stable owner that hired him often for mucking the stables and asked if they could stay in the stable for a few days until he could find them a home. He reluctantly agreed, and Dismas brought his mother and brothers to the stable that they would soon call home.

Dismas doubled his efforts to find work and save money to feed his mother and brothers. He knew that living in a stable would not be good for her health or for the baby's. He was certain that, while he and Jotham would not enjoy it at all, that they would be fine if they could stay warm and fed. Dismas had soon convinced the stable owner to allow him to build a small space onto the back of the stable where he could stay with his mother and brothers. The only problem was that he had to find his own materials and build it himself. Dismas had always been very persuasive and it was not long before he convinced, shamed actually, his old neighbor Jediah to help him find the materials and build a crude room for them. Serah was proud of what Dismas accomplished for them. It was crude and small, but it was a roof and a bed.

Little did she know this was the last home she would ever live in.

CHAPTER 2

A few miles away a small caravan made its way south on the road from Nazareth and into Bethlehem. In this caravan was a carpenter from Nazareth named Joseph, and his wife, Mary. She was a beautiful young girl, and she struggled greatly because she was very close to bearing a child. This journey would be very treacherous even for a healthy young woman, but this particular journey almost unbearable for her.

Weeks earlier, this carpenter from Nazareth was attending synagogue when he was informed that Augustus Caesar, The Emperor of Rome, decreed that a census must be taken in all of King Herod's lands. He was sure of one thing, and that was that Herod was probably was not very happy about it. It did not appear that Rome trusted Herod; otherwise this census would never have been ordered. He was sure it meant that Rome felt that they were not receiving the proper taxes and tribute due to them, and that they decided to take matters into their own hands by ordering a census to be taken. It was very typical of Romans to always want more power and control, so this was not unexpected of them. Inside, Joseph also knew the Romans were a cruel lot, and if

Herod Archelaus did not comply, he would surely be replaced . . . quite possibly by someone even more cruel and depraved than he was. The thought made Joseph shudder.

The Rabbi assured them that at least they had one small victory, and that was that Herod convinced the Emperor to allow the census to be undertaken in accordance to Jewish custom. This meant that the citizens would be required to travel to their ancestral homes to be counted. He was sure that it was not the most convenient method for Herod to conduct a census; especially with people all over the kingdom traveling back and forth. Not to mention all the disruption of trade it would cause. But at least it was a victory for God, because it allowed them to go forth in accordance to custom.

Since Joseph belonged to the House of David, he would be required to take Mary and travel to his ancestral home in Bethlehem for the coming census. He only wished that the timing had been much better. He did not think that the journey would be an easy one for Mary. Mary was so close to giving birth that he feared she may even have the child on the road to Bethlehem.

Joseph was very conflicted from the moment Mary told him she was with child. It was natural for him to doubt her when she told him that she had never been with a man yet she was with child. She insisted she was still a virgin. She told him the story of the visit from the angel and his message to her. She told him the story of her visit to see her cousin Elizabeth and what the angel told her as well. It was a lot for him to believe and trust. He truly loved Mary with all of his heart, and deep down he knew she would never lie to him. She was far too pious to do so in such a cruel way. It wasn't until Joseph laid his own troubled head down one night and the same angel visited him that he accepted this fate. It was then that he knew he must take care of Mary and the baby and raise it as his own child.

The timing for the census was terrible from the perspective of caring for her health, but he also knew that the timing for their absence would eliminate many more of the questions that were sure to rise from their friends and family. In his heart he felt fear for her but in his soul he knew that no harm would befall her on this journey. He was sure that this child was destined to be born in the House of David. How could the Messiah not be born in such a holy place to their people?

Mary was becoming more ill and he could tell the time was close at hand. He was grateful that they would reach Bethlehem in only a few hours. Ordinarily they might have stopped for the night and tried to push on to Bethlehem in the morning, but they were so close he could see the light of fires in the town and they pushed on. He was far too fearful of Mary having the child on the side of this road to stay longer.

The closer they came to the city, the more noise he could hear. There were campfires all around the outskirts of the town and even up on the hillsides. He never imagined that so many people from the House of David existed and traveled here for the census, but he also began to realize that many of them may have only been here to pass through on the way to their own ancestral homes. As they arrived inside the walls of the small town, Joseph and Mary made their way to the closest inn they could find.

When he inquired about a room the innkeeper laughed in his face and said "Look around you my friend. Does it look like anyone in this town has room available? I am blessed to have such good business right now."

Joseph furrowed his brow for he knew this was probably true and asked "Can you tell me then sir where I might be able to take my wife. She is about to have a child and I need a safe place for her. I don't ask for much."

"I am truly sorry, but I have people practically sleeping on top of each other now. There would be no room for your wife, and certainly not if she is having a child. I suggest you do what everyone else is doing and find a place on the hill and build a fire. There is no room here, nor at any other inn in the town I am afraid."

"Isn't there any other option? Do you know of any homes that might take us in for the night?"

"How in the world would I know that? Short of banging on doors in the middle of the night to ask, I have no idea who would take you in. I can say only one thing for sure that if you go banging on doors in the middle of night you will likely need attention yourself for the beating you will get. People that live here are very nervous about all these strangers" he said. "Now run along. I have my own business to attend to."

"I am sorry to have troubled you kind sir." The door was shut on him before he could even finish the sentence.

Joseph turned to go back to Mary and standing in front of him was a handsome boy of perhaps eleven or twelve years. He had curly brown hair, brown eyes and a very dirty face. "Well, hello there young man. I suppose you heard the kind gentleman educating me about the current housing situation in this town?" Joseph stooped down to one knee in front of the boy and said "I don't suppose you know where I could find a room for my wife and I do you?"

Joseph straightened himself up and wiped his hand on his cloak and then extended it toward the boy. "Goodness, where are my manners? I should introduce myself. My name is Joseph. What is your name young fellow? Are you from here or are you visiting like me?"

The boy smiled showing his dimples . . . it was quite an infectious smile too from Joseph's observation. "My name is Dismas sir. I live here in Bethlehem. I heard Cephus talking to you. You will have to forgive him. He is not normally so mean. He is normally very kind. He pays me sometimes to do chores for him because his wife gives him too many to do himself. He is just under a lot of stress. He gets nervous very easily around strangers."

"Well, my dear young Dismas. I don't suppose you can point me to the best place for my wife to have her child could you? The hour is late and her time will be very soon."

Dismas thought for a moment. "Sir, I don't think there is any place like what you are looking for, but I live in a small room with my mother and two brothers on the back of the stable on the south end of town at the bottom of the hill. There is not enough space for you with us but this particular stable is quite a good shelter and it is very clean. I clean it myself. I can move some of the animals and bring you some fresh straw to bed down on."

Joseph smiled and closed his eyes for a moment "Merciful Father in Heaven, thank you for sending this young man into my path." He looked back at the boy and with a sense of urgency said to him "Come Dismas, can you help me get my Mary to this stable quickly?"

Dismas smiled and nodded and then plodded quickly behind Joseph through the night to the place he left Mary to rest.

Mary tried her best to smile when she saw Joseph again, but he knew from the look on her face that the pain was growing. She tried so hard to be brave for him but inside he knew it was never necessary. He would always love her and protect her. He admired her for trying though.

He introduced Mary to the young boy Dismas. Dismas stood frozen. He could not explain it, but this girl was the most beautiful he had ever seen and he did not even have words to describe it. Until now his own mother was the most beautiful woman he had ever known, but there was something strange drawing him to this girl. It was if he was a moth and he was drawn to her as if she were a flame. He had an overwhelming feeling that he needed to find a way to protect her at all costs. Her smile seemed to melt away all his cares and fears.

"Dismas, don't just stand there like a tree, help me lift Mary up onto the donkey." Dismas instantly snapped out of his frozen stance and helped Joseph to lift her.

Joseph gestured forward with his arm. "Lead the way young man. We will follow." And then Dismas led them through the maze of streets to his home on the edge of town.

As they approached the stable, he ran ahead of them and led two very thin cows outside of the stable and tied them to the post out front, He then raced in and tied the two lambs he was watching up in a corner out of the way. He grabbed his rake and hurriedly mucked the stable then raced outside. Mary was already off the donkey and Joseph was helping her to sit on the ground. "What can I do to help you Dismas?"

Out of breath, Dismas replied, "I've made room and mucked the best I can for now, but if you want fresh bedding I could use some help to spread some fresh straw for you."

Joseph grabbed the other rake and began to thresh straw around with Dismas in a comfortable corner by the wall. It actually was quite warm and cozy, just as the boy described it. You could sense that he had great pride in his responsibilities there. They would be comfortable here and he knew it. It was not a fancy room at an inn, but it would do. He did not know what he would have done if this boy not been placed in their path and he was incredibly grateful to God that he provided this place.

Joseph grabbed all the blankets off of their donkey and laid them in the corner on top of the newly strewn straw. He then carried Mary to her new bed and he laid her there.

Dismas went to awake his mother and tell them of what he had done. She was still so very weak from her illness but she gave birth to three boys and knew that this young girl in the stable next door would likely need her help. She lay Aram next to his brother Jotham, who barely stirred, and then hurried with Dismas to the corner of the stable where Mary was about to give birth.

"Joseph, Mary," he called, "this is my mother Serah. She is very sick but she says you may need her to help you with the baby."

Mary looked at Serah and said "Why are you ill Serah?" Serah knew it was the first question a mother giving birth should be asking of her ill caretaker and she would have asked it herself. It was not a delicate question but she was certainly not offended by it.

Serah smiled comfortingly at Mary and said "Nothing to fear my child. I gave birth myself to a child a few months ago and the pregnancy and childbirth were very difficult for me. I fear I have not been able to fully recover from it. My husband is gone from us now and my son Dismas, whom you've already met I see, has done a remarkable job caring for me and his two younger brothers. He is my blessing from God."

"Tonight, he is our blessing as well." Mary said as she laid her head back to rest.

Without delay, Serah begins to bark orders to Joseph and Dismas to help her prepare for the imminent birth of this child.

Soon, and throughout all of time, this simple stable would never be the same.

CHAPTER 3

Months earlier and far away to the East of Bethlehem sat a beautiful temple on steep hilltop overlooking the sea. It became home over the years to a sect of Zoroastrian scholars and astronomers known simply as the Magi. The greatest of these scholars was an elderly gentleman named Melchior. Even though he had no official title or responsibilities in this place he had always been referred to as 'Master' by those that studied the stars and signs with him. The rest of the men in this conclave were other scholars that too studied the stars above and read the signs, made calculations, and also, on occasion, made predictions.

The brightest scholars from the entire known world came here to study and learn the art and the sciences of astronomy. Most did so to enlighten themselves about the world around them. Some did so to help them find meaning in the life they lived, yet, still some only came to learn with the hopes that they could return to their home countries and become valued advisors to the kings, rulers, and rich men of this world, and by doing so, become powerful and influential themselves.

Melchior could easily have become the wisest man in his entire home Persia, and have sat aside any king he so chose, perhaps even the Emperor of Rome if he so desired. However, he never really had this kind of ambition, and it seems these days his tired old body probably would not be able to handle more than sitting and studying, or perhaps engaging in discussions of philosophy and theology with his two closest colleagues, Gaspar and Balthazar.

Of all the scholars in this temple, those two were by far the brightest. Gaspar was here with him the longest and was perhaps the closest to him now in age. Gaspar had a slight frail frame and hailed from the lands they called India. He had frequently been the perfect foil to every one of Melchior's brilliant revelations of the past. He had his absolute admiration and respect but he always seemed to make the counterpoint to Melchior in any conversation and Melchior likewise did so with Gaspar. Outsiders would think they hated each other but nothing could be further from the truth. In fact, they cherished the arguments a great deal because it forced each of them to work harder and think harder to stay a step ahead of the inexorable arguments that would follow.

They had an unspoken language between them that they doubted anyone would ever understand . . . until that day years ago when Balthazar, the large man with the dark skin strode into the temple and upset the balance of things.

One would assume that Balthazar would be seen as a troublemaker as often as he challenged the two great masters of the temple. One would also assume wrongly that since he was their younger by better than 20 years, that he was not as wise as they . . . however, Balthazar had proven himself to be the best and brightest new mind the temple had ever seen. He brought with him new ideas and new thoughts on old problems and had challenged the status quo that had threatened to make this temple a relic of the past. In a sense, he brought new life and new passion into this place, and Gaspar and Melchior could not help but love him for it. What a joy it was for them to see his excitement when he spoke of his learnings and discoveries!

This particular day he did not smile as he greeted his two colleagues. He seemed to be troubled. He approached Gaspar and Melchior shortly before morning meal and gave them a customary greeting. Melchior looked at him and said "What troubles you this morning my friend? Normally when you come for the morning meal you are smiling because you are about to eat more than the rest of us combined! What on earth makes you frown so and what makes your brow seem so heavy?"

Balthazar paused for a moment to compile his thoughts and said "Brothers, this night I had a disturbing discovery and it baffles me still. I have been studying the movement of the stars for some time and I have always found them to be quite predictable, yet last night when I studied them I found a star that I had never seen before."

Gaspar said with a conciliatory tone "Brother do not fret seeing this new star, perhaps the nature of the sky had not made this star reveal itself before. Perhaps in previous studies this star seemed too dim to notice and it is now that the conditions are right to see it better. Remember, it is not normally so cold this time of year, and this can make the skies seem clearer to us."

"Gaspar, I am aware of this phenomenon but in this case it simply cannot be the truth of the matter." Balthazar approached the two men and sat in front of them. "The star I spotted this night was the most brilliant star I have ever seen in my life. It could not simply have been dim until the conditions of the night sky improved. It was the brightest in all of the sky!"

Melchior looked amazed. He said to his colleagues "Then we should be sure to study this star in much greater detail tonight. Perhaps all three of our minds together can determine the cause of this phenomenon."

Balthazar looked troubled still. Gaspar reached for his hand and said to him "My friend something still troubles you. What is it?"

Balthazar pursed his lips and then looked at Gaspar intently. "The location of this star is going to be even more troubling to you my brothers. The location of this star is at the base of the constellation of the Three Crosses. My calculations show this star to be at a perfect intersection of all three of the crosses in the constellation! I calculated the exact direction from here and plotted it on a map and it intersects directly with a small town in Herod's Kingdom called Bethlehem."

Melchior was visibly shaking and Gaspar was frozen in contemplation of what this meant. Melchior jumped to his feet and grabbed Balthazar and kissed him firmly on the forehead, much to Balthazar's surprise. "Brother, this is no time to be troubled! This is a time to be filled with joy! He is coming! He is coming at last! We shall see the new King! Oh joy! Oh joy! Ha ha ha! Joy to the world!" He scurried as fast as his frame could carry him to the central chamber calling everyone who could hear to come forth. "Come! Come Brothers! Come all you faithful! Here the news!" His shouts trailed off in the distance and they could see the aroused interest of everyone that could hear him. They were all murmuring and running to the central chamber to join him.

Balthazar looked to his friend Gaspar to inquire what on this earth Melchior was talking about. Gaspar seemed on the brink of running away shouting as well but seemed to know that it would be wise to tell Balthazar why this place would soon be filled with excitement. "My dear friend, there has long been a prophecy that a new King will be born that will deliver us all into a new age; an age of peace and enlightenment. There are many prophecies in many lands that herald the birth of the great King of Kings. Many of them say that a star will be born that will guide the enlightened to place of his birth . . . but dear Brother, there is one in particular that says 'And you, Bethlehem, in the land of Judah, are by no means least among the rulers of Judah; for from you shall come a ruler who is to shepherd my people Israel. And that his birth will be in Judaea in a city called . . . Bethlehem.' My brother, you have revealed to us this moment that the prophecy is being fulfilled!"

Gaspar turned to run down to the central chamber behind Melchior, and then turned to Balthazar, who stood there in awe at what was just revealed to him. "Come brother, we have much to do if we are to greet our new King!"

CHAPTER 4

I t seemed like just yesterday the star first appeared to Balthazar in his studies, now it has been almost two full months of hard travel following this star. He knew how far Bethlehem was on the map but he wondered how long it would take them. There was a time in his life that this journey would have been much easier for him. He had traveled like this before. But it seemed to him that he had gotten much softer in his time spent studying at the temple . . . at least he was sure his bottom had. He was not at all certain how his older Magi brothers were able to bear it. Perhaps their excitement at the prospect of witnessing the new King's birth had dulled their senses somewhat.

Balthazar looked around him at the caravan. He was certain that they did not need nearly as many men and camels as they took, but the scholars at the temple insisted that they have ample supplies for them and an ample number of guards and servants as well. The reputation of the temple was great but they were all certain that it would diminish if any of the three great masters were not able to return. They needed them to make this journey safely and without trouble.

They had paid a number of men to join them as guards should they run into trouble on the road. They knew that Judaea was a troubled place under Herod. The cruel and savage way he ruled his people along with the governance of Rome had given rise to a very disenchanted population of persecuted Jews. One of the results was a great increase in the number of highwaymen. These were men, and sometimes even women and children that lay in wait along the roads of the kingdom and were content to rob and harass any and all travelers they encountered. The soldiers of King Herod and the Roman Procurator did their best to control these growing populations of bandits, but for every one they arrested it seemed two more would spring up in their place. These savages knew the land and all of its hiding places far better than the soldiers ever would. This is why they would be hard to eradicate.

Balthazar was shaken from his drifting thoughts by his dear friend. "Oh Judaea" said Gaspar, "If ever there was a land that needed deliverance from persecution, it is you."

Melchior used this comment from his friend to bring forth a thought in his mind that was not unrelated. "We should give some thought in how to avoid persecution ourselves. We are about to cross the border into Herod's lands and we need to make a decision on how to proceed."

Balthazar had pondered that question himself earlier and looked to him and said "What are the options you recommend Melchior?"

"It seems they are quite simple answers, but all of them are fraught with a generous share of danger. We could turn back, which I think we would all agree is not a choice given that we have traveled so far already."

"I would not relish the thought of all this effort to go back empty handed," said Gaspar, "We knew we would have to deal with this. Our options should be in how to face it. Not to turn from it."

"Agreed," said Melchior. "Then it is clear that if we go forward, we must either inform Herod of our intentions and hope that he does not stop us, or go forward in secrecy and hope that we are not caught, for we will surely be put to death if we are."

Balthazar bought up another point to consider. "My Brothers, if we do proceed in secrecy, there is no way we could do so with this caravan in tow. It would surely attract attention and Herod would find us. My servant spoke to a woman at the well and she told him that Herod had decreed a census would take place in all of Judea and according to the custom all must return to their ancestral homes to be counted. This would mean that a greater number of people will be on the roads, and I fear this would increase our risk of exposure."

Gaspar placed his index finger in the air as if to call attention to his pause to gather a thought. "Perhaps that could work to our advantage. If we were to send away parts of our caravan and dress a bit more like the locals perhaps we would fit in with all the other caravans traveling the roads to their ancestral homes for the count. Would that not be a good option? It would certainly reduce our exposure."

Melchior was clearly the one they both looked to for the final answer on this matter. And their silence to him meant that they awaited his response to both issues.

"My Brothers, I am particularly fond of any ideas that reduce our danger, for I am old and fear my heart would fail me at an inconvenient time," he smiled. "However, there is one thing that I want all three of us to consider very strongly as we continue on this quest." He paused a moment. "We must consider that the very reason for this quest is to seek out the new Messiah foretold by prophecy. Every teaching and prophecy we have read and studied as part of this quest reveals him to be a wise and just King that will deliver us all from evil."

Balthazar said to Melchior, "but he will only be a child, surely he has no power yet to do these things."

Melchior's response was terse. "Balthazar, do you think for one moment that if we use lies and deceit just to reach him that we are any different than the very people he is meant to deliver this world from? Although our intentions are good, we have to remember that a great many of the worst decisions in life start with a good intention."

Balthazar countered, "But surely no one will be harmed by our intentions."

Melchior let out a short sigh and continued, "Balthazar, you are a very wise man and as such you are very welcome to counter any decision I may make in this matter, but I must say this one last thing before you do. Who is to say that no one will be harmed? If we go forth in secrecy and are discovered, you, Gaspar, and myself included, may be prepared for the consequences, but what of the servants and guards and their lives? Have you considered that anyone that goes with us could be harmed by this? What if Herod decides that because we went in secrecy we have something great to hide and it makes his fear and distrust in Jews grow? What if he takes it out on his people and innocents are killed to find out more 'secrets' that we made him fear in the first place? Does it sound to you that good intentions can save all from harm?"

No one said a word. The wisdom of Melchior's words was not lost on his fellow wise men.

Gaspar was the first to speak. "Then I recommend in this case that we dispatch an envoy to Herod's palace to request permission to enter his lands, and we should do so with haste for I fear that the time is growing short to reach Bethlehem. We should send some of the gifts we bring to Herod as tribute to soften him to our purpose. I think that we should of us each keep back our most prized possession to give tribute to the new King when we eventually reach him in Bethlehem.

CHAPTER 5

"So you are trying to convince me that the great and wise Magi are requesting MY permission to enter MY lands to seek out the prophesied Messiah who is to be born here? Is this Messiah soon to be my King as well? Are the Magi so anxious to seek my replacement?" Herod became suspicious of this request even though it was made openly and with gifts as tribute to him as well.

Poor Mathias, the Magi's chosen envoy, began to fear that Herod would have him killed when he started this rant and approached him so closely that he could smell the wine on his breath. He bowed even more deeply in deference to the mad king. He chose his next words wisely. "Oh great and wise Herod, my masters no not of politics or their intrigues, they are but simple scholars and are following a suspicious alignment of the stars. It is said in many prophecies that a new King will be heralded. This particular one has been more intriguing to them than most because the stars aligned closely to a prophecy regarding the birth of a Messiah. My masters merely felt it appropriate to show you, the one true king of Judea, that they mean no ill will to you at all and that they only wanted to continue their quest to see what lies at the end of their journey. Perhaps it will be nothing your Majesty. The Magi are nothing if not persistent in their pursuit of knowledge. Perhaps this is why people regard them so highly. I can assure you my lord that they only care about the pursuit of knowledge and nothing more."

"Very well then, you have given me much to consider and I shall think on it and give you an answer soon that you can take back to your masters. Until then, my servants will see that you are fed and rested." He motioned to the manservant next to him to escort Mathias away.

As Mathias was led away, his royal advisor Castor approached Herod and stood beside him. Herod leaned toward him and quietly said to him "Should I be worried that these Magi might find what they are looking for Castor?"

"Sire, there are great many prophesies among these people and it is easy to believe any of them you choose. It has been my observation that the people will make up whatever they want to achieve their purposes. As to whether this will be a Messiah or just another one of the many prophets that have plagued this kingdom, I do not know." He paused before the next comment. "The Magi have openly requested this permission and have graciously extended many gifts to you as tribute. I do not feel there is any ill will from them or they would have not been so open with you."

"But I do my dear Castor. I do." He now looked directly into his advisor's eyes. "If the Magi are allowed to continue this journey they will likely stir the people into believing there is a true King amongst them. Even if they do not find one, the people will, as you eloquently put it, believe whatever they want to believe to suit their purposes. I cannot allow this."

"I agree with you my lord but may I offer a solution to you that may solve this problem?"

"Go ahead Castor, I listen."

"Allow the Magi to continue their journey with your blessings and I will have them followed. My men will report back to me on their travels and we will have them report to us anyone they believe the Magi have identified as this so called King of Kings. After you know the answer, you can have this problem 'eliminated'."

"You realize that the Magi themselves must be 'eliminated' as well, or they will spread the news to the world of what they have discovered. We cannot have that."

"Which is why my lord you should invite them to return here at the completion of their journey to share these wondrous findings with you. Simply tell them that you desire the company of such fine scholars on their journey home and you wish to repay them for their generosity and respect they have shown to you."

With a wry smile Herod replied, "Castor, I am not sure having a man so devious and dangerous as you this close to me is such a wise idea." "Let the messenger rest a bit and call him back to me."

"Yes my lord" was the reply of Castor and he made his way out of the king's chamber.

CHAPTER 6

"And all Herod wants us to do is grace him with a visit on our return?" was the reply of Gaspar to Mathias' report.

"Master, he sent his blessings to your journey and only asked that you share your findings with him when you return." Mathias licked his lips and held back trying to determine what he wanted to say next.

Mathias knew his duty was to report to the Magi what Herod had said to them but this last part, while appearing to sound innocent, was so ominous in the way it was delivered that he wanted to tell the Magi what he thought of it. He wasn't sure if he dared to speak his mind.

"Mathias you hold back something. What is it? What troubles you? Speak freely; you are a trusted man in this company. You have nothing to fear." Melchior said as he moved closer to put his hand on the shoulder of Mathias.

Mathias was relieved to hear this blessing to speak his mind from his Master and blurted the next part out. "Masters, he says also that he wants you to tell him where this Messiah is so that he may also fall down and worship him. He's lying, I know it. It was the way he said it. Don't believe him Masters! If you return he will have you killed!"

It was Gaspar's turn to speak. "Melchior, we cannot say we did not know this would happen. Herod is a cruel tyrant. Mathias is correct that Herod will have us killed."

"Yes Gaspar, of that I am sure, but I am also certain now that he will expect our return since we have been so open from the beginning. This will allow us to finish our journey unhindered. We should plan to return home on a much different path than he is expecting so as not to be discovered until it is too late."

Balthazar said, "What of the Messiah? Who will protect him from Herod?"

Melchior turned to Balthazar and said, "There is no greater protector for the Messiah than God himself. Right or wrong, we have inadvertently alerted Herod to the prophecy and he will be looking for him even if we returned now. We should consider using any opportunity we can to warn them of the danger and protect him with whatever resources we can muster."

"Agreed" said Gaspar.

"Agreed" said Balthazar. "Can one of you loan me a pillow before we leave? I don't think my bottom can take another mile of this."

Melchior laughed heartily at his friend's pending misery. "You young people are so soft these days." Then he turned silently cursing himself because he knew Balthazar was the only one of the three of them brave enough to admit this. Oh how he longed for an extra pillow himself . . .

CHAPTER 7

B ack in the stable Joseph mused to himself whether or not men could handle the kind of pain women went through when they gave birth to a child. Then when Mary screamed again and tightened her grip on his hand he suddenly realized that they absolutely could not. He was almost in tears himself from the throbbing in his hand. Where did this little girl get such a strong grip?

"Joseph! Where is your mind at?" said Serah in an unexpectedly loud voice. "Mary is here, you need to be here too. Look her in the eyes and calm her. She needs your full attention now more than ever." She went back to mopping the sweat from Mary's brow and under her breath she said "This is your child too you know." To which Mary and Joseph both looked at each other knowingly and chuckled. Of course Serah would think that. How could she possibly understand what she was about to a part of? She was about to help this young girl give birth to the Messiah. As weak as she already was, she would probably faint if she knew.

Dismas was a curious boy and had wanted to stay, but his mother Serah had begged him just to sit outside and listen for her to call if she needed anything. He was sure she knew what was best for him; she always had, so he did as he was told. Truth be told he was excited to see his mother feeling useful again. She was so weak that she felt herself a burden on everyone and of no real use to anyone. He could see in her eyes that purpose is what she needed and now she had one; one that she was extremely good at.

Back inside, Mary could feel she was getting closer. Serah knew it too and she began to feel fear because she felt herself fading and she was certain that she was about to fail at the time when Mary and Joseph would need her most. She sat for a moment to gather her strength while Joseph relieved her mopping the sweat from Mary's brow and keeping her calm. Serah clasped her hands together and went directly to the Lord in prayer. "Father I am not worthy of you but I beg of you give me the strength to help this girl and her child. They need me and I am not strong enough."

For Serah, everything went suddenly black and her first impression was that she had fainted. Then suddenly she was blinded by a bright warm light, almost like sitting in the window of her old home and basking herself in the morning sun. She opened her eyes and sitting right in front of her, with legs crossed, was a man bathed in white light. He was the most beautiful man she thought she had ever seen and now she felt as if she were dreaming. He spoke. "Serah, blessed servant of God, You are not dreaming. I am Gabriel and I have been sent by our Father to bring you a message. Our Father wishes you to know that his light is to enter the world this very night and you have an important task to fulfill."

Serah felt in her heart that there was nothing to fear from what Gabriel told her. She was always a true believer of God and she knew that God spoke to believers, but she never felt that she was worthy. She looked to Gabriel with tears in her eyes and cried, "Tell me what I must do. I will do anything for the Father if it is within my strength, but please know Gabriel that I feel I am near my end and may not have the power left in me to do his bidding."

Gabriel reached to her and whispered in her ear, "Tonight the Messiah is to be born, the one who will deliver us from sin and bring light into the world. The Virgin Mary is to bear him. You Daughter, blessed servant of God, have been chosen to bear witness to his coming and to help Mary bring him into this world, so that he may be blessings to us all."

"Oh Gabriel, you bring a joyous task to such an unworthy servant of God. I am truly humbled. I will give my last breath for him if necessary. Will I have the strength to help Mary?"

"Daughter, you need only to hold the face of the Virgin Mary in your hands and you will receive what you need. The Father commands it."

And then, just as suddenly as the vision began, she realized she was in this stable next to a young girl in much pain and about to give birth. She lifted herself up and kneeled in front of Mary and held her face in her hands. "I know child! I know! I know who you are! The angel Gabriel spoke to me and commanded me to bear witness with you to the birth of the Son of God!" She shook with joy and tears were streaming down her face as she looked into Mary's eyes.

Mary knew without reservation that God had blessed this woman, not unlike the blessing she and Joseph had received when Gabriel came to them with his messages. She looked back in her eyes knowingly but had no words to say. She pressed her forehead to Serah's. It was then that she knew God was giving Serah strength through her. She could feel it, and in moments she could see it. It was as life was being poured back into Serah and Serah was positively beaming with the energy.

Poor Joseph . . . Mary was sure of what was coming next when she saw Serah's strength returning. Serah turned to face him. "Joseph, what's wrong with you? Can't you see we're out of water! Stop daydreaming and go fetch some more! We've got a baby to bring into the world!"

Mary couldn't help but smile a bit as Joseph sheepishly ran outside to find Dismas to help him bring more water.

Then the pain became almost unbearable . . . the time was at hand.

CHAPTER 8

D ismas positioned himself in the doorway when he heard the baby cry. He had hoped that someone would see him and invite him to come and see the child. He was there clearing his throat for about the fourth time when Serah finally looked at him and invited him to come and join her side and to see the baby. He made no waste of time reaching her. Secretly Dismas wanted to see the child as well for he was particularly drawn to Mary and Joseph, but in reality he was much more excited to be by his mother's side while she felt so good. He began to have hope that her health would be back to normal soon. He longed for this with all of his heart. He welcomed any chance to spend time with her for he loved her so much.

He looked at the child and asked Mary what she planned to name him. Mary glanced at Joseph with a look that implied she was asking permission to say something which they both already knew. When he nodded back to her, she looked to Dismas and said "We will name him Jesus."

Serah smiled so much she felt her cheeks starting to hurt a little, but what a joyous event this was! She held her son Dismas very tightly and told him "Behold son, you are looking at a child that will deliver all of us someday. He is very dear and special to us and great care must be taken to protect him."

Very little of what Serah had said to her son was actually understood. Dismas was so intently staring at the child that heard almost nothing. What was it about him? What made him so different? He didn't look that different, except that he probably had the most piercing blue eyes he had ever seen. He saw nothing overly special about him, yet he had this overwhelming sensation of belonging when he looked at him. He wondered if that was even the right word. It was as if they had some kind of bond, and he lacked the ability to explain for he had never felt this before.

Serah began to weaken rapidly now and Dismas could see it. "Mother, you must go and lie down. I will see that Joseph and Mary get what they need."

"Very well Dismas. You take such good care of your mother, I should not disobey you now" and then she smiled. "Can you help me son? I fear I no longer have the strength to walk this night."

"Come Dismas," said Joseph. "I will help you get your mother to her destination. It is the very least I can do for a woman who treated me so kindly tonight." That last bit of irony was for the benefit of Serah, for he knew exactly it would make her smile, and he was perfectly right, for she did.

When they reached the floor of the room behind the stable, Dismas stepped inside and moved his sleeping brothers just a bit so that his mother could lie down. Joseph helped Dismas to position her properly. Joseph was only beginning to realize how much this night had taken its toll her weakened body. He leaned in to her as he lay her down and spoke into her ear. "May God richly bless you Serah for what you have done for us this night."

She looked behind him as Dismas' face came into her view and said to him, "Thank you Joseph, but as you can see, he already has." Dismas approached his mother as Joseph backed out of the doorway and he covered her with a blanket to keep her warm.

"Rest Mother. I will sleep nearby in the stable and see that Mary and Joseph and the baby are taken care of. I will check on you in the morning." She pulled him to her and hugged him tightly and kissed him on the forehead, then drifted off to sleep with a joyful smile on her face.

Dismas returned to the stable and he could see that Mary was becoming very tired and that Joseph was practically sleeping already. He noted that the manger was very close to where they lay and he made his way to it with an armful of fresh straw and filled it. He looked to Mary and said, "Jesus can sleep here if you are tired. I put fresh straw in it and it is clean."

"Thank you Dismas. You have done so much for us. Can I just take a moment to thank you for everything you and your mother have done tonight?" Mary held his hands in hers. They were very warm. "You are a wonderful boy and we are very blessed that God helped us all to find each other. I hope that we can someday repay you for all that you have done."

Embarrassed, Dismas said, "You don't have to thank me at all Mary. I did nothing special. My mother taught me that God commands us to help one another. It's in the Torah. I'm just doing what I am commanded by God to do."

"Well Dismas, the reason you are so special is that many people in this world are taught exactly the same thing, but they are not obedient to God's word. You are obedient, so you are therefore special" she said as she touched his nose.

"What happens to those people that know what God commands them to do but they don't do it?"

Joseph decided to answer this question for Mary and said to the boy "Dismas, every single one of us are sinners. We all fall short of what God expects us to be, however, God teaches us that when we do fall short of his expectations and we allow sin to enter our lives, we must humble ourselves before him and ask for forgiveness with a heart that is truly sincere and truly penitent."

"And he will forgive us?" queried the boy.

"Certainly he will, my dear Dismas. If God did not forgive us of our sins none of us would ever be able to ascend to heaven. But remember, to truly be forgiven the sinner must ask forgiveness with a sincere and penitent heart." Joseph then patted the boy on the shoulder. "Dismas, you seem to be one of the smartest and brightest young boys I have met and I am certain you have nothing major to repent. What troubles you to be so concerned?"

"It's my father sir. He used to take me to synagogue with my mother and Jotham, my little brother. He taught us all about the Torah and about God's teachings. He used to be a very good man, but now he has left us all alone so he could go drink and gamble every day. We never see him anymore and he does not provide for us. Will God forgive him too?"

"Dismas, God loves us all and I know that if your father will someday realize his sin, he too can ask God to forgive him and his sin will be washed away and it will be as if he were truly a new man. Now, go rest yourself young man. We will pray for you and for your father too. God will reward those who are faithful. You must not lose hope."

"Yes sir," was the reply of the very sleepy Dismas. He trotted off to corner by the entrance of the stable and dove into the pile of fresh straw and pulled his cloak over him. This day truly was a tiring one. He looked over one last time at Mary and Joseph holding their new baby and smiled at the look of adoration in their eyes as they gazed at him. He wondered if his father and mother used to look at him that way. He started to miss his father all over again. He hoped that what Joseph said was true; that his father too could be forgiven by God. It gave him a good feeling inside to know that if you are truly repentant that God will forgive you. He liked this message. He was glad to have met this Joseph. He seemed like a very wise man.

Dismas' thoughts went back to the happiness he saw in his mother's eyes earlier and he smiled as he drifted off to sleep . . .

CHAPTER 9

As Dismas drifted off to sleep in the stable, not far away, Balthazar was the first to notice the lights of Bethlehem and he immediately awoke Melchior and Gaspar, both of whom slept while sitting in the saddle astride their camels. As he looked in the sky he could see that the star shone brighter now than it had since it had first revealed itself to him months earlier. In fact it was so bright now that you needed not be a scholar to notice its significance in the night sky for it burned brighter even than the moon.

"Brothers, we are close now. Bethlehem lies before us" said Balthazar with more than a little excitement in his voice.

Gaspar said, "Have we thought about where to even start looking once we get there?"

Melchior replied "I believe we should start with following the same star we've been following and see where it leads us. Balthazar, can you direct us exactly to the home by charting it on a map?"

Balthazar looked at Melchior and very simply answered "No. I cannot. It is impossible to be precise at this point. We may have to knock on doors until we find the child that has been born."

Gaspar was first to reply by saying "I suggest that we take our caravan to that stable down there and refresh our livestock and have a short rest ourselves first. This could be a very long process and we must be very delicate about it."

Melchior agreed and then winced. Balthazar was about to try to be funny and ask him if the saddle made his bottom hurt again when Melchior suddenly let out a tremendously loud and violent sneeze. His camel was startled and immediately began to jump, dumping the wisest scholar in the world on his backside. Both of his friends were quickly by his side picking him up to his feet. Their concerns were alleviated when Melchior started to laugh at his predicament.

Gaspar, gripping Melchior's arm, said, "You really scared him Melchior!"

"Scared him? Nonsense, he scared me!" he said chuckling as he walked back over to the beast that put him on the ground.

Balthazar looked at him as he walked past him to retrieve the reins and said "How scared were you my friend?"

Melchior leaned to whisper in Balthazar's ear, "Only the servant that washes my loincloth will know how scared I was . . ." They both immediately let out a loud belly laugh, leaving Gaspar to chase after Melchior to see what conversation he had missed.

Melchior's servant lifted him back to his seat on the camel and clucked at the animal. It arose and Melchior was once again wincing, but this time because the pain in his backside. "Come brothers, we need to rest so we can begin early on our quest. Let us find the closest stable and bed for the night. Leave the servants and let us take only two guards into the city. We should not do anything to attract undue attention."

Gaspar barked orders to Mathias to follow Melchior's instruction and he knew that it would be done exactly as instructed, for Mathias was a very faithful man. Mathias was the servant of one of the old masters at the temple and when his master died he had been set free. The temple was the only real home he knew and he had decided to remain since he did serve a purpose, and that was to take charge of all the daily operations of the temple. Although he was not a scholar, his job was no less important, for he was the one that kept things running smoothly so that the scholars could focus all their attention on their studies. He obediently set about the task given.

After a few brief moments the three Magi made their way down into the city.

CHAPTER 10

The Magi approached the stable where they intended to rest their livestock. It was Dismas that first heard the voices outside the stable. He wasn't sure how long he was asleep, but he was certain it wasn't long. What could it be he wondered? He hoped that they wouldn't be too noisy because they might wake the baby. When he looked up he realized that the baby was already awake and that Mary sat near the manger cradling him in her arms and singing to him. Joseph was lying beside her with his hand on her waist and he was sound asleep.

Balthazar stepped in through the narrow doorway but had to duck to keep from hitting a wooden beam, for he was very tall. As anyone walked into the stable, the first thing they would see as they came in would be a small corner where a pile of fresh straw lay. This night Dismas was on top of it covered in his cloak and half asleep. They caught each other's eye at the same time.

Dismas was the first to say anything and he asked "May I help you sir?" as he scooted off of the top of the pile of straw and tried to guide the tall, dark man back outside to keep the conversation more quiet for his other guests.

Balthazar said, "We are truly sorry to disturb you at this hour but we are very weary and we seek only to rest our camels for a while and perhaps ourselves as well. Have you room for us?"

"Sirs, you are catching us all at a strange time. The entire city is full because of the census and there is no room at any of the inns in the town."

Gaspar arrived and inquired himself, "We are certain that the stable will be as comfortable as an inn. We only wish to sleep for a bit. We have a large task at hand. Can we sleep here?"

Dismas did not want to disappoint them. He was sure they were very tired. They surely looked it as well. But there was simply no good way to break the news to them. "Unfortunately we are full inside as well."

Just then Melchior joined his fellow Magi's side as Gaspar continued his inquiry. "My boy, would it be possible for you to move your animals to the outside for a few hours so we can sleep somewhere besides out here in this cold?"

Dismas replied, "It's not animals that we are full of tonight sir. We have very special guests this evening." He beamed. "A man brought his wife in here tonight and she had a baby, just a little while ago. My mother said he was a very special baby.' He beamed. "I think he is too."

The meaning of the boys words were not lost on him and he immediately looked to Melchior. "Could it have been this easy?"

Melchior said quietly to Balthazar, "We'll see shall we?"

Gaspar turned from listening to the conversation between Balthazar and Melchior and looked again to Dismas. "Young man, do you suppose the child's parents would allow us to visit for a moment . . . to pay our respects their new baby?"

"I can ask. Mary is still awake. I just saw her."

Dismas stepped lightly back inside the stable and whispered to Mary quietly so as not to awake Joseph, "Mary, there are three men outside that would like to know if they can come and pay their respects to you and the baby. Is it okay? They seem like very nice men."

"Of course Dismas. Please ask them to come in and join us."

Dismas jumped to his feet and ran outside to his awaiting guests. "She will see you. Please come in."

Gaspar asked Dismas kindly to tend to their camels while they paid respects to the woman and her child. He obliged them by taking the reins of their camels and leading them to the side of the stable so he could tie them and bring them some straw and water.

The three men stepped into the stable and the noise had awoken the sleeping Joseph, who immediately sat up to wipe the sleep from his eye to see better the source of all of this noise. As they approached Mary and her child, Balthazar and Gaspar stopped as if to allow Melchior to step forward and represent them all as their anointed spokesperson in this matter.

"Excuse me my dear lady. I understand from the young boy outside that you have just given birth tonight to a new son. Was he correct?"

Mary looked at him with the most beautiful smile Melchior had ever seen and said, "Yes I have sir, and you may call me Mary. This sleepy man here is my husband Joseph."

Melchior straightened his cloak and made a very humble bow toward Mary and said "Mary, my name is Melchior." His right hand made a sweeping gesture to the men behind him and said, "These are my fellow travelers, Balthazar and Gaspar. We are of the Magi. Have you by chance heard of our people?"

"Yes. My father has talked about your people many times when I was a girl. Your people are scholars and you study the stars and from time to time make predictions I hear."

"Your father was indeed a wise man," said Melchior. "He was absolutely correct." He swallowed hard before continuing, "It is about that last part that I must tell you. We began a long journey months ago following a star that foretold the birth of a new King. This King was foretold to be born in the city of David, here in Bethlehem. The star led us here . . . and on the night we arrive, we learn of your child's birth. My dear, sometimes I am not as smart as people would proclaim me to be, but I am convinced that this may be the child we have been seeking. The circumstances are far too remote for it not to be. Tell me please that I am not a fool."

"Melchior . . . my learned friend. You are not a fool. Our baby's birth was foretold to us by the angel Gabriel and he shared with us this very same message from God."

Melchior's breath suddenly left his body and he shuddered in immense joy and anticipation. He looked to his dear friends and they were holding each other tightly and tears were beginning to form in the eyes of both men. The joy threatened to overtake them. The scholarly gentlemen were all three reduced to tears.

"May we see him?" said an anxious Melchior.

Mary pushed back the blanket around the child so that the men could all see him. Jesus was awake and looking directly at the old man, and it looked to all who would see him, a knowing smile, as if he were greeting a dear relative. It was an expression uncommon in children at this age. His pale blue eyes were such an unusual color that they seemed to hold on to you, for you could not look away from them.

His face was at last revealed to the three wise Magi. Melchior fell to his knees, trembling in delight, and said "Behold, the King of Kings!" He leaned forward and laid his forehead on the boy's feet and then kissed them as his tears of joy fell.

He turned to Gaspar and Balthazar who were both holding each other and weeping openly. "Come here brothers, let us adore him. Born here in Bethlehem is the King of Angels!"

They both fell to their knees beside him weeping as he was and took their turns kissing the child's feet. Joseph had to step back or they would have fallen on him.

Melchior then asked, "What name have you given the child?"

It was Joseph that replied this time, "We call him Jesus"

"Jesus. Jesus is a fitting name for a King I think," said Melchior.

It was Balthazar that broke the revelry for a moment when he said, "Brothers, we should present our gifts to the new King."

Gaspar whispered into his good friend Melchior's ear, "We should also try to make haste our visit. I fear we may all be in danger."

Melchior whispered back to Gaspar, "You're right my friend, as usual."

Melchior turned to Joseph, "I did not get the boy's name that helped us. Is he still outside?"

"Oh, you mean Dismas . . . I'm sure he is. I'll go and fetch him."

"Thank you Joseph, and when you do, tell him on the side of one of the camels is a blue satchel. Would you have him bring it in please?"

Joseph nodded and stepped outside to summon Dismas to the task, and then stepped back inside as the boy retrieved the bag to bring in.

When Joseph sat back down with Mary and the baby Dismas was already bringing the satchel in to the men. He left it on the dirt floor in front of the men and then retreated to his corner of the stable and he eavesdropped on the conversation.

Gaspar took the item the boy left for them and opened it. Inside were three items wrapped in cloth to keep them safe from harm. Each man reached in and took an item.

Melchior said to Mary and Joseph, "We are bearing you gifts from afar." Melchior took unwrapped his item and set it on the ground in front of the child. It was a small box. He opened it and said, "I bring you gold, a true gift for kings." He then kissed Mary's hand and made room for Gaspar.

Gaspar unwrapped his item, which was a small wooden cup with lid. He opened it to show the contents. Inside were many small amber colored crystals. "Behold, I bring you frankincense, which is more valuable even than gold. The people of my country value it most for it is used as an offering to God." He then kissed the hand of Mary as well and made room for Balthazar.

Balthazar kneeled before the child and he unwrapped his item, a small vial of oil. He said "Behold, my gift for you is myrrh. Among my people it is treasured as a holy oil for anointing." He laid the item at the foot of the child, and just as his fellow Magi before him, he took the hand of Mary and kissed it and rose to his feet and joined his brothers.

In the corner of the stable Dismas' sat wild eyed and silently calculating all the things he could buy if he had all of that money. The first thing he would do is buy his home back and put his, mother back in the home that she loved so much. And at last the four of them would have real beds to sleep on. They would no longer have to worry about food and he could even buy his mother the medicine she needs to get better. Heavens! He could even hire a servant to help his mother until she got better!

Alas, he realized that the money wasn't his to spend and he felt guilty about even dreaming that it was. He knew his mother would be ashamed of him for even thinking about taking it.

Melchior looked very somber for the first time since entering the stable. "I must also give you something even more important . . . some advice. As we entered the kingdom of Herod he became aware that we were looking for the prophesied Messiah. I am certain that he likely had us followed here. He fears that your son means harm to him and I am certain he intends to have all of us killed. You must take the boy and leave this town immediately. Use the gold and secure yourselves whatever supplies you need and go . . . right away."

Gaspar stepped forward and said, "I'm afraid that is all we can do to help you. We could take you with us and try to protect you, but Herod's men will easily spot our caravan and we do not have enough men to protect you. We are certain he means to find us and kill us too when we do not return to him. Your best chance is to slip out of town quickly before anyone notices you."

Joseph looked at Mary and said, "We should return to Nazareth with Jesus. We can get supplies in the morning and be on our way if you are well enough." He meant this last part as a question.

Mary replied, "I have no choice. We must protect him."

"It's decided then. In the morning I will take Dismas and we will get the supplies we need and we'll be off when I return."

He then turned to the Magi and said, "You know you can't go back the way you came. You should make your way North on the road to Nazareth and then return East. I don't think he will expect that. You may have a chance to escape."

Balthazar said to Melchior and Gaspar, "He is right brothers. We should leave now to rejoin our caravan and have Mathias break camp immediately."

Melchior paused to take in the moment one last time. He sensed that he would never see the child again but he was not sad. He had enjoyed a very full life and this moment was a crown on it all. There would never be another moment that held as much fulfillment and joy as this one did.

He smiled one last time and walked through the dusty doorway for he could not bear to say goodbye.

CHAPTER 11

J oseph did not think that you could ask for a better morning, unless there were a good night's sleep to go with it. He surveyed the two fine donkeys in front of him with a discerning look on his face. He was sure that they would be just fine, but the old man with the weathered face and bad limp was just asking too much for them.

If it weren't for the sheer number of people in town practically buying everything in sight, he might have easily bought these same two donkeys for a fraction of the price he was just quoted.

Joseph did his best to make this man think he was selling him two of the worst donkeys he had ever seen, but the old man never budged. Joseph had no talent for dishonesty and therefore he was certain he would not get the man to budge on the price.

The old man, Piram, was the owner of the stable, and as such was also technically Dismas' boss. He was, on most days, a very kind hearted man. He wasn't always as tough dealing with people, but he was sure that the man was so busy these days that he probably was not sleeping well. Dismas also knew that Piram's family had come home for the census and his home was quite full.

It was possible that he also just needed money to offset what all of his guests at home were likely consuming.

Dismas had always wondered why the man had been lame in his leg, but he was too polite to ask him. One day he and his mother were discussing it and she told him a story about the day Piram's daughter, who was much younger at the time, was playing in front of her father's stable when a few of Herod's soldiers came riding into the city. She said that everyone who saw that day had said that the soldiers saw her playing in the open and as if to play a game, tried to run her down. The soldiers terrorized her and when she screamed, Piram came running to her rescue as any father would. He swung his rake at the soldiers wildly to save his little girl, hoping that they would just leave them alone and ride away. Instead, it angered the soldiers and they took it out on him by knocking him to the earth with their horses and repeatedly riding over the top of him.

His mother said that Piram nearly died that day. His wounds were grave and almost fatal. But God smiled on him and he recovered fully, with the exception of his leg. It was so badly broken that it never truly healed. Piram's daughter was safe, Piram lived, and the townspeople thought of him as a hero for standing up to the soldiers of Herod. He became a well-respected man in the community.

Dismas did not need to hear any of the stories to know that Piram was a good man. He had always been very kind to Dismas, and now to his family. More than once he brought food to them that his wife had made. He always claimed that his wife always cooked too much, but inside Dismas knew that they were just being kind, but in a way that did not make them feel as beggars.

Joseph was still scratching his head trying to figure out the next negotiation tactic to try on the wise old Piram when Piram finally said "Listen, you are no good at this and you know it. You should pay me extra for wasting my time."

Joseph, always a quick wit, countered with, "You should give me a discount for entertaining you then. I don't work for free." He smiled awkwardly.

This made Dismas chuckle and he quickly tried to stifle it because he knew that Piram might not appreciate him interfering.

"If you are an entertainer, then maybe you should be in town singing or dancing, not wasting the time of a hard working man." He spit on the ground. "Are you going to take me up on the last price or are you going to go and try to entertain another donkey's owner?"

Dismas ran up to his friend Piram and tugged his arm to encourage him to lean closer so he could speak to him. He cupped his hand between his mouth and Piram's ear and whispered into it. Piram leaned away from him only a bit and made a sly wink at the boy as if he understood.

Piram said, "I'll make you a deal. If you are a carpenter like my employee here says you are I will give you both donkeys for half the price I quoted you if you will do me a large favor."

"I'm intrigued," said Joseph. "What is your offer?"

"I have materials to build two new mangers to replace the ones the donkeys have chewed on. If you will build them for me you may have the price I say. I am far too old to do the work and the boy here is far too small. Do we have a deal?"

Joseph grinned from ear to ear. "Ask and ye shall receive. Praise be to God. Yes! I accept. Show me the materials and I will start right away."

"Not so fast," said the old man. "I would like to be paid first if you don't mind. Sorry, but I have been cheated too many times over the years, and I have no forces to chase a young entertainer like you . . ."

"Of course," Joseph said still smiling. He took out three coins and promptly paid the man.

Joseph knew that he would be pressed for time with this new task, but it was important that he and Mary save whatever money they could for the trip back to Nazareth. He looked to his helper for the day, Dismas, and asked him if he could remember what supplies he was being sent to purchase for their journey to Nazareth. Dismas rattled off the list and Joseph was certain that he knew what was needed. The only thing he did not have was money.

"Dismas, I am going to give you two gold pieces. I want you to make sure that you pay no more than this for all the items we need. Can I trust you to do that?"

Dismas smartly said "Yes sir!" and put his hand out expecting the coins to be placed in it. He was certain he could do this.

"OK, here you go. Now be quick. We still have to see if there are any caravans leaving and going north today, preferably to Nazareth." Joseph gave him the two shiny coins that were given him to the Magi only hours earlier and then turned to follow Piram to his cache of building supplies.

Dismas set off into town to the market as fast as his two legs could carry him.

Inside the stable Serah sat with Mary and Jesus. She held the boy gently and sang a beautiful, sweet children's lullaby that she had sung to her own boys as babies. Jotham sat at her feet holding his little brother Aram between his legs. Aram leaned back on his brother and stared intently at his mother, enjoying the tune as well. Jotham held also in his lap a small drum that Piram had made for him to play with. It was only a small stretched piece of leather strung between four wooden sides but, but it had become Jotham's prize possession and he was very fond of playing his drum to this particular song when his mother would sing it. Jesus stared intently at Jotham as he played his little drum and seemed as if it made him smile.

Nearby Mary was washing up. She was grateful for the small break. She had not felt clean in very long time. Joseph had tried so hard to make a hasty trip to Bethlehem in fear that she would have the child on the side of the road that they had no time to wash up or even rest at any of the many streams they crossed on their journey. Now she was clean, fed, no longer in the pain and agony she had been in on the trip, and she was just . . . happy.

Joseph made his way into the stable and began to work on his new task of manger builder. He relished the opportunity to do this even though he never enjoyed rushing his work. There were so many things going on over the last several weeks that he had almost no time to work with the wood. Ever since he was a small boy he had always enjoyed building and making things. It calmed his spirit like nothing else he had ever done and he was certain that it was a gift from God this talent, for it had always brought him great joy.

The early morning went rather fast and Joseph finished his task in record time. Piram was quite impressed. Mary had taken Jesus into her arms and it was her turn singing as Serah and her two boys sat back and listened with great pleasure.

Dismas soon entered with another young boy in tow and the two of them were completely laden with the supplies Joseph had requested. Joseph quickly ran through the complete inventory with the boys and instructed them to start loading them on the donkeys.

When they finished securing the supplies on the donkeys, Dismas grabbed one of the loaves of leaven bread and gave it to the dirty young boy that helped him carry the supplies. He grabbed it and ran away so fast that Joseph was fairly certain that the boy wanted to get away with it before they changed their mind. Joseph started to object until Dismas told him that he had offered the boy a loaf of the bread if he would help him carry the supplies to the stable all the way from the market. One thing was for certain, there was no way that Dismas could have done it without help.

And being the kind man that Joseph was, he sort of enjoyed seeing the young man get some food. He was certain he probably had not eaten in a while judging by his appearance.

He looked to Dismas and said "God commands us to help those less fortunate than ourselves. It seems a very wise young boy said that to me once," he said with a half grin on his face. "You know there is one other lesson that I would like to leave you with on that topic young Dismas. God also says 'that which you do unto the least of yourselves, you do unto me.' That is God's way of telling us that we must treat those less fortunate with the same love and kindness we give to him, for when we do, we are demonstrating God's love to each other."

Dismas started to miss his father again. He used to tell him things like this too. "Thank you Joseph. I wish you could stay longer with us. You are a very good teacher." He paused for dramatic effect, and then quickly blurted, "And a good entertainer!" He chuckled and then ran back into the stable to see Mary and the baby one last time before they left.

What an odd site they saw next, for when they entered the stable it was Piram holding the baby Jesus and singing to him while the others all sat around and listened to him. Dismas had no idea that Piram had such a wonderful voice. The adoration the man showed to the child meant that he too was certain that there was something quite special about this child.

Piram finished his verse and gently handed the child back to his mother. He then looked to Joseph and said, "I found a caravan that is going to Capernaum. You should be able to travel with them all the way to Nazareth. They only left about three or four hours ago. If you leave now and do not stop to rest for long you will likely catch them by tomorrow."

Joseph was grateful for the news. He had hoped they would have a chance to rest a little more, but he was desperate to keep Mary and the child safe and the sacrifice must be made. He thanked Piram for everything and then helped Mary to her feet.

Joseph then turned to Piram and helped the old man to his feet. Piram reached into his cloak immediately upon standing and pulled the three coins out and placed them back into Joseph's hand. Joseph tried to refuse but the old man was insistent and would not have it.

Piram pulled Joseph close to him and said "I know who this child is and I will not take money from you. It is a humble gift to the child from a faithful servant of God. Now, hurry and go before it gets too late."

Joseph hugged the man and thanked him profusely for the gift.

Piram said his goodbyes to everyone and made his way slowly back down the hill and into the town. He was still singing the same song.

Serah and Dismas arose and Serah also said her goodbyes to the young family as Dismas continued outside to help Joseph load Mary and the child onto one of the two donkeys. Before Mary could be raised to her seat she gave Dismas a long and loving hug. She had grown very fond of the boy and had imagined that it was likely a great joy for Serah to be his mother. She was certain she would miss him and hoped that someday she might see him again.

Once Mary was seated, it became Joseph's turn to say goodbye to the boy. Like Mary, Joseph gave him a hug as well and thanked him profusely for being so helpful. He truly hoped that the boy's father would again find God and come back to him. He clearly loved his father very much and even though the man had gravely injured this beautiful family with his actions, he was quite certain that they would all forgive him and take him back if only he wished it. He feared that having to grow up so fast and become so responsible at such a young age would not be kind to the boy over time. A child needed to be able to play with other children, not earn a living for his family and care for his sick mother. He also feared what would become of all three of the boys if Serah succumbed to her illness.

There were a great many things for him to pray for. This much was certain, but he was sure he was up for the task. He vowed to lift the boy up in prayer often and hoped, like Mary, that he would be able to see him again.

He pulled away from Dismas but kept his hands on the boy's shoulder as he spoke. "Remember our lesson Dismas. If a man has sinned or fallen short of the grace of God, he need only come to God in prayer with a true and repentant heart, he will be forgiven. Will you remember that?"

Dismas obediently said, "Yes, sir. I will."

Joseph took up the rope on the lead donkey and made his way down the road. After a few moments, he looked back and saw

Dismas still standing there. He smiled and shouted to the boy, "Check your cloak Dismas!"

The boy did not understand and Joseph shouted once more, "Check your cloak!" while making a gesture to him hoping that he would understand what he meant.

Dismas then understood that Joseph meant for him to check his cloak. He reached all around himself and had no idea what he was checking for when he felt an unfamiliar lump. As he fished his fingers into the fold of his cloak three shiny coins fell to the ground. He bent over to pick them up certain they were the same three coins that Piram had just given back to Joseph. The boy raised them into the sky so Joseph could see had them, not certain really what it was about. He was simultaneously trying to determine when Joseph could have put them there and then he realized it had to have been when he hugged him and talked to him about forgiveness.

Joseph stopped in his tracks while noticing the boy was raising the coins in the air. He made a very deep bow in Dismas' direction as if he were demonstrating his thanks and then stood up, gave him a huge smile, waved, and then turned back around and began his long journey back to Nazareth.

Dismas could not believe his eyes. This was a lot of money! With it he could keep his family fed for quite some time and still have money left over. He knew exactly what he would do with it too. He would get his mother some good medicine to heal her and get a better roof over their head. All he needed were the materials and his good friend Jediah.

He was determined to get out and spend it now. He could not wait. His mother would be so happy and so proud of him. He tucked the coins back into the small fold in his cloak and headed to the marketplace as fast as his two legs would carry him. This would be a great day!

As jubilant boy made his hasty departure to the town's market, he was unaware that his father Benjamin sat not more than two hundred meters away up on the hill watching his son run into the town. Dismas also did not know it but he had been sitting there all night and part of this day. He watched his family and tried to find the courage to approach them to ask forgiveness. He had not consumed any wine this last two days. Not since the dream where the angel came to him and told him that a time of great peril was before him and before his family. The angel told him that he must find the courage to act when the time is right, for God commanded it. Benjamin awoke trembling and for the first time in months, his head was clear. He knew that he had wronged his family and left them vulnerable. He was not certain if they would forgive him, but the fear that they would not paralyzed him. For now he would have to be content watching over them until he did. He knew that the angel was clear that they were in danger. This was the only thing he knew to do, and that was to sit here and watch over them.

He silently wished he had a bit of wine to calm him but he knew that it was the wine that helped to get him into this situation in the first place. He would have no more of it. Soon he would have the courage to walk down the hill and face his beloved Serah . . . but not today.

Unbeknownst to the boy, on this night, the three coins in his pocket would set him on a course that would change his life forever.

CHAPTER 12

Meanwhile, Herod brimmed with an unmitigated fury when Castor informed him that his messenger had reported that the Magi had disappeared.

"I want them found! I want them found now, and I want them brought to me so that I might kill them myself!" said the angry Herod. His face was red and spittle flew from his mouth as he spoke.

"No one dares to defy me! This is MY land, MY kingdom!" He looked to Castor who remained in front of him calmly as if he not a care in the world. This was not the first time Herod had shown this ill-tempered side of himself. As often as it presented itself he had no doubts it would not be the last time he would see it. Castor had learned very quickly in his role as Herod's chief advisor, and that was when Herod was angry, it was best just to placate him and agree with everything he said. This fact was lost on his predecessor, which was precisely why Castor was now the advisor. Castor knew when to keep his mouth shut and avoid the wrath of the mad King Herod.

"Castor, did I not allow them access to my kingdom?" said Herod.

"Yes my lord you did. You were a most gracious host."

"Did I not accept their tribute?"

"Yes, my lord. A truly generous act on your part."

"Castor, did I not allow them to continue their journey with only one request, to return to me and report their findings?"

"Yes, my lord. You made only a humble request in return for your kindness and the Magi betrayed you."

He sprang to his feet and pointed his chubby finger to the sky. "Then I command you to send our men to find them and have them brought to me immediately!"

Castor knew that Herod was not as smart as one would hope a king to be and it was necessary to preserve the kingdom at times by carefully guiding the actions of the king. It was a delicate process that required great skill and tact. If one were to suggest a course of action contrary to what the king's wishes were, one had to do it with great skill so as to keep one's head on one's shoulders. This was one of those times. He knew that it would be a waste of time to send soldiers to search the country side for three old men when the true danger was that a prophesied Messiah had been born in Bethlehem. If only they could find this child they could end this mess. He did not like the thought of having a child killed, but if it preserved peace in the kingdom it may save a great many more lives.

Castor carefully weighed his next words. "My lord, if I may?"

With a wave of Herod's hand Castor continued, "My lord, perhaps it may be simpler to send our men into Bethlehem and find this child and have him brought to you instead. It will solve the immediate problem of crushing this prophecy the people fantasize about. This is a greater danger to you my lord than three cowardly old men."

He could sense that Herod contemplated the wisdom of this thought when he continued, "Also my lord, I can think of no grander punishment than allowing these men to know that they led you to the prophesied Messiah. The shame will be carried with them all of their life. Surely this would show them that you will have power over them not just for days but for all the years remaining in their life. You will have shown the wisest men of this world, that you, the mighty King Herod, are truly the wisest of them all."

Herod grabbed onto this idea and indeed he looked to Castor as if he liked it. Castor felt a rush of confidence that he made the right choice.

Herod raised a finger in the air as if to declare this his idea and said, "Indeed I AM wiser than all of the Magi! Let them go Castor. I will allow them to live with this shame for the rest of their cowardly days."

"My lord, shall I send your men to Bethlehem to find the child right away and have him brought to you?" Castor was relieved that he had carried influence with Herod.

No sooner had he calmed himself, Herod turned red again and he immediately knew something else still bothered him.

Herod angrily blurted, "I am sick to death with always feeling that the people are looking for someone else to lead them! And I am growing weary with all these so-called prophets and Messiahs, and Zealots causing trouble for me! Don't they understand how hard it is to be their king while Rome watches over us and controls every move we make as if we are puppets and they are our puppet masters?"

Castor knew it was not the time to speak. It was best to let Herod continue this angry rant until he became a little calmer.

Herod continued, this time rising to his feet. He appeared at this moment to have even more angry thoughts swirling in his head. "No, I must crush this once and for all if I am to break the yoke these Jews and Rome are trying to put on me."

In all of his memory he had never seen Herod so angry. He feared what he might say next. "Castor, we must crush this prophesy immediately! Send our men to Bethlehem and kill all male children under two years of age! We cannot be sure when this Messiah was born but we should crush the dream of a Messiah very quickly. Perhaps the people will finally see the wisdom of not pursuing these fantasies any further!"

Castor was absolutely horrified at this thought. He had no problem with handling the one child, but to kill ALL of the young males in Bethlehem? That would be unconscionable! It wasn't just a revolting thought; it was also a dangerous one. Herod was already unpopular in the kingdom. He genuinely feared this one decision would bring great peril not just to Herod, but to the entire kingdom. He knew he had to protest.

"My lord, I beg you, let us search for the one the Magi sought! I am confident that we can find him and we can bring him here. It will serve no purpose to kill all the male children under two except to rally even more anger toward you." Castor was desperately making this plea but he was certain that it only made Herod focus his angered attention on him. He knew he needed to tread lightly with his next comments or Herod would surely have him killed, just as he had done with Castor's predecessor.

"My lord, I will take charge of this quest personally. I will bring you this child."

Herod was intently focused now on showing Castor that he was the one who made the decisions. "And if you do Castor, what will stop the Jews from saying that another child in the village was the prophesied king and that we took the wrong one? You know that is what they will do! It is not enough to take only one child if you are to crush this fantasy. You must crush it once and for all! The message will be clearly understood and the people will see the peril of continuing with this false dream of theirs. It must be done!"

At great peril to his personal safety, Castor begged one more time, "But my lord . . ." and he was instantly cut off by Herod.

"Not another word from you Castor or so help me your head will join that of your predecessor's! Since you are so intent on making sure I am protected, you will go with the men to Bethlehem and oversee this yourself."

Herod sat back on his thrown, confident in himself and in this decision. It did not matter what Castor said. He knew he was right and it had to be done quickly and brutally. Otherwise the people would think they could continue with their little rebellions that continued to tear this kingdom apart. He would have no more of Rome constantly telling he had to act or they would do it for him . . . This was his kingdom and he will rule it in his way.

"Go now Castor and see to it that it is done. You must personally insure that every single male child in Bethlehem under the age of two is killed. If I hear that any were missed by you, you will be executed yourself." He followed with a final comment in his most ominous tone, "Make no mistake. If you fail me, your death will most assuredly NOT be quick and painless. Do you understand me Castor?"

There only was one reply he could have given in this moment, "Yes my lord."

Castor bowed to King Herod and backed away from him. As he was clear of the king's sight, he sighed deeply, still trembling from this encounter, and departed the king's chamber with haste. He hurriedly walked down the corridor to the outside courtyard. Inside his mind screamed "What have I done?" He knew it was his job to keep the king from making decisions like this and he was a complete and utter failure at it this night.

Perhaps his predecessor had not been a fool, just smart enough not to let himself be part of decisions that would cause so many innocents to die.

Castor wondered just how long it would be before his head truly did join that of his predecessor's as he mounted his horse.

CHAPTER 13

Dismas began to make one of several trips into the market to bring supplies back home to his family. It wasn't that he had that much money to be spending, for things were still quite expensive with the extra visitors in town for the census; it was just that he wasn't big enough to carry much at a time without help. He thought it best not to spend more than he had to in order to get help when there was truly no hurry. He was really looking forward to tonight's meal. His mother had promised to make him his favorite lamb stew. He was happier that she was having a good day than he was about the meal, but having both made the day even more special to him.

His mother was particularly loving toward him since Joseph and Mary left with the baby. She told him that she had truly been feeling the spirit of God since their visit and she was repeatedly telling him how grateful she was to have him as a son. He did not feel that special himself. He had only been doing what he thought was right, but it was still nice that she was proud of him. He began to feel like he was becoming more of a man. That was until his mother spit on a cloth and wiped the dirt from his cheek and then kissed him on the forehead before he ran off to the market again.

"I love you my son! Be careful! Hurry home and I will start your dinner!" she said to him as he trotted quickly down the hill and back into town. She then turned and ushered Jotham back into their modest room on the back of the stable while carefully setting Aram down on his mat as she entered the room.

On the hill, Benjamin was in prayer all morning and he knew that he finally had the courage to speak with her. With Dismas off into the town, he seemed like a good time for him to speak with Serah. He knew that it was very likely that she might just send him away, but he at least would be able to take the first steps to clearing his conscience by apologizing to her. He was sure that if the Angel was correct, they would need him again. How could they not? God would not lie to him. That much he was certain of. He started his journey down the hill to the stable.

It was then that he heard a noise that immediately filled him with terror. The sound of men, women and children screaming mingled with the sound of soldiers shouting and the hurried hoof beats of their mounts as they rode into the town. Was his mind playing some cruel trick on him? He closed his eyes as if to believe that when he opened them again, the objects of this terror would be gone. When he did open them again, his terror became even more real, for the scene playing out before his eyes was quickly becoming an unholy one. He saw the soldiers riding up to a family on the rode selling their goods, when one soldier suddenly stopped and without warning, jumped off his mount and ripped a child from the arms of his mother. What he did next could not be comprehended, for surely no man have done such a horrible thing. He drew his sword and without so much as a word, slew the child in front of his terrified family. The child's father could not restrain his fury and was struck down dead by another soldier behind him while his wife lay on the ground stricken in grief.

Benjamin was wild eyed in fear. These were Herod's men! He might have expected this from Romans, but this was far beyond what he expected from Herod. The king was mad for sure, but this, this was truly evil.

The men were back on their horse and he saw them heading toward the stable as several of the other soldiers immediately rode down into Bethlehem, swords drawn. Benjamin was no longer standing there frozen in fear. He knew what he had to do and leapt off of the rock he stood on. He ran as fast as his legs would carry him to the stable below. The memories of what had happened the last time this occurred drove him on even faster. He would not fail his family again.

Piram haggled with the potential buyer of one of his lambs when he saw the commotion on the road. He too was in shock, transfixed by what just occurred, and without thinking he left his buyer and hobbled as fast as he could to the stable. The soldiers were riding there quickly. He shouted ahead to Serah to take the boys and run but he was sure she would not hear him in time to take action. He made it in to the stable just before the soldiers arrived and he could hear them shouting to him to stop.

He knew he could not get around the stable in time to help, but he get THROUGH it in time. He lunged his body into the corner of the stable and tore the old dirty blanket down that partially separated the stable from the small dark room where Serah and the boys lived. Serah was startled by all the noise from outside, but became even more terrified when the old man tore through the wall behind her.

He said, "Serah, the soldiers are coming and you have no time to run. We need to hide you and the boys! Come with me quickly!"

She knew she trusted Piram and that was all she needed to know as she handed Jotham through the wall to the old man. As soon as she had done so a figure burst through the door of the room where she stayed with the boys and she was certain that this was the end. A flicker of recognition and she knew, "Benjamin? Is it you?"

"Yes my love. We need to save you and the boys now!" was his impassioned plea.

Piram had hurriedly shoved Jotham under a large pile of straw and furiously threw more on top of him to insure that he could not be seen. Jotham whimpered and sobbed loudly because he was so afraid. Piram warned him to be as quiet as he could until the soldiers were gone, and then turned back to get Serah and Aram. As he was about to turn, one of the soldiers ducked in to the stable. Piram turned back to face the man. It was then that he heard a man's voice in the room with Serah and he was certain that it was too late for them. It was as if the wind had suddenly left his lungs. He had spent most of his life in the service of others. It was God's will that he do so. And now, in the end, he would give his life for others. He knew he had to save Jotham even if it meant his own death.

The soldier clutched the old man's arm and dragged him closer to his face. He shouted, "Why did you run old man? What are you trying to hide from us?" It was then that Piram decided to fight with the only weapon he possessed, and he swung his crutch at the soldier's head with all of his might. It was a good swing and connected hard with the soldier's temple. The soldier's head snapped sideways on impact and he immediately fell to the ground unconscious. Piram had only a brief moment to savor his victory when another soldier stepped in. He looked at the scene before him. On the ground lie a soldier bleeding from a wound to the head and standing over him was an old man with a crutch still clutched in his two hands. He drew his sword and without saying a word, thrust it into Piram's side. Piram dropped to his knees and fell backward onto the pile of straw, further obscuring the boy from their sight.

As Piram lay gasping, unable to breathe, the soldier helped his wounded companion to his feet. Piram mouthed the words, "May God forgive you," and then drew his final ragged breath.

Benjamin was unaware of the struggle in the stable. He was still clutching Aram in his arms and he ducked in to the stable through the hole in the wall. He immediately caught the attention of the two soldiers. He froze. He saw his old friend Piram lying dead at their feet. He turned to duck back into the room but it was too late, they had already seen him and started pursuit. He pushed Serah back into the room so they could make their escape out of the other door. He felt a sudden burst of warmth and looked down to see a sword protruding from his chest. Serah screamed. He stared at the sword in disbelief. He knew that he was dying. He slowly and carefully handed Aram to her to protect him one last time and fell to his face at Serah's feet.

The soldiers both ducked in to the small dark room over the top of Benjamin's still form. Serah shrieked and turned toward the door to run. The first soldier grabbed her by the arm and twisted her to him. The other soldier tried to rip the screaming Aram from her arms. She would not have it. She was weak, but she knew that she had to give every last ounce of strength that God could give her to save her son, and she held him tight. She held him so tightly that the first soldier had begun to beat her in the head with his fist until she could hold no more and then she fell to the floor. She lay there fading from consciousness, crawling toward him as they carried him away. She willed herself to try and find the strength to fight more. She could hear Aram screaming as the soldiers carried him outside, and then he screamed no more. She sobbed in despair for she knew her son was dead. She looked next to her and saw Benjamin lying dead and she slowly crawled to him. She laid her body across his. She kissed the head of the man she once called husband and the world went black.

Across town everyone in the market scattered when the soldiers rode in. Some were just trying to hide from the soldiers for they knew not what their purpose was. They only knew it was dangerous to be around them. The rest were trying to make their way home to protect their own families. When they realized what the soldiers were doing to the children a great many of them came out of their hiding to fight, but it was a futile attempt to do so, for the soldiers had horses, weapons, and skill. The people of the town of Bethlehem did not. Many citizens of Bethlehem died trying to stop Herod's men.

Dismas had already dropped everything he had and tried his best to make his way back to his mother without being seen. He hid just inside a doorway but he was certain that he would be spotted soon because there was no room for him to hide any better. He tried to bang on the door hoping that someone would let him duck in, but they either were not home or they were too afraid to open. Either way, he was too exposed and he would have to make a run for it sooner or later.

He spotted two soldiers about to ride past him. One of them had a large gash on his head. They were heading into the center of the town toward the market. He pulled himself in tight to the door and prepared himself to run as fast as he could if they spotted him. They passed him and did not even notice him. Apparently they were too focused on their task to notice. When they were completely out of view, he looked around once more and then when he realized that it was clear, he turned and ran as fast as he could back home.

Along the streets he followed back out of the town he saw one scene after another that was eerily similar. There were many mothers and fathers screaming in despair because the soldiers had murdered their sons. It became clear to him now that the men were killing all the young boys but he could not understand why. What he did know is that he had to protect his brothers and he ran even faster back to the stable.

Out of breath, Dismas finally neared the stable. There did not seem to be anyone nearby except a woman on the road screaming over the bodies of her son and her husband. He was very afraid now. Had they already been here he wondered? He hoped they did not think to look for his family in the stable. Perhaps they were safe. He cautiously rounded the corner on the back of the stable and he saw it. Nothing in his life could have ever prepared him for what lie before him. Lying in the dirt was a small child's body. He was certain it was Aram. He feared that Jotham and his mother were dead too because he knew that his mother would not have left Aram out here like this if she were alive.

He trembled hard. He had never been so scared in his life. Not even when the Roman soldiers came last year had he felt this afraid. He stepped in to the small room cautiously and saw his mother lying across a man. She had a still oozing wound on her head but he could see she was still alive. Where was Jotham he wondered? He gently cradled her head to his lap when he noticed that the man lying next to her was his father. He was clearly dead. He could tell from the huge wound to his back. He wondered why he was here. Had he come to save them again? Dismas realized that he would never again have a chance to be together with his father and he began to cry.

Dismas tore a small strip of cloth from his cloak and held it to the gash on his mother's head, hoping to stop the bleeding. It was then that she slowly opened her eyes and saw him. When she realized it was her beloved son Dismas, she cried, but not because of pain. She cried because she was relieved that he was safe. She reached up and without words she stroked his face.

Dismas said, "Mother, I saw Aram and I saw Father. The soldiers killed them."

Serah took her hand from Dismas' face and held it to her mouth. She clenched her teeth and then cried "Aram . . ." She sobbed silently for a few more moments, and then looked Dismas in the eyes.

"Your father came back to us. He tried to save us and they killed him." she sobbed. "Please tell me you can forgive him now."

Dismas looked again to his father and with tears welling up in his eyes, he said, "I forgave him Mother, a long time ago." He sobbed a bit and continued, "I knew he would come back. I knew God would bring him home."

Dismas asked the next question not knowing if he really wanted to know the answer. "Mother, what did they do to Jotham?"

She realized at that moment that she did not see him with Dismas and said, "Piram tried to help us hide and he took Jotham into the stable. I saw him putting him under the pile of straw. Oh Dismas, go now and see if he is safe!"

Dismas lay his mother's head on the ground and ducked quickly through the hole in the wall and into the stable. He wasn't quite prepared to see his friend Piram lying on the straw. He cried out "Piram!" and ran to him hoping he was still alive but he could tell instantly that he was not. He heard sobbing from underneath Piram's body and heard Jotham say "Dismas are we safe? Are the soldiers gone?"

Dismas moved Piram's body to the side and then he dug wildly to pull his brother from his straw prison. He tucked Jotham under his arm and led him back to the room with his mother, careful not to let him see his father's body. Jotham cried out "Mother!" and ran to her. Dismas used this opportunity to cover his father with a blanket so that Jotham would be spared seeing the face of his dead father.

The boys huddled around their mother. Jotham cried and Dismas tried to care for her the best he could. Serah knew she was dying and she also knew it was coming fast. She put her hand on Dismas' cheek and said softly to him with ragged breath, "I am dying my son. I want you to know that you have made me so proud. Be true to God and follow his word and we will see each other again in heaven. Promise me you will take care of your brother. You must protect him."

"I will Mother. I promise I will." Dismas sobbingly replied.

His mother then gave a sigh and winced in pain. Her eyes then looked to heaven and she whispered her last words with a soft smile on her face, "I'm going to be with your father now . . ." and with that she died.

No sooner had her last breath left her lips; they heard the hoof beats of the soldiers riding nearer. Dismas immediately snapped into action and grabbed Jotham and quickly made his way back to the pile of straw beside Piram's body. He quickly covered up Jotham and then did his best to cover himself before the sound of the soldiers became dangerously close. He gave Piram's body a quick tug and pulled him over onto the top of himself to give him a last measure of protection from view. He had not counted on the fact that Piram's face would be directly in front of his. It unnerved the boy a great deal when he realized that he had to look into his friend's dead eyes. He wanted to look away but it was the only way he could see what was going on in the stable.

Outside he heard the soldiers stopping. He heard the sound of footsteps getting nearer and then they entered the stable.

"Nothing in here sir, just the old man. He must be the one that struck Ector earlier. They said they had to kill him."

The soldier that had clearly been the one in charge of the others said with a great deal of irony in his tone, "They must have had a terrible battle with this poor crippled old man." He looked almost sad to Dismas.

"Go look around quickly just to make sure there are no other male children. Have one of your men account for all of our soldiers outside. When they are all here, we will leave."

"Yes sir!" said the soldier and he quickly departed. The leader remained behind and he looked around him and looked to the body of Piram lying before him. When he was sure he was alone,

Castor started to wipe tears from his own eyes and he slowly sobbed. He then fell to his knees.

"Herod, what have we done here today?" he said to himself angrily. "God will never forgive us for this!" He sat silently on his knees for a long moment. His voice trailed off, "He will never forgive this . . ."

Castor rose to his feet, wiped the tears from his eyes, and took one last look around, briefly gazing on the body of Piram. He then put his helmet back on. A moment later a soldier walked in and gave a final report to him. "Sir, there are two dead adults and one dead child behind the stable and I've just been informed that all of our soldiers are accounted for."

"And you're sure that all the male children under two were taken care of? Because there will be heck to pay if we missed any. It will mean we all lose our heads. Are you ready to bet yours that we got them all?"

"Yes sir. We were very thorough. We may have actually taken care of a great deal more than just those under the age of two." The soldier clearly wasn't proud to say that, but he knew it to be true and there was no sense for him to hide what they all knew.

"Very well then, we leave immediately." He then walked outside and mounted his horse. "I'm certain we will be remembered throughout all of time for what we've done here today." He paused, "I hope we can all live with that . . ." With a kick to his horse they rode away.

CHAPTER 14

D ismas waited until he was certain that the soldiers were far enough away and when they were, he crawled out from under the body of his friend Piram. He hefted him up and then laid him over on his back, then with his hand brushed Piram's eyes closed. He turned to unbury his little brother from the pile of straw and then gave him his hand to pull him up. Jotham and Dismas both were completely drained of emotion. The shock of what they just survived, along with the accompanying crash after such an enormous adrenaline rush took its toll on the two young boys. Neither of them had the courage to look at the bodies of their dead family, so they sat.

Alta, Piram's wife, approached the stable screaming out his name. Dismas crawled to his feet and stepped into the doorway where he could see her. She immediately saw him and ran to him. When she reached him she grabbed his shoulders and said "Dismas, have you seen my Piram?" Dismas just stood his ground and looked down. Just then Alta saw the body of her husband lying on the ground. She screamed his name and ran to him, falling immediately to her knees beside him.

Dismas helped Jotham to his feet and the two of them walked outside and sat again. Dismas had no forces to go any further and he was quite certain from his appearance that neither did Jotham. He could not bear to be inside with Alta as she grieved her husband. He knew that he probably should be doing the same with his family but he could not bring himself to face such a terrible sight again. He certainly could not force it on his little brother. So they waited. What they were waiting for he did not know, but he knew that he needed time to think, so they would sit until he knew what to do.

After what seemed like an eternity, Alta stepped back outside wiping tears from her eyes and she sat next to the boys. "Poor boys . . . I was so blinded by my grief that I did not ask of your mother and Aram. Can I assume that they are dead also since you are here alone?"

Dismas nodded without looking up from his gaze at the earth beneath him. She pulled both of them close and cried again. He felt comforted by this and began to cry again himself. The emotions flooded from him as she held him close.

After a while, the tears stopped flowing and they knew they could not stay any longer. Alta stood and said, "Come on boys, you must come home with me. We'll send someone here to help take care of the bodies so we can bury them. Right now we need to get you two inside and get you taken care of."

Without a single word the boys stood and followed behind her like two little ducklings following their mother.

Alta and Piram lived just the other side of the market place. As they were beginning to get closer they could hear the voices of many people crying and wailing. They also heard a lone voice shouting, followed by many more loud voices.

A few more steps and Dismas saw the crowds gathering around a couple of men that appeared to be the leaders of this rabble. People were all shouting over each other but occasionally someone's voice could be heard over that of the others. "Why did Herod send his men for this?" What are we going to do about this?" "We have to fight back! We can't let him kill our children!"

Then one of the two men in front of the crowd said "Herod's men were told to kill the male children under two years of age. I heard them talking about it!" He continued, "They were looking for a child that Herod said was dangerous, a prophesied Messiah!"

Another person from the crowd shouted "Why were they looking here?"

The crowd murmured some more and then a lone voice shouted out a reply that caught the attention of the entire crowd. "Herod has a spy amongst us!"

Everyone shouted over each other but they could tell that most were asking only one word . . . "Who?"

One older woman with a ruddy face and a hawkish nose looked around and started staring at Dismas. He recognized her as the woman he had purchased medicine and food from earlier in the day just before the soldiers rode in.

She pointed her bony finger at him and shouted "You! Boy! You had gold coin earlier buying things here! Where did a boy like you get that kind of money? Tell me! Are you a spy?"

Every head turned to see the boy that had gotten her attention. They too wanted to know where he had gotten the money and it seemed the same question came at him from hundreds of different directions. He and Jotham were both beginning to be very afraid, and sensing this; Alta stepped between them and the crowd as if to protect them.

Just then another voice rose from behind the boys and Alta, "I know him! He works at the stable. I just came up the road and saw the leader of the soldiers come out of the stable just before the boy stepped out! He's the spy! He's the one that that brought this terror on us!"

The crowd moved in closer, clearly intent on getting their hands on Dismas. He and Jotham were terrified. Alta pulled them in tighter behind them and backed to the nearest wall with the boys behind her.

Alta shouted in her loudest voice, "STOP! I know this child and he would never do harm to anyone. His own family was killed by the soldiers, why would he help them?"

A majority of people began to shrink back after hearing this. After all, he was just a boy and if his own family were killed, surely he was not the spy. Still, there were a large number of people so blinded by anger, rage and grief that they refused to back down. For those people, only payment in kind would do. They would not be satisfied until they had their revenge.

During the confusion and the bickering that started to occur within the crowd, Alta slipped with the boys through the alley directly behind them and when they made it around the corner they ran. Alta was not very fast but her fear drove her faster and she clung tightly to their hands as she went. She slipped with them around a wall and before they knew it they stood in a small courtyard of Alta and Piram's home.

Alta wasted no time and immediately gathered a sack full of food and a waterskin. She ran back out of the home to the boys and put the strap of the food bag over Dismas and handed the waterskin to Jotham. She led the boys to the fence where she had one of the Piram's donkeys tied. Normally it would not be here, it would have been at the stable, but Piram had used him to bring a load of fresh straw to their home earlier intending to use it for a fresh change of straw in their mattresses. He had no time to return it, because when he saw the soldiers killing the male children, his first thought was to go to the stable and protect the boys.

Alta pulled the donkey closer to the fence and had the boys step up on it so she could boost them up on to his back. They could hear the crowd shouting. They were getting closer. Most people knew Alta and she was certain that was how they closed in so quickly.

She looked into Dismas face and said, "You must leave now! Go north. Try to make it to Jerusalem if you can, but go fast! You are in danger. You must go now and never return here! Do you understand me?"

Dismas could only nod. He was still in shock from what just happened. He probably would not have had the time to respond anyway, for Alta had slapped the back of the donkey hard. Startled, he ran. Jotham held him so tightly that both of them almost fell off of the animal as it began its startled run.

Dismas gained a better grip and finally had the confidence in his seat to look back at Alta who still stood staring at them as they rode away. He wondered what would happen to her. He knew the crowds would be angry with her for helping the boys escape.

The terrified animal ran quickly into the night with two even more terrified boys on his back.

CHAPTER 15

Morning came and both boys were near freezing. They were ill-prepared for a journey like the one they just began. The donkey had long since stopped running and it seemed that he was near exhaustion. Dismas had not allowed them to stop and rest for he feared that the men from the crowd would surely be after them. Jotham was still clutching his brother tightly, afraid that he might fall off.

"Brother, I want to stop. Please stop." Jotham pleaded. As much as Dismas felt they should continue, he knew for certain that the donkey could go no further without rest. He also feared that Jotham would fall asleep and lose his grip and surely fall. With all of these rocks around them, he was certain it would injure the young boy of he did.

Dismas slowed the animal to a stop and dismounted. He was feeling a bit sore and stiff after an entire night of riding. He turned slowly, his body aching all over, and helped his little brother off of the mount as well. Jotham plopped to the ground and promptly laid his head down right there and closed his eyes. Dismas knew that it was cool enough for him to know that now, but in about an hour or so things would begin to become unbearable when the sun spread its full measure out on the terrain before him. He looked around. There wasn't a single tree or any source of shade in sight. He knew they would be in trouble soon and he did not know what to do about it. They had only a little bit of water to share and hardly any food. He knew that the donkey would have no water and no food. There wasn't a thing in sight.

What should they do? Dismas mused in his head. They certainly could not turn back and he did not know where else to go because he was totally lost. They rode through the night and he was not certain even which direction they had even traveled. He had a feeling they were traveling North, but was not sure exactly. He searched all around them and saw no one and no roads. He started to become afraid but his body was not allowing him to do anything about it. Something was wrong. He was not feeling right. He became a little bit light headed and then suddenly, the world dissolved around him.

He was not sure how long he slept but when he awoke he was so thirsty he swore he would have drank water from a muddy hoof print if he could find one. His face was burned and his lips were dry. The sun seemed to be a full mid-day and Jotham was seated next to him holding his cloak over both his head and Dismas'. He too looked as if he were about to die from this terrible heat.

He looked around to take a drink from the waterskin that Alta had given them but did not see it. Not only did Dismas not see the water, he did not see the donkey. He looked at Jotham as if he would know the answer and said, "Where is the donkey Jotham?"

Jotham turned his head very slowly. His head seemed to feel to him that it was in mud, and he said, "I don't know Dismas. I woke up and he was gone." Jotham began to cry. "It's not my fault Dismas. I did not let him go. I was so tired. He ran away."

Dismas started to realize the full gravity of the danger they were in. He surveyed the landscape around them and still he saw nothing. There was not a single home, tree, body of water, or even a large rock close by, much less signs of a donkey. He wanted to follow his tracks but there were so many rocks surrounding him that it would be impossible.

He knew they were in great danger if they did not find shelter and water. He had to make a decision and he had to make it fast. He thought for a second and then he decided that the only logical thing they could do is try to make it to the road and follow it north to Jerusalem. The only problem with this plan was that he wasn't exactly sure where the road was. He only generally knew which way was north.

Dismas pulled his brother to his feet and helped him tie a bit of his cloak over the top of his head to protect him from the burning sun. He then did the same for himself. It wasn't going to help them for long, but maybe all they needed was a little time. He held Jotham's hand and then headed in the direction that he had chosen. He was not sure where they would go but he did know that if they stayed here they surely would die.

A few hours later Jotham began to really struggle to stay on his feet. Walking for him became very difficult. Dismas had always admired the fact that even when the boy was clearly suffering, he never complained. He hardly ever said a word. He had been this way since the Roman soldiers attacked last year. From time to time he would become emotional. You could see it in his eyes sometimes and it would be evident when he cried, but he would rarely ever say anything. Jotham had not said a word; he simply just started to fall behind. Dismas had long since let go of the boy's hand, but he never let him get more than a few feet behind him.

He tried his best to encourage Jotham to keep moving, but he too began to have great difficulty, and he was several years older than Jotham. He could not imagine how hard this was for him. He was too young really to even understand what was happening to them. This last two days would be a challenge even for a full grown adult, much less a five year old boy.

Jotham faltered and fell. Dismas tried to get him up but he would not rise again. "I can't" he said, and then he fell back down again. This time, Dismas, completely drained and exhausted sat back down next to him.

"Maybe we will rest for a few minutes Jotham. Will that help you?"

The small boy only nodded his head before passing out and his limp body leaned over into his big brother's lap. Dismas cradled Jotham's head in his own lap and tried to cover his brother from the blazing sun as best he could. Maybe a rest really would help and then they could start again. His mind began to slowly drift. He tried hard to fight it, but the sun took its toll on him, and soon he himself passed out falling over on to his brother.

Something more dangerous than the desert sun would soon be upon them.

CHAPTER 16

D ismas awoke first, not sure where he was. Had he been
dreaming? When he finally came to, it was almost
sundown and he found himself surrounded by people
he had never seen before. His heart raced. For a moment he
thought he and Jotham were caught by the crowd in Bethlehem,
but these men did not seem familiar to him at all . . . Jotham!
Where was his brother? He looked around frantically until he
saw his brother sitting just a few feet away. Jotham drank thirstily
from a waterskin with a short squat man sitting in front of him.
The man noticed Dismas sitting up and took the waterskin away
from Jotham and brought it to him.

Dismas had barely begun to drink when an older man said
"Enough!"

The man was tall with a medium build and a slight paunch
in his belly. He had shoulder length black hair with streaks of
white around its edges. His beard was similar, mostly black, but
with streak of white in it. He had a rather loud gravelly voice.
It sounded like the kind one might have if they spent a lot of
time yelling loudly. He was clearly the leader the way he moved

amongst these men. It wasn't that hard to tell when the men around him made a clear path for him wherever he walked. It was as if they feared even touching him. Whoever he was, Dismas was grateful that they had been found, for if they hadn't, it would have been a sure death for the boys.

The man looked at Dismas and said, "Come here boy!" The loudness and the sense of urgency in his voice compelled Dismas to move quickly. He could not move very fast, but he did his best. It was clear that making this man mad might be perilous for him and Jotham.

Dismas stood directly in front of the man and said "Yes sir."

"What's your name and how did you two get all the way out here in the middle of nowhere?" said the man.

"My name is Dismas sir. This is my brother Jotham. We were riding in the night and we got lost. Our donkey was missing this morning and we became lost in the desert."

Agitated, the man said, "Well Dismas and Jotham, I am Tiran. These men are my 'business associates'." With a slight whimsical tone of voice clearly meant to be ironic, complete with grand gestures, he continued, "We are free desert spirits and we prefer to travel the lonely desert helping to 'redistribute' the wealth of fellow travelers. Do you understand what that means Dismas?"

Dismas was too tired to be politically correct and answered truthfully, "Yes sir."

"Oh you do! Tell me lad, what does it mean to you?"

"It means you're all highwaymen!" He blurted. He wasn't sure it was so smart to have replied this way but Tiran did not seem at all to him like a man that would take too kindly to a boy that does not know how to tell the truth either.

"Tsk, tsk, young Dismas, the real thieves are the rich men that make their fortune off of the labor of slaves. Slaves that should be free men, and be their own masters!"

Tiran suddenly took a more serious tone with him and grabbed his cloak and pulled Dismas close enough he could smell his stale breath. "Now listen here you little desert rat with a smart mouth; the ONLY reason I didn't just continue on and let you die is because of this!" He reached his hand out in front of himself and opened it. Dismas looked down and in Tiran's hand he saw a shiny gold coin in it. That could mean only one thing, that Tiran had found Dismas' last gold coin.

"Would you tell me where I found this coin," said Tiran. Dismas knew full well that lying now was pointless for the man clearly found it on Dismas when he was unconscious. That meant that they were likely just going to rob the boys and then leave them. The coin must have intrigued him in some way.

Dismas nervously replied, "On me. You found it on me."

"And how did a little desert rat like you come to have a nice shiny gold coin? Are you rich? Maybe your daddy will pay nicely to have his two little boys back home safe and sound. Maybe he will pay more if he gets you both back in one piece and unharmed. Tell me! Where did you get it?"

Dismas did not answer. He was afraid. He did not want to put anyone in danger. He especially did not want Joseph and Mary to be hurt.

When Dismas did not reply, Tiran motioned to one of his men and said "Abba, take the small one."

The man that Tiran called Abba pulled a knife out of his waist and then grabbed Jotham by the hair and lifted him up. He then drew the small knife with the curved blade up to Jotham's throat. Jotham's eyes were wide open in fear and he began to breathe very hard and very rapidly.

Dismas shouted "No! Stop! Don't do anything to him, I'll tell you where I got it. Just don't hurt my brother; he's all I have left."

Tiran feigned surprise and said "Well, well, well, isn't that sentimental? If it's all the same to you, Abba is going to leave that knife right where it is and you're going to tell me now or I'm going to order him to slit his throat. Are we clear?"

Shaking, Dismas said, "Yes sir." He tried to think as fast as he could what to say when suddenly it occurred to him . . . he needed to be useful. If he wasn't they would kill him and Jotham both and them leave their bodies out here in the desert for the animals.

He thought for just a moment and then blurted out, "I stole it. I stole it! We ran away because we got caught. Please, I told you! Now please let my brother go!"

Tiran had a rather strange look on his face and Dismas could not tell what it was, but it almost looked like he was excited. "So you are telling me that a little rat like you lifted this gold coin and managed to make a good escape?"

"Yes sir. That's what I did." Dismas lied, but because he was sure that it was right thing to say in this moment, he had a little more confidence. Apparently it was convincing enough that he though Tiran was starting to believe him and his story.

Tiran stood up straight and then motioned his head with a slight nod toward Abba and he dropped the boy to the ground. Tiran then paced a few steps as if pondering the next question before saying, "I would like to know who the benefactor of this shiny gold coin was. Perhaps we should go and help him 'redistribute' his wealth to the poor . . . namely us!" he said and everyone laughed with him.

"What do you say you take us to where you found this coin and show us who you stole it from, huh? If you do I may decide to let one of you live. Who knows, if there is enough wealth to redistribute, I might feel generous and let both of you live. What do you think men?" Tiran's band of highwaymen all cheered.

Dismas realized his new predicament. He could not say he took it in Bethlehem, for returning there could get him caught and the townsfolk would surely kill him. If he told them he got it from Joseph, the highwaymen would surely try to track down their caravan and they would be in danger. He couldn't do that. Suddenly he thought he knew the perfect answer.

"I took it from some rich old men in a large caravan on the road. They had a lot of guards. You could probably never get close enough to steal from them without a fight." Dismas was proud of himself. He had found a way to keep the highwaymen from attacking the Magi and their caravan too. He just was not sure that he had proven he could be useful enough to keep alive yet. That was when Tiran gave him the opportunity without even knowing it.

"Well then how did you get away with it? If they are so well guarded how did you do it? Be quick now! Don't lie to me!"

Without much thought, Dismas said, "I am small and quick. I snuck in while they were sleeping and I took it."

Tiran smiled and said, "Well then, we are so lucky to have such a good thief in our presence. We should take you with us and let you repeat your performance. Now tell me . . . where can we find these rich old men?"

Dismas replied, "They have a caravan going north from here but they are at least two days ride ahead of us."

Tiran pointed his finger in the air and made a quick signal that apparently was signaling his men to mount up and then they all scattered towards their mules, donkeys and camels.

Dismas was still standing there and Jotham had run to his side holding him. He looked to Tiran and said, "What about us? I did what you said. Aren't you going to take us too? You said you would let us live if we were useful. Didn't I just prove that? Won't you need me to help you steal more gold?"

Tiran sat back on his camel and sighed, then looked back at the boy. He seemed to have a little compassion in him from the look he gave. "Yes, I believe there might be some use for you for a few more days. But I'm warning you right now. The second you or that other little desert rat brother of yours becomes a burden in any way; we'll slit your throats and leave you for the wild dogs. Am I clear?"

"Yes sir." Dismas replied. He was pretty certain that the old man would do exactly that. He was determined to keep them alive, even if it meant that they had to rob someone to do it. He promised his mother he would keep Jotham alive and although she would not be happy, there would be time to repent later.

Tiran looked over to a tall thin wiry boy perhaps only a couple of years older than Dismas, and clearly the only other person even close to his age in this band. "This is my son Gestas. He'll get you a mount to use. We just so happen to have had a 'vacancy' recently from someone who was no longer useful to me. You can use it until I kill you."

That last statement clearly startled Dismas and he was afraid to move. Tiran could tell he had terrified the boy perhaps a little too much and said, "Relax boy. If you are useful I may let you live a little longer. Now get mounted up, we have a hard ride ahead of us."

Dismas was about to turn around when he suddenly got a fist to the side of the head. His head was swimming. He looked up to see Gestas standing there with an angry look on his face and his fist still raised. He said to the older boy, "Why did you do that?"

Gestas replied with indifference, "Because I don't like you that's why. Now get on that donkey before I beat you again."

Dismas gave Jotham a big push and then Jotham in turn helped him get a leg up and over on the donkey they were given.

They then did their best to catch up. The two young orphans now had a purpose. They were on a mission to rob the Magi . . .

CHAPTER 17

I t was an incredibly rough few days for the boys. It seemed like one indignity after another. What both of the boys needed was just a little time to rest and absorb everything that had just happened to them. It was clear that resting would not happen anytime soon. In fact, it appeared that their predicament would likely get much worse before it got any better.

The band of highwaymen were making good time heading north. It was clear to Dismas that they traveled very light and very fast. They had good stock and carried very little. He was also keenly aware that another reason they seemed to travel very quickly is that they knew these hills very well and it allowed them to take some little known roads and paths to get north. It was clearly the main reason why this caravan seemed to be getting north much faster than the normal travelers would have made it.

One of Tiran's riders, a man named Thomas, had been used as a scout for the main group. He was able to move around very quickly because he had the only horse amongst the bunch. It wasn't common for anyone to have a horse after the Romans increased their numbers in the region. If they saw a horse they would just take it from the owner. It was much easier for them to get around on one and to the Romans it added a certain amount of dignity to an otherwise undignified assignment. Tiran was wise to allow only this one because to have more than that would clearly have attracted a lot of attention to them. Thomas' horse helped him to get around very quickly and the man seemed to be a very experienced rider. He was the clear choice for the job of scout.

Thomas came back to the group early on the second morning and reported to them that he had spotted a large caravan. Tiran was certain it was the one that Dismas had described to them and called Dismas up to the front of the highwaymen's caravan so he could confirm it with him. Dismas made his way to the front as quickly as he could. He did not want to do anything that might make his and Jotham's situation more precarious than it had already been. When he reached the front of the column, Tiran had Thomas relay to him what he had observed in this caravan he had spotted. Thomas also added that the caravan was moving very slowly and that they had quite a few men keeping guard as they traveled. He was certain that unless they had a stealthy plan, that the well-armed men would mean great trouble for Tiran and his band of highwaymen.

Dismas was certain it was the Magi from the description and he relayed this confirmation to the leader of the group of bandits. Tiran ordered Thomas to ride ahead and keep an eye on them and then when they stop to make camp, he was to ride back to them and report it. Thomas also did as he was told. Even though he seemed to be the most trusted of Tiran's men, he still feared the man and did not want to put himself in danger any more than he had to. That was something Thomas had in common with Dismas and Jotham's predicament.

Tiran gathered his men around and discussed the plan with them. He had decided that the best course of action would be for the men to wait until the caravan had bedded down and then send a few men in to incapacitate the guards quietly. Then the rest of them would ride in quickly, disarm the remaining men, and steal the gold and whatever else they could get their hands on.

It seemed to be a solid plan, but Dismas worried about the possibility of violence, or that the kind old Magi would be harmed. He pondered all the choices available to him that might avoid any chance of blood being spilled and he could think of none. At least he could think of none that allowed him and Jotham to live. It seemed that fate had dealt Dismas and his little brother a very cruel hand and they must soon accept their lot in life. He doubted very seriously now that these men would ever just let them go. He knew that if they were to escape they would be caught and killed. No, his only hope of keeping them alive is to become 'useful' as Tiran had phrased it, and hope that he would allow them to live. If an escape could be made, he would have to wait until a much better moment . . . if it ever came.

The highwaymen were gathering around to have a rest and to have a meal. They had been riding very hard this last two days and Tiran wanted them to be fed and well rested before they attempted to take on these men of the Magi's caravan. He was sure that the plan was a solid one but he did not want to take any chances. Being cautious is why a man like him had been able to survive so long in the first place. He would not throw caution into the wind now. This was especially true on this occasion. If these men had the money he thought they did it would mean that they could all take a much needed rest for a while. After all, what good was it to make money if you never took the time to spend it?

He used to look forward to making it back into Jerusalem every time he was free. A few years back he had met a beautiful woman named Mira and she had stolen his heart. For many years he used every opportunity he could to make it back there to see her. She had married poorly in life while she was very young. Her husband was many years her elder and he died not long after they were wed. During her marriage to this man she became pregnant and bore him a son. She had no one else left in her life and her son, Gestas, had been her pride and joy. She truly loved this boy with all of her heart.

Mira met Tiran not long after Gestas was born and they had immediately been drawn to each other. Were it not for the fact that he made a living as a highwayman, he probably would have married her. Just as well that he did not though, because he knew that he had rambling blood in his veins and could never stay in one spot for very long. Fortunately for him, she knew this and accepted it. Maybe that was one of the reasons he loved this woman so much. Because she knew what he was and did not judge him. Tiran was drawn very close to the two and he loved

Gestas as if he were his own son. He never failed to give money to Mira to care for him and to take care of herself. On one of his visits home he found that Mira had taken ill and he stayed with her for months to try to nurse her back to health. Even after he realized that it would do him no good, he stayed with her because he did not want her to die alone. Gestas was a very loving child to her and was always there when she needed him. This was a difficult time for the two, watching her die slowly.

One rainy morning she never woke again and Tiran had never loved another woman since. He knew that Gestas would probably have been much better off if he had been left for a loving family to take care of, but he selfishly wanted to keep the boy with him. Not only did he truly love him, he knew that Gestas was the only piece of Mira he had left. He chose to take the boy with him. The life was hard for them, but Gestas had always had an impressionable boy's interpretation of what life would be like as a highwayman and he was drawn to the glamorized view he had in his head of the life he would live. He soon found out that it was not easy to be thought of so lowly by others or to be known as a killer. It wasn't easy for everyone to be afraid of you or to live in fear of being caught and crucified by Roman soldiers every single day of this miserable life. Tiran was tough with him, and gave him no special favor in this group. He knew that his men would not respect Gestas if they ever felt that he had not earned his place amongst them. In fact, Tiran went to such lengths to avoid the appearance of favor with the boy, that he often treated him much more harshly than he did all of the rest of his men. It was this reason that Gestas always seemed so bitter. How could someone possibly love you if they treat you this way?

This was one of those days when Tiran had been particularly harsh with Gestas. He thought it odd that Tiran was so amazingly accommodating to the two young boys that had just joined them. What had they done to earn his favor? Surely it was not because they led him to this caravan that was nothing. Gestas imagined that they probably would have spotted them on their own even without them. At least the little one had the decency to act like he was afraid and keep his mouth shut. He was starting to like him a little, but Dismas he could not stand. He did not know why, but he felt that his father favored him more than he did his own son, and this truly bothered him. That's why when the boy walked past him he had to stick his foot out and trip him. Dismas fell to the dirt hard. He stood up quickly as if he wanted to fight, but then took a moment to think and walked away wiping the dirt from his lips. Gestas knew that he could be provoked very easily and made it a personal goal to get Dismas to fight back. It was in that moment that he hoped he could put him in his place with everyone watching. Maybe then he could win their respect . . . maybe then he could win his father's respect.

The men soon had eaten their meals and had laid down for a short sleep. It was fortunate for them that the clouds were out this day or it would truly have been a miserable one, for this location was a bit more exposed to the elements than most. They had to stop here because if they were to go further, they would risk being detected by the Magi. Soon they would begin their assault on the caravan and would have a lot of riches to show for it. Tiran knew there was one thing he could count on in this moment, and that was that every man was dreaming in his head about how to spend his share of the money. Good for him, he thought. Greedy men worked harder and were easier to manage. He understood greed. He lived with it his entire life. Never one to work, he would just let someone else do it for him. Plus, he really enjoyed the freedom he felt. Yes, it was dangerous, but even that was a small reward in itself, for it made him feel even more alive.

The men were just starting to arouse from a late afternoon slumber when they heard the hoof beats of Thomas' horse returning to their camp at a full trot. The old horseman relayed the news to Tiran that the caravan made camp for the night and he gave a full account of the positions of their livestock and all their guards. It sounded like easy pickings.

Tiran rallied the leaders of this bunch and gave them all their assignments. As they started to disperse, Dismas approached him and asked Tiran what he wanted him to do. He patted the boy on the head and said, "I still don't trust you yet but I will let you do something very important. When my men reach the camp, they will dismount and many of them will walk in quietly to begin the attack. These men will need someone to hold their mounts for them for when they return. Do you think that you and your brother can handle that? Because if you can't I'll just have Abba deal with you right here and we'll be done with you."

"We can do that sir." Dismas knew that no other reply would be acceptable. Even though he was just guarding the mounts, he knew that Tiran trusted him to do something very important, which meant that maybe; just maybe, they had a chance to live. Perhaps if the riches they stole from the Magi were great enough, he might be inclined to not only let them live, but live without the constant threats of throat slitting. Dismas only hoped that no one would be hurt in this night's raid.

Tiran then gave the familiar signal to mount up and the men quickly made it to their mounts and then began the ride north.

Dismas grabbed Jotham and ran to their donkey. They were the last to mount and were already being left behind. Dismas kicked the poor donkey's flanks hard and he began to run. This would be a rough ride again, he could tell. The pace they were traveling at would be difficult for the donkey to maintain even if he did not have two scared boys on his back.

Dismas began to think of his mother again. He wondered if she would be ashamed of him for what he was about to do or if she would be proud that he was able to keep them alive this long. He suspected it would have been a little of both. He remembered Joseph's lesson and he prayed that he would have a chance one day to ask God to forgive him. For now he would have to live with his decision . . . or die with it. Only time would tell.

CHAPTER 18

The Magi's caravan had found a nice spot down in the bottom of two hills that offered a natural break from the cool wind that kicked up all afternoon. Indeed it had been nice to have clouds this day for the sun was particularly unkind to travelers these last few days. Unfortunately the clouds brought much cooler weather, which at times in the desert, could be almost as uncomfortable as full sun. Finding this place was fortunate because the two small hills on their flank offered them a respite from the wind that dogged them all afternoon and made them feel uncomfortable. This had truly been a long trip and these men were all but certain to want it to be over with soon.

When the caravan had unloaded the stock for the night, the servants set about preparing the evening meal for everyone. Two men set up the fire while two other men took all of the livestock to tie them up at a small tie line set up between two trees. The men hired to accompany the Magi as personal guard set up their nightly watch and the rest of them searched for a comfortable place to bed down for the night. The guards were on a particularly high alert since being informed by the Magi that Herod may be sending men out to get them. After a few days of traveling, they became more lax about this task, thinking that the worst was now over since they were able to make it so far north. Little did they know they were being stalked by men equally as dangerous to them.

Melchior had spent the better part of the last hour arguing with Gaspar about the usual topics of philosophy while Balthazar did his best to hold his tongue since he had a completely different view. He did not do this because he did not want to argue, it was simply that he was just too tired to argue at that moment. Right now he just wanted what all of them wanted, some food in their belly and a place to sleep.

Soon after the meal, the topics went those more of reflection on days past. The two older men were merrily recalling people they used to know. Many of their past acquaintances were long gone before Balthazar had even been born. All the same, Balthazar reveled in these times because he would usually get a turn to tell stories of his own. The stories were of his home and some of the tales he had been taught as a child. The older men were often mesmerized when he did. They had a deep appreciation for learning and they enjoyed hearing new tales and new stories to add to the repositories of their mind. These three men had grown very close over the years. Indeed, they had all three become like brothers and shared a bond that went beyond friendship. They were very close before they started this journey. The countless miles they travelled to find the Messiah had brought them much closer. The days since discovering him had all been magical. The joy that meeting him had brought into their lives could not be measured. They were not sure what changes that the child would usher into this world but they all prayed that they would live long enough to see it. Soon they were all asleep. Little did they know that death was stalking them and tonight he would visit . . .

Melchior was not asleep for long when a familiar uncomfortable feeling began to rise up in him. He always hated this time. Alas, it was something he had been dealing with for several years now and it was common for many men his age. The urge to have to relieve himself several times in the night had become all too often for him and it was time once again. This was one of the reasons why the old man always made his bedroll close to where he could make a quick exit to a convenient place to do his business and get back without waking everyone up. He slowly rose to his feet and made the trek to the tree line where he could relieve himself again. He had just done his business and was about to make the return trip when he looked up and saw a large man with a scarred face standing directly in front of him, knife in hand. It was that brief moment Melchior was grateful he had finished his business because he had an immediate urge to do so again. The scarred man made a quick back and forth motion with the knife as if to signal to Melchior to be silent.

As Melchior looked over the man's shoulder he could see several other men stealthily were disabling the guards and others coming in behind them and taking up station near the clumps of men bundled up on the ground. Melchior began to feel a real fear that these men were about to kill and he let out a quick shout

"Brothers!" That was all he could get out before the scarred man struck him over the head.

Melchior awoke with his hands tied behind his back and lying right where he was so unceremoniously dumped on the ground moments earlier. His faced was half buried in the dirt. He arose when he heard the shouting of someone that had a very loud but gravelly voice. It was not a voice that was familiar him. He realized it had to be one of the bandits. As he sat up he noticed that both Balthazar and Gaspar were tied up next to them and that they and all of their men were bound in a similar fashion and surrounded by about twenty men brandishing knives and swords. Both Balthazar and Gaspar appeared to have been beaten.

Tiran noted that Melchior was now awake. "Welcome back to the world of the living old man. I thought my man Abba had struck you too hard and killed you."

Tiran approached Melchior very menacingly and said "Perhaps you are smarter than these other men. I was asking your friends here where you were hiding the rest of your riches at and they don't want to seem to answer my questions. Maybe you will be more cooperative. The only thing we've found is this small cache of coins, and from the looks of your caravan and your fancy clothes, I'm thinking you probably have more."

Melchior steeled himself for a beating for he was sure that his answer would not please this man. "We are but simple travelers passing through sir. We have no more."

Melchior was correct. This man was not pleased with his answer and he swung a fist at the man's face striking him hard.

"Wrong answer grandfather! You see, these other men have already told me who you all are, and I already know you are no simple traveler. Perhaps you have noticed the bruising on their faces? They tried to tell me the same thing the first time I asked. They became more obedient after my gentle persuasive techniques." He leaned into Melchior's face again and said, "Now, one more time 'Magi' . . . Where are you hiding the rest of your riches?"

Melchior steeled himself bravely again and said, "You are correct, we are of the Magi, but if you know anything of us, you must know that we are simply scholars. We travel much in search of knowledge. That is why we find ourselves in this place. As much as I we hate to disappoint you, there are no other riches."

Again, Tiran was not pleased with this answer and struck Melchior square on the face, this time even harder than the last. "Well then grandfather, can you tell me why three simple scholars are traveling with such a large caravan and you have so many servants and guards. That is surely not what one would expect to see if you truly were scholars. Who are you?" He then struck Melchior again.

Gaspar, fearing Melchior's stubbornness would only lead to all of their deaths suddenly shouted "Stop! Don't hit him again. I will tell you what you wish to know. But only if you promise not to harm anyone."

Both Melchior and Balthazar turned to their friend, not quite sure what he was about to say, but they knew he was smart enough not to endanger them or the child Jesus with his reply. He was very quick witted and they were certain a solution had just come to him. All the same they knew it had to be convincing so they had to make it appear as though he were about to betray them. They both shot hard looks at him and said "No Gaspar!" in unison.

Tiran approached Gaspar and said "So you are the smartest of the smart men, eh? Let's hear your song old bird, but I'm warning you. If it does not make me feel like dancing, I might just kill you."

"I understand" was Gaspar's reply. He swallowed hard and readied himself for his attempt at saving their lives.

"Well, start singing old bird" said Tiran as he stood back up.

Gaspar was clearly feeling more comfortable now and began his story. "You see kind sir we really are of the Magi. We are indeed scholars as we have said. The man you have been calling 'grandfather' is our top scholar, although I don't know why," Gaspar scoffed, "he hasn't had an original idea since before my friend Balthazar here was born." A couple of Tiran's men chuckled at the comment, which immediately drew his attention. When he turned to shut them up, Gaspar whispered through the corner of his mouth "Just play along" to his brothers.

Gaspar straightened himself up again and continued. "Well, you see, a while back he began prattling on about how the earth was round and that if you were to get into a boat you could sail actually sail around it. Of course it was a completely idiotic theory and I disagreed with it."

"I don't 'prattle'" shot back Melchior with indignation.

Balthazar took his turn and smiled at Melchior, and said, "Oh yes you do. I've been silent for too long about this but, YES, you do prattle, you prattle morning, noon and night, we are all sick of it . . ."

Before Melchior could retort Tiran said "Shut up!" He looked around him and almost every man chuckled now at the exchange between the Magi. He looked back to Gaspar and said, "Tell me how the old man's prattling led to you being here and be quick about the answer."

"Well sir, as I was saying, Melchior had this idiotic theory about how you could sail around the world and of course we all disagreed with him. But despite that he kept prattling on about it constantly. Finally he had convinced several of our fellow Magi to allow him to take a caravan to the east, secure a ship, and then confirm his theory. They were especially fine with it when he said he would use his own money . . . you see he comes from a very wealthy family and occasionally he consults royal persons and other persons of interest and they pay him well. In reality, I think they really just wanted him to shut him up about it. I know that many of our order wanted only to see him return in shame . . ."

Tiran interrupted, "So why are you two here with him then?"

Balthazar, certain where Gaspar was going with his story, said "We volunteered. There was no way we were going to let this mad man disappear into the desert with all that money. We figured as old as he is the trip would probably kill him, and why not keep all that money for ourselves?" Gaspar nodded in agreement.

Melchior added his touch to the story about him being old and crazy and interrupted with his indignation "I do not prattle!" The comment solicited raucous laughter from Tiran's men, and even Tiran himself smiled. This gave Gaspar some confidence that his story was working.

Tiran quickly took a more serious, threatening countenance on his face that immediately struck that new found confidence in Gaspar. "So, I get it. You intended to rob the old man. I personally would have just slit his throat as soon as I got out of sight of your other Magi friends and just taken his money then. It certainly would have saved you having to listen to this for as long as you probably have. It still doesn't answer my main question . . . where is the money? You certainly could not have secured a ship with no more than we have found here. Tell me where you are hiding it and we may let you all live . . . albeit a little light of valuables and perhaps an exchange of livestock."

Gaspar prepared himself to continue with a more serious tone. He had thought of something these men would completely understand and he hoped that by sharing a common enemy it might generate some favor from them and keep them safe from further harm. He really did not care about any of the personal belongings; he just did not want anyone to be harmed. After meeting the child Jesus he was certain now that earthly belongings had much less meaning than they ever had before. He was certain that his colleagues both felt the same way.

Gaspar continued, "You see kind sir, we were about to cross over into Herod's lands when a patrol of his men caught up with us. We had a similar experience with them as the one we experience tonight. So you can see kind sir, that we are all too familiar with our current predicament."

Tiran's face betrayed his feeling of mutual understanding with these men now. Gaspar was certain he had made the right choice of action. He continued his tale. "His man Castor, the leader of these men, threatened us with execution if we did not pay tribute to King Herod."

Tiran recognized the name and said "You met Castor, that slimy little parasite?"

"You know this man too then?" was Gaspar's reply.

Tiran shifted uncomfortably at the thought of this man and said "You could say that. I have crossed paths with him before. He has been working very hard to make sure they don't cross again. A goal he and I both share. Continue . . ."

Gaspar was encouraged by the reply and he continued. "Well, as I was saying. He threatened to have us executed if we did not pay tribute to King Herod, so we paid them, very handsomely I might add. We thought that would be then end of it, but not long after we entered the Kingdom of Herod, they caught up with us again and robbed us of the rest. We had only very little left after they were done. We have been trying hard to make our escape north because we fear crossing paths with them again . . . And here we are . . ."

The story suddenly gave Tiran a revelation that Castor was perhaps not as 'clean' as he made himself out to be, that indeed he was a thief too, just like he was. Only Castor got to hide behind the cloak of the King of Thieves himself, Herod.

"Ok, so that may explain why you three really smart men don't have much to show right now, but I hope you don't mind if I try to confirm a little more of this story do you?"

"Certainly kind sir," said Gaspar.

Tiran turned and shouted "Dismas! Come to me!"

The boy's name struck absolute fear in all three men for now they truly felt they were in danger of being revealed. But, even worse, the child Jesus could be endangered now as well. The three men sat petrified in fear as the boy approached. They were even more so as the boy's face slowly came into view from the light of the fire. Had he been listening to their story?

Tiran placed his hand on the boy's head and said, "Dismas do you know these men?"

"I don't know them, but I have seen them. I cared for their camels once when they had a rest a few days ago" was the response of the boy. He was very nervous when he saw the men, for he was afraid that they would reveal his lie to Tiran. He was absolutely terrified that they might have said something to Tiran that would put Mary and Joseph and their baby in danger. The expression on his face was a mirror of the terror they had on theirs. Somehow he sensed that they were probably in the same predicament he was in and had to resort to lying to this dangerous group of men to stay alive.

Tiran, looked to the men and said, "Do you recognize the little desert rat? Is he the same boy you caught stealing some coin from you? Pardon me, almost caught, since he and his little desert rat brother apparently stole from you and got away from you 'highly' intelligent men." Tiran smirked and continued, "Do you?"

Now the men sensed that, similar to them, the boy had likely been caught in a lie as well to save his life. They knew that if this band of men had Dismas and Jotham, that something had to have happened to their family, which could only mean one thing. Herod's men must have been following them and now they had placed the child Jesus in danger. Did they make it out in time? They could only hope. They needed to go along with the lie to save the boys' life, and maybe even their own.

"Yes he is" said Gaspar. "We thought he got away. I suppose you caught him instead. I'm sure you won't let us have back what he stole, but I don't suppose you will let us keep the boys and make sure that they are appropriately punished would you? We have been cooperative."

"What, and leave him with a crazy old man and two of his thieving friends who would rob one of their own? You must be crazy to think I would allow that. No, I have started to grow fond of the little vermin. They are much better off in the company of Herod's finest citizens. We represent our beloved king in the truest manner for we are trying our utter best to be exactly like him . . . this is why we roam the deserts and exact our 'tribute' from other travelers. We wish to be more like our beloved King Herod."

Tiran looked again at the boy and said, "No, I'm thinking about keeping them. Besides, without him I would never have found you three. Although, we have found so little of your riches left that it was hardly worth the effort."

Only a few feet away from the men, and just out of earshot, Mathias had managed to get his hands free of the ropes binding them. He was not about to let these men get away with everything they had. If they took what was left it would leave them with no means to return home. He feared that they would be hunted down by Herod's men and killed and he knew they needed a means to escape this dreadful land and its miserable people. He would make a move the first chance he got.

Now seemed to be the best time he would ever have. He did not know who the boy was but he appeared to have some kind of connection with the leader of this group. Was it his son? He could not hear what was being said between the man and his Magi masters but he sensed danger for all of them. He leapt to his feet and overpowered Tiran's man that stood next to him and took his dagger from him. He crept forward in the dark and quickened his approach to the boy when he knew that the light of the fire would expose him. He grabbed Dismas by the hair and put his dagger to the boy's throat. He was careful at this point not to expose his back to anyone that might get close to him.

Tiran stood just far enough from the boy after Mathias grabbed him that he was in no position to take action. All the same, his dagger was instantly out and ready for action if the right moment presented itself to him.

Mathias was clearly nervous but he was already committed to this action so he knew he needed to see it through regardless of the outcome. The real predicament he was in was that both he and the Magi knew that he would do no harm to the boy and the Magi were now certain that Tiran was not a man to back down, especially since the boy he held probably meant nothing at all to him.

"Everyone just drop your weapons and leave and I won't kill the boy!" Mathias nervously shouted.

Mathias clearly did not expect Tiran's reply of, "Go ahead and kill him, he means absolutely nothing to me." He was confused by this. It made his next choices more difficult for he had not counted on this answer.

Gaspar hoped to diffuse this situation by trying to talk Mathias into letting the boy go before anyone got hurt. "Mathias, let the boy go I order it!"

"No master. I have to save us all from these bandits. We can't let them kill us."

Gaspar pleaded, "Mathias, let them boy go, you won't hurt him, you know you won't. Don't put him at risk. Let him go."

Mathias became more agitated because now he clearly did not know what to do. This was a dangerous moment for Dismas because, in shaking, the man had begun to cut the boys neck by accident. A dark red trickle began to run down his neck and they all knew he was in trouble.

In Dismas' desperation he knew only that he was about to die and he was afraid. Without thinking he made a grab for the hilt of the knife and it startled Mathias. Mathias had been so concentrated on protecting himself from Tiran's men that he did not realize that the boy might be the one to take action.

Tiran detected the brief moment of surprise and made a quick grab for the boy. The sudden movement of the man prompted Mathias to step back, and in doing so, he tripped on a bedroll behind his foot. Tiran had a hold of Dismas' cloak. When Mathias fell he was still clutching the boy. It was just enough to twist Dismas around where he faced Mathias with the hilt of the knife now in Dismas hand. The weight of the boy falling plunged the knife deep into Mathias' chest. He let out a gasp of air and breathed no more. Death was quick for the man.

To all who had seen this, it appeared as though the boy had turned on the man who held him and pushed him to the ground and put a knife in him. When Dismas stood up he looked at everyone. He was in shock. What had he done? It was an accident. He had not meant to kill the man, but here he stood, over the man's body and his death had been his fault.

Tiran, clearly surprised by what he witnessed, was the first to speak. "Well what do you know? The boy's got talent. Can't say I saw that in him, but I am impressed." He looked at the Magi. The event clearly distressed them a great deal. They must have been close this man. "How about you three telling me know where the rest of the money is and we'll be on our way."

Balthazar directed the man to a hidden pocket on one of the saddle bags on the ground to his right. In there, Tiran found what was left of the money the Magi were hiding. The hidden pocket was designed to protect the last of their money in case they were ever robbed. Apparently it served no useful purpose this time.

Dismas was still in shock over the death of the man they called Mathias and he stood in the same spot without moving. It appeared to everyone who saw him that he was a cold blooded killer and that his intention in just standing there was to strike fear in all that saw him. Nothing could have been further from the truth. As he looked at the Magi still on the ground he could see they were all looking at him with contempt. He was ashamed. He turned and walked away. He retreated back to his assigned post with the livestock. Jotham looked at him in terror. He had seen what just happened and now he was terrified of his own brother. As Dismas approached him, Jotham grabbed Gestas and hid behind him as if to protect him from his own brother. Gestas said nothing, but held the boy's shoulder to comfort him. As Dismas passed him, Gestas looked him in the eye and smiled. At last, they had something in common. They were both killers.

CHAPTER 19

The highwaymen concluded their business by rounding up all the other valuables they could find and loading them onto their mounts. Some of the men saw fit to exchange their mounts with the mounts of the Magi's caravan. Tiran allowed the Magi and the rest of their men to live. He saw no need to provoke further revenge on him and his band of highwaymen. Robbing was dangerous enough for them for they would surely be executed for this alone, but killing would only encourage greater numbers of Roman troops on the roads trying to catch them. That simply would not do. Still, occasionally in this line of business someone will press your hand on the issue and he was left with no other alternative. He did not blame the boy for killing the man. It was self-defense. Also, Tiran firmly believed that the Magi would be so focused on avoiding any further entanglements with anyone of authority that he doubted they would report their man's death.

He did choose though to leave them all tied when he departed. He figured that they would manage to get themselves untied soon enough, but a slight delay might discourage any further stupid heroics from any of their other guards that might want to seek revenge. He couldn't have that.

The plan was to go back to the same spot that they had camped out earlier in the day and camp there for the night. They had left a couple of men there with some unnecessary gear so the rest of the main group could travel lighter in this raid. At some point they would likely split the spoils in a manner that Tiran would obviously control tightly. They would all then make their way back to Jerusalem for a respite from the highways for a while. He was sure that when the money was nearly gone, these men would be itching to get back out on the highways again to make some more.

As the men were leaving, Jotham had still not found a way to get over his fear of his brother. Who could blame him though? He had just witnessed him murder a man. Self-defense or not it must have been terrifying to the young boy. It did not help matters that Dismas was still standing there looking like a mad man. If he were Jotham he likely would have felt the same way. The most bothersome part to Dismas was that Jotham tried to protect himself from his older brother by hiding himself behind Gestas. As they were leaving Jotham mounted up with Gestas and Gestas seemed to be very careful with him. Perhaps Gestas did have a redeeming quality or two about him. Dismas only hoped that he were able to find more before one of the boys wound up killing the other.

Soon they reached the old campsite and everyone started dismounting, and finding a place to put out their bedrolls. A guard was placed out on the perimeter to keep watch and two other men were posted to guard all the spoils of the night's raid. No fires were lit. Dismas was not sure what was going on. It was if nothing had happened. He half expected a night of drunkenness and debauchery to celebrate their success and for everyone to divide their spoils. As he tied his donkey on to the tie line he asked the old man Thomas why the men were not excited.

Thomas replied "Oh, don't think that they aren't excited. Every man is down there right now dreaming about how he's going to spend his share. Tiran is making them wait until tomorrow morning before he does anything. If we were to make our fires, get all drunk and making noise we might attract too much attention and give away our position." He continued, "Tiran is a smart man and he didn't last this long being foolish. If you want to live, I suggest you pay very close attention to what the man tells you and never, ever disobey him."

The old horseman started to give the boy some more advice but the silence was soon broken by Tiran's voice. "Someone tell me who the man was that was responsible for guarding the poor idiot that got himself killed tonight?" There was no immediate reply.

Tiran raised his voice again. "Well come on now, speak up. Don't make me come find you. It will only make me angry."

The short, squat fellow that gave Dismas and Jotham water on the day they were found rose up from his seat on his bedroll and was shaking profusely. He said, "It was me sir." He trembled even more and his head moved from side to side as if to find someone who would stand with him or maybe support him.

Tiran was historically unkind to men who exhibited any signs of incompetence. If one looked around there were a great many of these men with a scar to prove it and perhaps a missing digit. He was sure it was his turn tonight.

"Well, don't just stand there, come here and visit with me Gerah, you fat slob." Tiran said with a look on his face that said he wanted to get this over with.

Gerah approached his leader nervously and slowly. Dismas was thinking that it reminded him of the way a dog would approach his master when he had beaten frequently.

Gerah did not waste any time apologizing repeatedly for his failure. He was certain that the only apology that Tiran would accept was one that was given while screaming in great pain. This made the poor man almost pass out. He had probably been the weakest of the men in this bunch and it would make sense if Tiran wanted this one to be gone. He was out of shape and constantly relying on others to help him. All the men here smelled very badly, but this man stood out amongst them as the worst and none of the other men liked him. It was evident to Dismas that a man that consumed resources in this band that did not pull his own weight would not be here long.

Tiran tried to put the man at ease by speaking to him in a comforting tone. To anyone else listening it was an extremely condescending one. Gerah was just too scared to understand it. "Come now Gerah, I like you, why are you afraid of me? I just want to hear your account of what happened, that is all. Poor Dismas was nearly killed by that man and I was only a step away from danger myself. More than that, I was terrified that the man had killed you. Were you hurt?"

Gerah made his next mistake by trusting Tiran. He sheepishly replied with his usual half-witted smile, "Well, now that you mention . . ." and no more. A blade across the man's throat silenced him forever. He fell to the ground. The man who silenced him stood in his place. It was the man with the scar on his face, the one they all referred to as Abba. Abba wiped the blade across the cloak of the dead man. He then replaced it back into his belt and walked away.

Tiran looked at the dead Gerah on the ground and said, "Will someone get this stinking corpse out of this camp right now please. He smelled bad alive, I don't want to think about how badly he'll smell dead." Two men closest immediately obliged their leader and scrambled to pull the dead body of Gerah out of sight.

Tiran, looked around at his men and said, "This is the reward for dereliction of duty. This idiot almost cost Dismas and I our lives and this is his reward . . . oh well, more money for the rest of you to split right?" To which all the men smiled.

"Now, on to another task . . . It seems that one of us has become a killer tonight. Come here to me Dismas." He looked deadpan straight at the boy. Dismas shook in fear too. He thought that he might have somehow earned a spot for he and Jotham in this band with the murder of the Magi's guard, although it had only been an accident. Now he feared that he and Gerah were about to share a similar fate this night.

He approached the man slowly. Although he was afraid, he still had more dignity about him than the slimy fat man Gerah did.

"Well Dismas, I must say seeing you disarm and kill that man tonight was quite a surprise to all of us. Who knew you had it in you? Did you Abba?" He looked at the scarred man, who was still close by. Dismas was careful to keep a close watch on where Abba stood lest he share the same fate as the last man he stood behind.

Abba did not answer. He only shook his head as if answering with a no.

Tiran turned back to the boy. "You know I told you a couple of days ago that I would only let you live if you proved yourself useful. Tonight we are sitting here with a lot of money thanks to your help; albeit, not quite as much as we hoped, it was still a very generous day for us. For that I am thankful. I believe I may allow you and your brother not only to live, but to become part of our family if you choose to. Would you like that?"

Dismas nervously replied "Yes" but he sensed something a bit more ominous in the way Tiran had presented this.

"Good. Then it's settled. You will stay with us. But I warn you. If you disappoint me or become less than useful to me; like Gerah did. You will share his fate. I trust we understand each other, yes?"

"Yes sir" was Dismas' relieved reply.

"There's just one more problem that we need to deal with. No one here likes being hunted by Roman soldiers and when someone is killed while our band exacts its 'tribute' it only encourages them to send greater numbers out to find us. No one gave you permission to kill that man so you must be taught a lesson." He nodded to the men approaching behind Dismas and they grabbed him by the arms.

Dismas was terrified of what would happen next and he was sure that it wouldn't be good, whatever it was. He steeled himself for it. Tiran then turned his back and he saw Gestas approaching him. "Your turn my boy" Tiran said to Gestas, "Make sure he knows his place."

Gestas had a look of satisfaction on his face as he approached Dismas. Dismas struggled but it did him no good. These men had him held firm and he knew he would just have to endure. Endure he would. At least there was a small measure of comfort that he would not be killed, at least not now, and that he and Jotham would be safe, at least for a little while. No one could take that from him. The blows came fast and furiously. He felt the rage of Gestas in every single one of them. He was certain of one thing though as he was pummeled into unconsciousness. The rage wasn't directed at him. It was clearly rage this young man had been holding onto for some time and Dismas just happened to offer him the most convenient outlet tonight. Dismas was determined to take it like a man and he was doing better than the other men had expected. Gestas may be just a young man, but they all knew that he was as tough as any one of them. They knew Dismas was taking a huge beating.

Dismas struggled to raise his head after the last blow, but he did. He was surprised at what he saw in Gestas' eyes as he delivered the last blow Dismas would remember. There were tears welling up in them. And then all went black . . .

CHAPTER 20

D ismas opened his eyes and noticed that it was daylight all around him and he was tied unceremoniously over the back of the donkey that he and Jotham shared. Jotham wasn't able to ride it with Dismas tied across it and he ran alongside the donkey trying hard to stay up as the caravan of highwaymen were heading south. Jotham grabbed the waterskin from the saddlebag next to Dismas and poured some water onto a cloth and daubed at the trickle running from Dismas' broken nose. The pain in his head was excruciating. He had to get off of this donkey now and get into an upright position before it exploded.

"Jotham, stop the donkey. I need to get down." Jotham immediately grabbed the lead rope of the donkey and held him hard to make him stop. He did. Jotham set about trying to untie Dismas but he struggled to do so and could not. Dismas was clearly not in a position to do so and he began to panic. The pain in his head became much more intense. Suddenly he noticed a pair of sandaled feet below where he hung suspended from the side of the donkey. It was Gestas. Without a word Gestas untied him and helped him up off of the donkey. Dismas collapsed onto the ground and Jotham handed him the waterskin again. He drained it completely. Gestas pulled his waterskin from his saddlebag and gave it to Dismas to have some more. He motioned for Jotham to hand his rag back to him and he poured a bit more water onto it before taking the waterskin from Dismas and placing it back into his saddlebag.

Dismas wiped his brow. He was not surprised to find that his face was caked with sweat and dirt. He was more than a bit surprised at Gestas' gesture. It struck him as odd that he had beaten him so ferociously the night before and now he seemed as if he were trying to atone for it. Perhaps he really was angry at someone else.

Gestas helped Dismas to his feet and gave him a boost back on to the donkey. "Come on, they'll leave us behind if we don't hurry."

He turned to get back on to his donkey, but before doing so he held his hand out to Jotham and said, "Come on little man. You ride with me. Give your brother some space. He's not feeling well."

Jotham was still terrified of Gestas and was afraid to go with him. He looked at Dismas as if he were seeking his direction. Dismas nodded his permission. Jotham looked at him one last time before taking Gestas' hand and said, "I'm glad you're not dead Dismas."

Dismas smiled and said, "Me too little brother."

A little later in the afternoon the caravan approached a stream crossing that they frequented whenever they were in the area. It was a good place to have a rest and bed down for many travelers coming through on this road between Jerusalem and Nazareth. The area had an abundance of dates and olive trees that offered shade and sometimes a little food. A traveler also had the luxury of good fresh water throughout most of the year. It was an ideal rest stop on this road. However, for the band of highwaymen it was a perilous crossing for precisely that same reason. So many travelers used this area that it made it difficult to pass unnoticed, and if there happened to be a patrol of Roman soldiers in the area there would be trouble. Because of the high hills surrounding the stream that had cut its way through them over the centuries, the nearest crossing to avoid this particular place was too far away to have made it worthwhile. This trip Tiran had decided to just pass through quickly and hope for the best.

By the time they got to the crossing they were surprised to find that they could see only one small caravan in the area. With the census going on there were people everywhere on the roads. It was a bit unusual, but Tiran supposed it was possible. Tiran's rider Thomas had just come back to the highwaymen's caravan to the north of the stream. He reported that he had been south of the stream a few miles and he saw no one coming north at all. This gave Tiran a small measure of comfort that they could actually take some time to rest up and get some water. He still thought it best to do so and then push on further south before resting for the night. This stream, being in such a low area gave no visibility more than a mile north or south on the road and the hills surrounding this little roadside oasis made it a very indefensible place to be caught at. No thanks, thought Tiran. Better to take their chances where they can defend themselves.

One thing that Tiran took a particular liking to was that this little caravan certainly looked promising. There were several donkeys that looked like they were laden down with goods for trade and that was always appealing. That usually meant money too. Why not? Tiran thought . . . They could rob these men easily and be on their way in no time. There was no one anywhere close on the roads and there did not seem to be any guards at all. It would be much easier than the previous night's trappings.

Tiran called up his leaders and gave instruction and soon the men descended upon the stream and the unsuspecting travelers that were just now trying to unload and bed down for the night. In moments they were surrounded.

Dismas was still feeling shaky but he was ready to take his station of guarding the animals with Jotham when he noticed two particular travelers with a baby in this caravan that he recognized immediately. Dismas was frozen with fear. He was afraid that they might expose him to Tiran and this was a terrifying thought to the boy because the memory of the knife sliding across Gerah's throat the night before was still vivid in his mind. More than this he was genuinely worried for their safety as well. He was sure that if Tiran found the gold, frankincense and myrrh on Joseph that he would hurt him. Joseph was a good man and he did not deserve that, but he was certain that Joseph, like most men, would lay down his life to protect his family. His own father redeemed himself to Dismas by doing the same not more than a few days ago. Dismas was determined not to let Joseph share this fate.

Dismas thought for a moment and then he came up with a brilliant idea. He just needed to take action right away to make it work. He leapt over the tie line for the livestock and stopped only long enough to tell Jotham to keep an eye on the livestock until he returned, then he continued his run across the stream to the caravan. Tiran's men had already made themselves known to these travelers and they were caught completely unawares and unprepared.

Joseph was the first to spot the boy as he ran directly to them. Joseph did not recognize him at first but realized who it was instantly when he heard Mary's voice saying "Dismas?" It was then that he knew who approached them. He was perplexed at why the boy was here. Was he with these bandits?

Dismas, upon hearing his name, raised a finger to his lips imploring Mary not to say another word. He finally reached Joseph out of breath. Mary looked at him worriedly and said "Dismas are you okay? What happened to your face?"

"Quick, I don't have time to explain, but I need the gold, frankincense and myrrh that the Magi gave you and I need it fast!"

"Dismas, are you robbing us? Are you one of them?" said Mary.

"How could you? We trusted you!" Joseph said to the boy with a very disapproving look.

"No sir. My mother and Aram are dead and these men have taken Jotham and me. I need that gold, frankincense and myrrh now Joseph. We have no time to waste. I'm trying to save your lives. They'll kill you if they find it on you."

Joseph trusted his feelings and knew that the boy would not have put himself at risk like this if he meant harm to them. He said "In the basket, on that donkey there." He motioned to a donkey that was tied to a low tree next to where he had just lain down their bedrolls for the night.

Dismas bolted to the basket and quickly rummaged out the riches left to them by the Magi. He turned to Joseph and said "You mustn't act like you know me or it would be dangerous for all of us." As he turned about, arms full, he saw Jotham standing there before him staring at Mary, who held Jesus in her arms. He had not expected Jotham to recognize them as well. Now he had another problem to solve.

"Jotham, what are you doing here? I told you to stay with the livestock and guard them for me."

"I saw Mary and Joseph and I wanted to come and see the baby." said Jotham innocently. "Are you stealing from them Dismas? Are you going to kill them too like you did that man last night? Don't kill them Dismas, don't kill them!" the child implored. That stung Dismas far worse than the beating he took the night before. Joseph and Mary again looked at Dismas, this time with a look of aberration. They wondered how in the world they could have misjudged this young man so badly.

"Jotham no! I'm not going to hurt them. I want to save them. Help me put these things in that basket over there." He motioned to a basket of trade goods heaped near a few donkeys belonging to one of the traders in the caravan. The boys ran to the basket and heaped the Magi's riches into it and threw a few valuable looking trinkets over the top of them. His intention was to carry them back to the highwaymen's caravan as if he had liberated them himself. Since Thomas had told him they do not split riches immediately, it would be a while before they figured out there were some particularly valuable items here. By then it would be too late and they would not risk going back to see if there were more. He was quite certain that Tiran would call it a lucky find and count his blessings that he were not caught while 'liberating' it. It was a great plan, but it would only work now if they were not exposed.

Jotham and Dismas turned back to the couple and their child and said "I am so sorry. Please forgive me?"

Jotham was completely oblivious to their situation and when Dismas turned he found the boy standing in front of Mary and the child was holding his finger. It was as if Jotham and Jesus had some sort of supernatural connection. Jotham made drumming sounds with his mouth and Jesus was apparently enraptured by it. He approached Jotham to pull him away but could not resist looking at Jesus one last time. He peered into the swaddling cloth and the child looked directly at him as if his eyes were reaching right down into his soul. He felt that he was suddenly and completely overwhelmed with shame. He couldn't look at him any longer without fear of losing himself. He finally took Jotham by the shoulder and said "Come Jotham, we have to hurry."

Jotham lifted his finger away from the hand of Jesus and looked back at him and said "We're sorry", then turned to leave with Dismas.

The two boys had no time left to get up the hill with the basket, because as they turned they saw Thomas standing there. They weren't certain how long he was there or what he had observed, but they were afraid and just froze there in front of the man.

"What are you two doing down here? You supposed to be on the other side of the creek guarding the stock" said the old horseman. Something about the way he spoke to them made them feel they had nothing to fear from him.

"We wanted to make ourselves useful. Since the stock is all tied up and there are no guards here, we thought if we helped out Tiran would be pleased."

Thomas looked back over his shoulder to the spot Tiran stood barking orders. He looked back to the boys and said, "Good initiative boys, but very bad judgment. I know you both want to please him, but what pleases him most is obedience, not initiative. Best you scoot back across the creek before you get caught. What were you just doing here anyway?"

"All we had time to do was search this couple with the baby and they didn't have anything, but when we started searching the baskets belonging to the trader we found all these trinkets in the big basket. They looked like they might be worth something and we were going to take them back across the creek and start loading them."

Thomas smiled at the boys and with a slight nod of understanding he said, "You boys go on back and I will take it from here. Your secret is safe with me. Just don't do anything stupid like this again."

Dismas nodded and grabbed Jotham and set off at a dead run back to the tie line before they got caught. He was beginning to like this Thomas. It might be worthwhile to try to stay close to him when he could. Perhaps he could teach him how to stay on Tiran's good side. He looked back once more and saw Joseph staring at him as if he was disappointed. Mary was otherwise preoccupied, for Thomas had approached her seeing that she had a child and had begun making cooing sounds at the baby. It looked like the old man truly did have a soft heart and he wondered how he had come to be with this lot. He did not seem at all like the rest of them.

A few moments later he picked up the large basket and slung it across his shoulders and started carrying it back to the center of the caravan as if to meet the men from the front that were working their way toward him searching everyone. This apparently was the signal that they were done and they all carried their 'liberated' treasures with them back to the tie line where Jotham and Dismas appeared to be waiting eagerly. Except for Thomas, no one was the wiser that they had temporarily deserted their post.

The men all mounted up and began the journey south to a small hidden grove the men had used before and they bedded down for the night. Apparently all had gone well because that night all was quiet and to Dismas' relief, no one was killed or beaten.

As Dismas fell asleep that night his thoughts kept taking him back to that moment at the stream when he looked on Jesus. How had this child affected him so? He tried to fathom it. Perhaps everything he heard the Magi telling Mary and Joseph was true. There was something special about him. Maybe he was the Messiah they mentioned . . . whatever that is . . . Dismas had never heard the word before. He did know one thing. His mother was filled with joy when Jesus was born and he remembered her telling him that one day he would deliver all of them. He didn't know what he was delivering them from, but he held on to hope that it might be he and Jotham . . . if they lived long enough.

Something else troubled Dismas. He could not protect Jotham unless he could find a way to get him away from these men somehow. His mother made him promise to look after him and right now he was fortunate enough to keep him alive. He also knew that his mother had meant to protect him from all the things this lifestyle would bring him. Dismas had to find a way to save him. He did not know what it would be or when he could make it happen, but he vowed then and there that Jotham would never live as a thief. He hoped with all of his heart that neither of them would die as one . . .

CHAPTER 21

Daybreak came and apparently Dismas had slept through Tiran's discovery of the all the gold, frankincense and myrrh that were found. The man was clearly in a great mood. You could see it all over his face. Tiran had already put Abba to the task of dividing the spoils with the men. He had also tasked Gestas with helping him to do it. Dismas was pretty certain that he and Jotham would probably get nothing and did not bother to attend to the crowd gathering around Abba and Gestas. It turned out he was right because when they were done, he and Jotham were left empty handed. He wasn't sure how they were going to survive when they got to Jerusalem, but he did know that he could beg if he needed to or find work. He had done it before and he saw no reason why he could not do it again.

Tiran approached the boys and tossed them some bread that he had brought with him from the sack he carried. "I didn't see you boys at breakfast; I thought I would bring you something" and then he tossed it to them. Jotham descended on it like a locust and began eating it. Clearly he was very hungry. Dismas reached over to tear off a piece for himself but he was a bit afraid that he might draw back a stump instead of a hand as ravenously as Jotham attacked it. "I'm not bringing you food again, do you understand? If you can't carry your lazy bottoms down to get food, you starve. In this outfit, you have to fend for yourselves."

Tiran continued, "I told Abba not to give you anything when he divided things up." Dismas had figured as much. To him it was clear he did not think they deserved anything.

"Well, don't you want to know why?" Tiran continued.

Dismas answered, "Not really sir. You don't owe us anything. We've been a burden."

"That's not it at all young man. I told him not to because I had your share with me." He looked at Dismas expecting him to understand why.

Dismas was perplexed by this. He could not understand what he meant.

Seeing the confusion on the boy's face he reached into his belt and pulled out the coin he had taken from the boy days ago and flicked it over to him. "Do you recognize that?"

"Yes sir. It's the coin I had."

"It's also the only reason I didn't let you die out there in the desert. If I hadn't found it on you I wouldn't have bothered even taking you on. That coin saved your life. You should probably keep it as a reminder. Don't spend it. It will bring you luck."

Tiran reached into his belt one more time. He pulled out a very small leather pouch that clearly had a little jingle to it when he did. He tossed it to the boy. Dismas caught it clumsily with his free hand. The other one was filled with the remains of his bread.

"I like you boy, you've got something in you and I can sense it. That is a reward for you. I'm keenly aware that without you guiding us to the Magi we would not have all these spoils we are carrying away today. I've come to think of you as a bit of a good luck charm and I'd like you to stay. You'll need money to live off of for a while. Next time you take part when we divvy up. You will have earned it by then I'm sure."

"Thank you sir!" was Dismas' excited reply. He had never had this kind of money in his life and he was sure he and his brother could be comfortable for quite a while on it. Most importantly though, he thought he might be able to find a way to hide some back and find a way to escape with Jotham someday.

"One more thing . . . I want you and your brother Jotham to stay with Gestas and I for a while in Jerusalem. We've got some business associates that put us up while we are in town and the place is pretty big and pretty comfortable. There will be room for you. If you want you can make a little extra coin working as a servant for the house master. I'll see to it. You interested?"

How could Dismas say no to that? "Of course we will! Thank you sir!"

Tiran looked at Jotham who was still steadily devouring the rest of his bread. "Looks like you're going to have to get a full time job just to feed him" he said laughing.

Dismas looked at Jotham and started laughing as well. It was a funny sight to see someone eat that way. Jotham looked up at both of them when he sensed they were speaking of him. He looked up innocently, bread still hanging from both his nostrils, and said "What?" Both Dismas and Tiran laughed even harder. Tiran walked away still laughing.

Dismas smiled and watched him walk away. He wasn't entirely sure he knew exactly what to feel right now. He just knew it felt good to be alive.

CHAPTER 22

Ten years later . . .

The guilt of not having the courage to run away after all these years now weighed heavily on Dismas. He had promised himself many years back that he would find a way to get he and Jotham away from this life, but alas, it never materialized. So here they were, on the road again with the band of highwaymen, roaming the country and exacting 'tribute' as Tiran liked to refer to it, from poor unsuspecting travelers.

Sure he had a few chances, but when he had those small windows of opportunity opened for them, there would always be something that would happen and make him doubt their chances of success. One such time was when they found themselves alone in Jerusalem while Tiran and Gestas were away on business. Dismas had saved some money for a getaway if such an occasion ever arose. However, in this occasion Jotham had become very ill with fever and he felt it was unwise to depart with him doing so poorly.

Another such occasion was on a recent trip that Jotham and he were sent on. Tiran had trusted them enough to leave them with a lot of money and instructions to buy new mules and supplies with it. The thought entered his mind that it would be easy to just take the money and keep on riding and never turn back. In the end Dismas had decided not to risk it because he hadn't given enough thought into where they could go and how he planned on avoiding Tiran's grasp. He may be a very bad man but he a great many friends everywhere and one could never tell where his reach ended. It was safest to just assume that he could just reach you anywhere you happened to be. Nothing was beyond his reach.

Dismas recalled that a couple of years ago, the horseman Thomas found out the hard way the extent of Tiran's reach. Thomas was a trusted member of this band for a great many years; in fact, no one knew exactly when he and Tiran first joined forces. They only knew that no one could remember being a part of this band of highwaymen before him. This meant that Thomas had been with Tiran a very long time. A couple of years back Thomas had met an old woman and had fallen in love with her. He was married before, in fact, he was married several times but this one woman made Thomas fall foolishly and madly head over heels in love with her. While out scouting on one of his typical excursions, Thomas made a point to go back home to his wife without so much as saying a word to Tiran. His wife had been begging him to stay with her and quit this life of thieving and everyone knew Thomas was not the hardened criminal that many of Tiran's men were. Perhaps Thomas had finally decided that the lifestyle he lived was no longer important to him or perhaps he was henpecked by his wife into staying home. No one would ever know what his motivation was because when everyone returned to Jerusalem they heard that Thomas and his wife were found dead with their throats cut.

Tiran would never admit to having them killed but it was not hard to imagine that it was his order. For one, Tiran did not tolerate a lack of discipline. Thomas never so much as said he wanted to leave. One day he was there and the next he wasn't. Tiran never said a word about Thomas' disappearance, nor did he grieve when arguably the man he knew the best of them all was murdered. Tiran would not be a man to have taken the murder of one of his own lightly. He would have sought revenge. Another reason to suspect Tiran was because of the method of killing. Both of their throats were cut. Tiran had shown over the years that when someone needed to be killed it was his preferred method of execution.

Dismas did not have to imagine hard that if it were two young men he trusted and called 'family' that had stolen money from him and ran away, they would likely suffer a much harsher fate. Dismas would not risk it but it was no longer because he feared death. It was because he feared for his little brother Jotham. The promise he made his mother to protect him all those years ago was still weighing heavily on Dismas. He could never burn the memory from his mind when his mother made him promise this with her dying breath.

Dismas was worried more and more about Jotham. He was no longer the scared kid that hardly ever spoke. Now he had fully embraced this highwayman lifestyle. Now he drank and swore just like the rest of them despite the warnings of his older brother that he should resist falling into the lifestyle. Dismas supposed that if he did not find a way to get Jotham away from this lifestyle that he would surely lose him. He could not let that happen.

Dismas and Gestas over the years became much more tolerant of each other and even though Dismas would not exactly call them friends he knew that if he ever needed help, Gestas would be there for him. Dismas sensed that they were growing further apart again in recent days, and that Gestas' growing friendship with Jotham may have been to blame. Jotham, like Gestas really embraced the life of a highwayman and this truly worried Dismas. He felt that his influence over Jotham waned and if he did not act soon he would lose Jotham to this life forever. He knew what he had always known, and that was that if he were to save Jotham he would have to save enough money for him to make an escape. Now Dismas even doubted that his little brother would even consider it. He had to act soon.

Gestas was very kind to Jotham, perhaps because they were closest in age besides Dismas, and Jotham and he had much more in common. Dismas also felt that there was a bit of jealousy on the part of Gestas too because Tiran seemed to pay more attention to him than he did his own son. Dismas had always been smarter about a great many things than Gestas and he guessed that Tiran saw him more as a perfect replacement for him someday than he did his own son. Dismas was always serious, where Gestas was the one who wanted to be carefree. He lacked in self-control and discipline whereas Dismas excelled in them. Gestas was rash, where Dismas was thoughtful and deliberate in his actions. Tiran appreciated this approach and indeed felt easier communications between he and Dismas than with his own boy. It became clear to Dismas that Gestas was jealous of the relationship his father was building with Tiran.

Gestas had fallen even more out of favor with his father when they were recently robbing a few traders on the road. One of the traders had a beautiful daughter near Gestas' age and he had taken a particular fancy to her. While the men were dealing with the particularly delicate matter of trying to rob her father and his colleagues, Gestas went about trying to talk to her and when she rebuffed him, he struck her hard. Her father did what any father would have done in this situation and he leapt to his daughter's defense. In seconds Gestas had drawn a blade and killed the man. Of course Tiran had a very firm rule in this matter and that night Abba was assigned the task of punishing the boy. It was harsh. Tiran would have it no other way. If Gestas were to have been given special favor it would have gone against everything Tiran tried to build. Of course Gestas would be angry with his father for not showing any compassion to his own son.

There were a very unfortunate crossing of paths between the traders and a patrol of Roman soldiers just after the incident with the traders. The traders had still been grieving the loss of their friend as was their dear friend's daughter. They had not even the time to bury the poor man yet.

When the soldiers approached the men gave a full account of the events that had happened and they also gave their best account of the direction the men had gone and a description of them. The soldiers of this patrol were led by a young centurion that called himself Longinus. He was slightly taller than the other Romans with him in this patrol and he clearly looked like he had seen more action, although he did not look nearly as old as they were. There was something clearly different about him as well, for he had blue eyes and very light colored hair. It was a trait shared by people that migrated from the lands north. The Roman Empire was vast and with their size they often infused a great deal of other races into their own.

Longinus was the son of centurion like his father before him and his father before that. Longinus' father was a commander in the forces on the borderlands of Britannia. He had taken a young slave girl during one of the skirmishes and had fallen in love with her. They were together for a very long time until she died giving birth to Longinus. Longinus' father was a man of resources and of a wealthy family and he knew that if he took this child back to Rome that he would never be accepted as noble by them. He made a pact with one of his dear friends that served with him in the borderlands of Britannia and had known for many years. He gave the man a small fortune to take the boy back with him to Rome and have him taken care of by relatives that could keep him safe and get him an education. His friend honored Longinus' father's wish. Longinus never got a chance to see his father again, for he had been killed shortly afterward in a battle with the Britons. Longinus had however been told the full story of who his parents were and he wanted to honor them by joining the legions himself. When he came of age he followed in his father's footsteps and became a centurion.

Longinus had always had a bit of a rebellious streak and he was one of the finest fighters many men had ever seen. The men he served with had all seen a lot of combat and were all well respected fighters in their own right. Longinus truly loved a good fight when he could find one and unfortunately for him he found them quite often even when he was not in combat. For this reason he was sent to this forsaken place to be forgotten. He did not like being here anymore than his fellow soldiers did, but he had always been a practical man and he did enjoy the occasional scuffle with the outlaws in this part of the country. They were good fighters and he appreciated that.

This particular band of highwaymen that the traders and the girl had described to him were a bunch that had been troubling the area for a while. It was clear from the way they moved and traveled and from all the stories that they were like a small disciplined military unit themselves. Hunting them had become an obsession for Longinus. He relished the challenge. He looked forward to the day when he would finally catch them but at the same time he dreaded it as well. The biggest majority of outlaws they ran into were not quite so talented at escape and quite frankly not much of a challenge. To take out this one band would surely lead to boredom dealing with the rest.

It was clear to Longinus that a different tactic would have to be used to catch this bunch because no matter how hard they tried to chase them down, they knew these roads and hills so well that the Romans simply could not keep up with them. Nothing they had tried before would seem to work. It was time to lay a trap for them and Longinus knew just how he would do it . . .

CHAPTER 23

T iran had given the task of scouting to Gestas not long after the death of Thomas. It was a good position for him to earn the respect of the rest of the men, and Gestas has always been good with a horse. Deep down Tiran knew there would never be anyone as good scouting as Thomas was. Gestas did well, but he was too sloppy sometimes and Tiran was sure that it would someday put them all at risk. Tiran had taken quite a liking to Jotham and he felt that maybe it would not be a bad idea to have Gestas train him to scout as well and he used the excuse that they could share duties. He was silently hoping Jotham would be able to do better than Gestas did, because Gestas had become very sloppy in his work in recent days.

There was one such occasion where Tiran had made the decision to send out Gestas and Jotham out together. It was a particularly bad time for all of them because the Roman patrols were becoming more frequent in the area and it was clear that they were stepping up their efforts to try and curb the highwaymen from robbing traffic on the roads. The people were complaining to Herod about the constant harassment by thieves, and Herod had requested the Romans to assist him by stepping up the patrols in this region. It was having an adverse effect on Tiran's wealth, for they were having a very difficult time these days.

Gestas and Jotham were out on patrol together and they were lost in conversations of what they were going to do with their money, who was the better rider, who was more handsome, and just about any other topic other than the one they were sent out to do. This is why when the small caravan of traders on the road were spotted, they failed to notice that they did not look like normal traders, and they failed to spot the Roman soldiers hiding in wait along the hillside surrounding the caravan. An observant scout would have seen this and known immediately that it was a trap. Instead, Gestas and Jotham rode right past them continuing their conversation as if they were travelers themselves. Yes, they had seen the caravan but no more had been noticed by the inattentive young men. They rode on to meet with Tiran and brief him on the caravan they had spotted and encouraged him to take action and rob them.

Longinus was in the caravan along with a few more of his men and they were disguised as traders in the hopes that the highwaymen would try to rob them. They would simply wait until the right moment and when they shed their cloaks it would be a signal to the rest of the men in hiding to join them in the fight to capture these thieves in the act.

He had seen the young men riding by and instantly knew something was off about them. For one, he thought it odd that both of them would have horses. Prices on horses were a premium because they were such a prized possession. There was also a shortage of supply because the Romans tended to take every horse they found for themselves. The fact that both of them were so young and in possession of such fine horses was odd by itself. Another thing that struck Longinus as odd was the fact that neither one of them had so much as even a bedroll, much less enough supplies to have lasted them all the way to the nearest town. There was something strange about these two and Longinus had the distinct impression that very soon they would see these two again. He would wait . . .

When Gestas and Jotham arrived back at camp they were both excited and hurried to find Tiran and tell him the news. He would be very glad to hear that they had discovered a small band of traders laden down with goods and apparently they had no guards. It should be easy money. Tiran was indeed very happy to hear this because for the first time in quite a few trips they were in danger of having to return home empty handed. Many of his men were thinking that they would have to return back to Jerusalem and take honest jobs just to survive. The thought was chilling to many of them, for they had never had an honest job in their entire lives. They would not even know what to do.

Gestas and Jotham were very pleased with themselves. They went to go rest up for a while before the rest of the band would dispatch to the caravan for the upcoming raid. Dismas followed them and had begun quizzing them on all their other observations. He had a habit of checking and double-checking everything they reported back because he felt that both of them were sloppy in their duties. Sometimes even a small detail could have a disastrous consequence if they did not spend their time carefully observing. Dismas began to think that if these two acted the same way on a scouting trip that they did when they were back in camp, Tiran would not be able to trust that they did anything other than talk. They always missed details or omitted them. They were becoming dangerous. Dismas was not a coward but he certainly did not want to die.

Jotham was the first to react to the line of questioning Dismas was rationing to them. "Dismas, stop worrying. We know what we are doing. What makes you so sure you know better than us on anything? You're no better than anyone else here. Go away."

Gestas just turned and chuckled because he knew Dismas would put up his usual weak argument and then just walk away. He just wasn't one that liked conflict and it showed. He always took the cautious side and the safe side of everything. He never learned to take risks. He was jealous that his father seemed to like that trait the most in him; which is why Gestas felt that Tiran was trying to groom him to lead when he was gone. Gestas could not understand why his father would be so foolish. Sure, Dismas was smart and disciplined, but he lacked passion and Gestas knew for certain that Dismas would never be capable of enforcing discipline with men like this. He never even tried. He never got into conflicts with anyone and that's why everyone liked him, but they would never, ever think of him as a leader. Someone would surely kill him. Jotham on the other hand was incredibly smart as well, and while he was still a little too young to really judge his character, Gestas felt him to be a better match. Jotham had never been a situation that tested him, but Gestas was certain he would do well. He was very brave. Gestas knew that Jotham's biggest weakness was that he loved his brother and all too often he really did listen to his advice. The two had a bond that was forged at a very young age and a very tough circumstance. It was a bond that would not be broken easily. Gestas did not hate Dismas at all. He actually liked him. He just did not feel that this was the place for him.

As predicted, Dismas made a weak argument with Jotham and then turned and walked away because he did not like to argue with his brother.

Dismas did not like the way his brother Jotham was becoming. He had begun to have a hardened heart about everything. He idolized Tiran and was quickly becoming more and more like one of them. Dismas had to put a stop to it soon. He had to buy his escape no matter what the cost. Dismas vowed that he would save every single bit of money he could to help Jotham escape. He did not want him to come to harm, but he was certain that the longer he stayed the greater his chances of being killed, or even worse losing his soul because he had become one of them.

Soon, Tiran gave the order to his men to mount up and prepare to raid the small caravan. They took up the usual positions and readied themselves to depart.

Jotham felt badly about the way he embarrassed his big brother in front of everyone. He came to Dismas and said "I'm sorry Brother. I shouldn't have been so harsh with you earlier. I know you were only trying to keep us all safe. I just wish you would trust me. I am almost grown now; you have to let me make my own mistakes."

"Jotham, you don't need to ask forgiveness. I forgave you the second the words came from your lips. I know this is not an easy life for us and I am still doing everything I can to protect you, but you have to understand that if you do make a mistake it could easily get someone killed, including yourself. I don't want to risk that."

"Brother, I know you want to protect me, but you have to start trusting me sometime. I am almost a man now. Treat me like one."

"Jotham, believe me I already think of you as a man, but no matter how old you get you will always be my little brother, don't forget that." He smiled a bit now because he knew the tension between them had gone. Dismas always had an incredibly strong bond with his little brother and even though Jotham occasionally got very hot headed with him he knew that they would never remain mad at each other for very long.

"Jotham, when we get a chance to talk alone next I want to discuss something with you. I want to discuss with you how we can make a better life for you. I know you are starting to enjoy this life just fine and to be truthful, that is why I want to find something better for you. Just promise you will hear me out, okay?"

"Brother I can't leave you here and go somewhere else. Who would look after you? Besides, Tiran has taken good care of us and you can't promise life anywhere else would be any better for us. I say we stay and we take our chances."

"There is no time to continue this conversation here Jotham. Just promise me to keep an open mind." Jotham mounted his horse. Dismas handed him the reins and said "Be safe."

"You too brother . . . You better hurry or you'll be left behind!" he said as he galloped away to meet up with Gestas, who had already been mounted and waiting for him at the head of the column.

Dismas looked at him wistfully as he realized it would be harder than he thought to get his brother away from these men.

CHAPTER 24

Longinus' men were getting very bored with this assignment. They were playing this role of 'traders laden down with riches' for two days now and not a single sign of the bandits. For that matter, other than a couple of old men and a string of camels that came through yesterday, the only thing they had seen were the two young men on horses earlier in the day. It started to get dark and they were all silently wishing they could go on about their regular patrolling. It was much more exciting to these men than staying in one spot so long.

Longinus would not allow it. The boys that came through earlier had set him on edge and he had ordered all of these me to be extra vigilant in case the two young men were scouts for the band of highwaymen they were looking for. They learned to trust him over the last few months of serving under him. He was very tough, but had always been very fair. He had a sense of honor about him that was rare for men sent here from Rome. It seemed most of the men sent here were misfits of some kind and deserving of punishment. So it was a rare trait to find many men you could trust in the legions here.

On the hill above this small stream Tiran looked down carefully at the small caravan below. Indeed, they certainly looked like they had a lot of goods worthy of taking. Gestas and Jotham had done well to have found them. What Tiran did not realize at that moment was that, because it started to get dark, he had not noticed the men in the tree line surrounding the narrow road crossing the stream below. Nor did he notice the fact that all of the traders in this caravan did not look like the normal men one would see as a trader in this country. These men stood up straight and walked around their camp with a stride that was purposeful. A normal trader would have looked much more worn down and would be drudgingly shuffling about. It was mistake that would soon cost Tiran greatly.

Tiran gave the order and the men immediately set out down the hill to take the traders by surprise. Gestas and Jotham were in the lead, but not because they were tasked with doing so, nor was it because they had the fastest mounts. It was because they felt this victory today was theirs and they wanted to be the ones that led the raid and to take credit for the day's spoils. Tiran had no problem with it this time, but he made a point to remind himself later to have a very stern discussion with them. Tiran remained a distance back where he could best survey the events unfolding and give commands as needed. When the area was secured, he would usually ride in and command more directly. His men knew what to do and they did it well. Dismas' place was by his side. Tiran had always said that he needed someone to be his bodyguard, but everyone knew he was just trying to protect him.

Longinus' men heard the commotion. Many other men would have become anxious and perhaps exposed themselves too soon, but not these men. Longinus had them well-disciplined. They were commanded to wait and not expose themselves until he threw off his cloak. It was only then that they were allowed to take action. They waited.

As Jotham and Gestas arrived at the caravan's camp site Longinus' men feigned being startled so as not to give anything away just yet until the rest of their band could be in close. This way his men could dispatch or capture the greatest number of them before they got away. He was confident in his men. He had trained them well and they were among some of the best fighters he had ever served with. They would hold their own this night and they would be victorious.

Gestas jumped off his mount and drew his short sword. Jotham followed suit. Gestas asked the first man he saw who was the leader and the man motioned to Longinus who stood still with his head down. This close, he was sure the young man would know something was amiss because of Longinus' unusual appearance. As both young men approached him afoot, the rest of the highwaymen were descending all around, and many of them were already dismounting. Fools . . . They were so confident that there would be no challenge here that many of them had not even drawn a sword or dagger. Longinus began to imagine to himself that this would be far easier than he originally expected.

Jotham felt a little emboldened as well and he was the first to approach Longinus. He poked Longinus in the chest with his short sword. Hard enough to make sure he got the man's attention, but not hard enough to harm him. It was, however, hard enough to make him very mad. Longinus slowly raised his head to look Jotham in the eyes. Jotham knew the moment he saw Longinus' face and his height that he was no ordinary trader and he immediately became afraid.

Longinus said in a most cold and calculating tone, "Big mistake boy." He then threw off his cloak, but did so in a manner that obscured from both Jotham and Gestas that he drew his own sword. Instantly there was motion all around them as the rest of the traders threw off their cloaks with sword in hand, and all around them the trees were erupting with motion.

Within seconds the highwaymen that were dismounted were in a fight for their lives. Jotham and Gestas were immediately engaged in a defensive fight with Longinus. He swung at them furiously and despite the fact that there were two of them he was sure to win this one. Both of the boys were excellent fighters but this man was different. He clearly had seen a lot of personal combat in his career as a soldier and he was fast and strong.

Dismas and Tiran watched this sudden change of situation unfold below them and it caught them by surprise. Despite the detachment they should have felt this moment as the men responsible for giving commands; they reacted just as any men would if someone they cared about were in danger. They rode in fast with swords already drawn. It took only moments for them to be in the thick of the action. They saw the large centurion that had been on the attack against Jotham and Gestas and both men were determined to fight a swath through to them and give aid.

Nearby, several of Tiran's men that were afoot had already been killed. They simply were not prepared, and even if they were, it was likely they would be killed anyway. They were simply no match for a well-trained and well-disciplined Roman soldier. The men that were on the scene but had the sense not to dismount, or the luck not to have gotten there as quickly as the rest, had already ridden away.

There was however one man in particular that saw this event happen and dismounted anyway to join the fight. That man was Abba. Even against a trained Roman soldier he was a formidable foe. He too was strong and fast, and had been a stone cold killer his entire life. He moved like a man not afraid to die and this made him dangerous. He saw Gestas and Jotham engaged in combat with the large centurion and he knew he had to get to them and help. He liked both of these boys a great deal and he knew that Tiran would want him to help. For Abba there was no decision making involved. He simply did what he had to do, and he would kill every man that got in his way.

A few feet in front of him Longinus had taken the first blow. He made a huge arcing swing at Gestas and had managed to connect hard with the young man's shoulder. It was not a clean cut. The bad angle of the blade spared him worse injury because Gestas was quick to duck it. He was not fast enough to keep it from smashing his shoulder and breaking his collar bone. The blade had connected just enough to have left a large gash, but not a life threatening one. He knew if the centurion swung at him one more time he would be done. Jotham tried to get in between them and the large centurion was too close to him to swing his sword and he shouldered the boy hard and he fell to the ground. Gestas had risen to his knees and attempted to pick up his sword with his good arm when Longinus stepped up and towered over him. He knew it was the end. This was it. He steeled himself for the blow that would end his life when suddenly he saw a blade arc between them. Longinus had not counted on Jotham being so quick to regain his feet. In his overconfidence did not see the boy raise his sword. The blade struck him hard across the cheek nearly taking out his eye. Longinus raised his sword to strike Jotham down and before he could swing, he felt a sharp pain in his back. He turned to see Abba standing in front of him with a dagger in his hand. The centurion let loose an elbow that knocked Abba to the ground and then another centurion was suddenly in between them. He had to scramble back to avoid being killed right there.

All around them, the battle had become decidedly one-sided. The soldiers had dispatched many of Tiran's men already and the rest were fleeing. Abba made his way to Tiran and grabbed both he and Dismas as many of the centurions had already descended on Jotham and Gestas. There was no hope for them now, they were hopelessly outnumbered. They could not save Gestas and Jotham. Abba, Tiran and Dismas just happened to be standing closely to two of the mules that were unfortunate enough to be tied too well to get away when the commotion started like the rest of the livestock had done. It was fortunate for the men because with a quick flick of blade they were freed and the three men mounted them without haste and rode off into the night. Tiran and Abba were on one and Dismas on the other. Dismas shouted Jotham's name as they made their escape.

The battle was now over and both Gestas and Jotham were the only two remaining alive. Everyone else either died or escaped. Now they were prisoners. Both of them knew it would be better for them to have been killed tonight. They knew what happened to bandits when they were caught. They had a slow and painful death on the cross.

Jotham knew now that his brother was right. He was always right. He was ashamed for being so arrogant when he dismissed Dismas' fears earlier. There was little he could do about it now. He only wished he could see him once more before he died.

Jotham looked up and saw the centurion standing over them. He was cut badly across his cheek and his eye was swollen shut. He knew this look . . . It was the look of a man about to kill someone. Strangely, both of the young men were relieved. For now, they knew they would get the swift death they both desired . . .

CHAPTER 25

The three men finally found a safe place to rest for they had been riding for some time now. They checked constantly to insure that they were not being followed. They were exhausted and could barely stand when they finally dismounted.

Abba spoke first. "No one has been following us. I think that they decided it was safer not to come after everyone at night."

Tiran had obviously been thinking of a plan this entire time because he wasted no time in giving commands. "Good, but you're only partly right Abba. They aren't afraid of us. They think they have scared us all off into the winds and they have no desire to try to come after us in piecemeal." He paused for a moment listening for any noise that might indicate they were not alone. "No. They killed several men and the rest ran. The arrogant animals think they have finished us off and no doubt will be celebrating. I would bet my life they are so arrogant that they would not expect any more trouble for the night! That's why we are going back right now. We have to see if Jotham and Gestas are safe and rescue them."

Abba countered, "Tiran, they're likely dead by now. You saw Jotham cut that centurion, and Gestas was already down. There is no way a soldier would let them live after that. I certainly wouldn't have."

Dismas was angry and upset and he was not doing a very good job hiding it. "I'm going back if I have to go alone! I will never leave my brother behind. Even if he is dead I will not leave him!" He mounted one of the mules.

Tiran grabbed him by the arm. "Dismas stop. You are not going alone. I'm going with you. Gestas is my son and I will not leave him behind, dead or alive. Don't listen to Abba. He isn't going to leave us to do this alone. Where I go, he goes." He then turned and stared at Abba as if willing him to answer yes.

Abba looked a bit embarrassed and said "I'm not leaving your side. Someone has to look out for you two." He put his hand on Tiran's shoulder and said "To the end."

Tiran then put his hands on both of their shoulders and looking Abba in the eye first, said "To the end."

Dismas looked at Tiran and he spoke next, "To the end."

Tiran said, "It's settled then. Let's mount up and ride back quietly and see what's going on." He then mounted up with Dismas this time and they rode back south to the soldier's encampment. Both Tiran and Dismas were not sure what they would find, but they both knew that they could not live with themselves if they didn't at least try to save the boys. They were the only family either one of them had left. They rode on.

Down in the Roman camp the soldiers had just finished dragging the bodies of the dead men to the wagons. The centurions had a small wagon for their own and the highwaymen's bodies were in one of the larger wagons. Longinus lost only three men tonight. All three were brave men and good fighters and they would surely be missed. The highwaymen had lost nine of their number. It appeared to be about a third of the men that rode into the camp earlier. It was hard to tell because of all the action and the darkness, but it was quite possible that several of them men may have even been outside of the soldier's view. By their best guesses it appeared that the men killed were equal to a third of their number. The rest had all run away.

The Romans had several slightly injured and two that were seriously wounded. One of the men that was fighting a large bandit with a scarred face had been lucky to survive, for he was stabbed in the chest very close to his heart. He would live, but the injury was still very severe and he would need great care to recover. The other man seriously wounded was Longinus himself. The large centurion sat on a large rock beside the stream with a bandage wrapped over the side of his head and face. One of the men tended to the wound in his back. He was fortunate that the knife that struck him in the back had hit a rib or he may have very well been killed tonight. He was very angry but it was not because he was injured. He supposed the thing that made him the most furious was that the person that marked him for life was nothing more than a boy. Longinus also was a bit ashamed because he knew he had his own share of the blame for being careless enough not to have watched the young man more closely. His arrogance overwhelmed him for thinking these two boys would be easy to dispatch. He had almost killed them both earlier. He had the sword in his hand and had begun to swing it hard enough to have killed the young man that cut his face, but at the last moment he forced himself to hold back. No. He had a much better plan for them. He would take them both back to Jerusalem and see to it that they were both flogged and crucified as bandits and highwaymen. These men were plaguing the travelers of the region for so long the people would cheer the Romans for a change just for bringing them in for justice. That was just a side benefit to what he really wanted. He really just wanted to watch the boys die slowly. They deserved far worse in his opinion but that would have to do.

"Bring him here" said the burly man.

"Bring who here sir?" was the reply of the man that bandaged him.

He stood up quickly and menacingly and shouted "Who do you think? Bring me the savage that cut me! Now!" and then he raised his knee and kicked the man away from him.

The centurion he barked at wasted no time at all running to the man guarding the two prisoners and then had the man dragged to the stream where the centurion stood, still fuming from this insulting injury to his face.

The two men dragged him to their commander and when they reached him they shoved him down to his knees. One man held him by the hair and pulled his head back so the larger centurion could look into his face with his one unbandaged eye.

"What is your name bandit?" He said with only a little bit more reserve than thought he would show. Jotham would not answer. He was defiant and determined not to say a word. Longinus struck him hard and shattered the boy's nose. His head reeled. The blow had nearly knocked him unconscious.

"I said . . . what is your name bandit?" Jotham looked back up at him, feeling like he might actually lose consciousness and defiantly stared back at him, then lowered his head and spit at Longinus' feet. "Wrong answer" said Longinus and then he bent over and struck the boy hard in his stomach. Jotham doubled over and fell face flat on the ground unable to catch his breath.

Longinus looked to the men next to him and said, "Bring me his friend." They eagerly shuffled back to where Gestas was held and brought him back. He was much more compliant because he was in so much pain. He had no fight in him whatsoever. He was dumped unceremoniously at the feet of Longinus next to Jotham, who was still lying on the ground laboring to breathe.

"Help him up." He said motioning the men to lift Jotham back up to his knees. "Now, you may be brave or you may be stupid, I'm not sure which one, but I did see how fiercely you fought to save your friend here earlier. Perhaps you won't mind if I hurt him instead if you choose not to tell me your name."

He stepped over to Gestas and put his large hand on Gestas broken collarbone and just the touch made Gestas wince in incredible pain. "Now, tell me your name," he said, pronouncing each word slowly and deliberately to add emphasis to his inquiry.

Jotham looked at Gestas. Gestas gave a slight shake of his head as if to signal Jotham not to talk. Jotham looked back at the centurion and said, "Never!"

Longinus' large hand squeezed Gestas' collarbone very slowly and increased the pressure until Gestas could no longer bear the pain and he screamed in sheer agony. Jotham began to sob. He could take a beating for himself but Gestas was his friend and he could not bear to see him hurting so badly. He had to end this now . . . "Okay, okay! Stop!! I'll tell you my name. Just don't hurt him anymore!"

Gestas looked at him and said "Don't you do it. They'll kill us anyway!"

Jotham paused just long enough to make Longinus think he had changed his mind. Time to try another tactic . . . The centurion drew his dagger out slowly from his belt and held it to Gestas' throat. "Now boy! Tell me your name now or I'll cut your friend's throat and leave his body here for the crows!"

"Jotham! My name is Jotham!" he cried out. Gestas slumped in defeat upon seeing his friend give in. "Let him go please! I beg of you, let him go!"

"Now your friend's name . . ." Longinus placed the point of the dagger against Gestas' throat to make his point clear to Jotham that he was not bluffing.

"Gestas! His name is Gestas . . ." Jotham had completely broken down sobbing by this point. The weight of their predicament had finally caught up to him. He knew they were going to die and he suddenly realized he was more afraid of death than he had imagined.

"Jotham . . . Jotham . . . This is a name I will commit to my memory forever. You marked me boy. I will never forget that. I would love to kill you right here and right now, but I have a special punishment for you that I believe is much more fitting. You see, I'm going to take you and your friend here back to Jerusalem and put you both in chains. Then I am going to watch with great pleasure when you are lashed so hard the skin literally flays right off your back. When that's done and you can't stand anymore I'm going to watch these men beat you unconscious. Then we'll drag you and your friend out and hang you both still alive on crosses and let you boil out in the sun while the birds pick your eyes out and the people of town laugh at your agony. That's what I'm going to do." Jotham and Gestas both were wishing they had both died fighting. "You will wish that you had never crossed my path."

The centurion had both of the boys dragged back to cart where they were being held and went back to his rock to sit for a while.

On the hilltop above the stream Tiran, Dismas and Abba watched this scene unfold below them. Tiran and Dismas both could hardly contain themselves when Gestas and Jotham were being beaten by the large centurion. If it were not for Abba restraining them, it is likely that they might be sharing a spot next to them at this very moment for they surely were outnumbered.

They had to come up with a plan and they needed to do so quickly. It was Dismas that broke the silence first. "I have an idea. Do you see where Jotham and Gestas are being held?" He motioned in the direction of the wagon they were tied to. "Do you see what is behind them?" Tiran and Abba strained their eyes and then they saw it. Brilliant! They knew exactly what he was thinking now. A few feet behind Jotham and Gestas was the tie line for the Roman soldier's horses.

"Dismas, you are a genius. If Abba and I can create a disturbance and draw the men away, do you think you can sneak into their camp and free them?" was the question Tiran had asked.

"I'm sure I could. I'll leave the mule and go on foot so I can get in quickly and quietly. When I get them cut free, we'll just steal the horse we need and drive the rest off into the hills. They'll never be able to catch us. They'll never know what happened." Dismas was rather proud of the idea because it was just bold enough to work. These men would never be suspecting the bandits to come back.

Tiran grinned from ear to ear. "Do you remember the spot where we took the Magi caravan years ago?" How could Dismas have ever forgotten that? It was the place where he had first killed a man. Nothing he ever did could dull that memory. Dismas could only swallow hard and nod yes.

"When you three get free of the camp then go straight there. Use the pass that we took that night to get there. If they manage to get their horses back and try to follow, the rocks in the area will mask your tracks. Get there as soon as you can. That's where we will meet you."

Dismas realized that this was a pretty good idea and said enthusiastically "We'll be there!"

"Well what are you waiting for? Let's go! Go get our boys!" He turned to Abba and the two immediately made their way back over the hill to where they had the two mules tied up. Dismas set off along the ridgeline staying low enough not to attract any attention and then when he got far enough down the stream to come down unnoticed, he made his way further down to the water and crossed it quietly. He was now on the same side of the stream where the horses were. He could see them up ahead. He would wait a few minutes for the distraction to start.

He no sooner had that thought when he heard the loud crashing of rocks tumbling down the hillside on the other side of the road. It had attracted the attention of the guard on watch and he shouted to wake the other men. Longinus was lying on the ground with his spear by his side and had just barely drifted off when he heard the alert. He sprang to his feet and heard more rocks tumbling from the side of the hill across the road.

The attention to the dark hillside was more than enough of a distraction for Dismas to creep up, dagger in hand, to the wagon where his brother and Gestas were tied. He whispered to catch their attention and begged them to be silent while he cut the ropes that bound them to the wagon.

Just then they heard more crashing on the side of the hill followed by the sound of a man moaning loudly as if he were injured. The guard that had alerted the men and had woken them up shouted "It's got to be one of the bandits that got left behind!"

Longinus agreed. That had to be it. One of the poor devils was left behind by his cowardly friends and was too stupid to stay quiet and stay out of sight.

Longinus gave the order for five of the men to scramble up the hillside to get the poor straggler. The men grabbed a torch from the fire and quickly obliged, then eagerly charged the hill. He was thinking that his two bandit prisoners would soon have someone to share their fate and turned to look at them. They were not there. It was a trick! The bandits were a smarter bunch than he had given them credit for. He turned to the rest of his men and said "Spread out! Find the prisoners! You men on the hill, get back here now! It's a trick!"

It was too late. Longinus heard the sound of hoof beats on the hill and he knew that whoever it was had gotten away. He turned immediately when he realized that their own horses were sounding as if they were spooked. Then he saw them. The three young men had made it to the tie line and were trying to steal their horses. He and two other centurions close to him were running to catch them before it was too late. He could just make out the boy Jotham already on one of the horses and another man he did not recognize was helping the wounded Gestas up onto the side of another. The man he had not seen before had turned to cut the tie line and scare off all of their horses when Longinus saw his chance. He was at a full run already and raised his spear up to his shoulder as he charged. He knew he would only have one shot at this and he was determined to make it a good one. He had always been incredibly talented with the spear and this night he was more determined to hit his target than he had ever been in competition. Dismas jumped on to the back of Gestas horse, for he knew that Gestas would not be able to hold on with his injuries. At this very same moment Longinus planted his left foot down hard and with his right arm, threw the spear with all of his might. His aim was true. It found its mark deep in the back of the man that had just rescued his bandit friends. He saw him slump over but he did not fall. As they disappeared out of sight into the night he knew that he likely killed this man. If he hadn't, the man would surely remember this night much the same as Longinus would, for he was now marked for life as well.

CHAPTER 26

The sun shone in through the window and onto his face. The profuse sweating resulting from the heat and from his broken fever conspired to wake Dismas. He slowly regained consciousness and his thoughts were beginning to re-assemble. He realized that he was alone in a room in a nice comfortable bed on a particularly hot morning. His head was still clearing and after a few moments he realized that he had absolutely no idea where he was. The light smell of perfume, the nice bedding, and the candles surrounding him on the shelves and window made it evident to him that he was likely in the home of one of Tiran's many women. But which one and where? Where was everyone, and how had he gotten here? He could not recall.

He thought hard to remember how he may have come to be in this place. His thoughts were starting to come back to him slowly. He started to remember helping Gestas to his horse and then he started to recall turning to cut the tie line for the horses and seeing the big centurion with his spear running at him with the other two centurions. He was terrified he was that they would catch up to them before the boys could get away. After he jumped onto the horse with Gestas he suddenly recalled feeling a shock of pain in his side and then . . . nothing. His memories of the events after that were a little too hazy to completely recall. He just remembered seeing faces. Tiran, Abba, Jotham and Gestas faces he did remember, but there were a couple of others he did not recognize that appeared to him. Maybe someone could tell him who they were; if he could find them that is.

He started to sit up. He felt a deep pain and tightness of the flesh in his left side. He looked down and saw that there was a carefully wrapped bandage around his side with the stain of his wound on it. He imagined he must have been wounded in the escape and he suddenly recalled that the big centurion had a spear in his hand when he had been running to catch the boys. Had he thrown it? It seemed to make sense. How else could this have happened? He had to find his brother and see if he made away safely. As he sat up he felt dizzy. His mouth was dry and he felt very hungry. He wondered how long he had been lying here. It seemed to him like forever. Just then he heard men laughing nearby outside. His first instinct after years of roaming the country as a bandit was to hide. He could never be sure if a new person was a friend or foe and he had no desire to have survived the night of the ambush only to die here in a bed. He tried to stand and couldn't. The voices got closer and he became desperate to move quickly. As he stood to his feet, he immediately fell to the floor. Just as he did, the men who were speaking entered the home. They had heard the sound and, like Dismas, became alarmed. Dismas looked up from the floor that he had so unceremoniously dumped himself onto and saw the faces of Abba and Jotham standing there with daggers drawn. Both of them were relieved not only to know that there was nothing to be afraid of, but that Dismas had finally woke up.

Jotham jumped to the floor and helped his brother up. Abba replaced his dagger back into his belt and reached over to assist Jotham in helping the boy back to the bed. Dismas smiled. His brother was safe and that is all that mattered to him. Tiran and Gestas then stepped in through the veil that covered the door to the room. Instantly a wide ear to ear grin appeared on the faces of both men.

"You're alive!" exclaimed Tiran excitedly. "Thank the Gods. We thought you were going to die."

Abba put his hand to Dismas' head and turning to Tiran said. "His fever's gone now. I think he will be fine. We should bring the healer to look in on him again."

Dismas smiled again, grateful for Jotham's safety. Other than two black eyes and an apparently broken nose, he looked okay. The other men looked like they had made it out none the worse for wear. Gestas looked good but the injury to his collar was not visible. His armed was wrapped to his side to prevent it from moving. This was the only outward sign that he was injured. Dismas was certain that he had been in pain. He had seen men with this kind of injury before and he was familiar with the pain and suffering that went with it. But they were all alive. This was good. They would heal and life would go on.

"What happened? How long have I been here? I don't remember anything after we got on the horses except for feeling a pain in my side and then waking up here." Dismas hoped that the men could help fill in some of the holes in his memory.

Jotham spoke. "After you cut the tie line and jumped on to the horse with Gestas the big centurion threw that spear of his at you. He got you good. Fortunately it hit far enough left on your side that it only tore a good sized hole in you and did not stick. If it had it would have killed you for sure."

Gestas enthusiastically chimed in "That's for sure. The spear was thrown so hard it went through your side and even stuck me." He pulled his cloak up to his thigh showing off a bandage wrapped around his injured thigh.

"What happened after that?" Dismas quizzed the men.

Tiran jumped in at this point as he walked all the way in the door and motioned Abba away from his seat on Dismas' flank. He sat in the spot that Abba vacated for him. "You three barely made to the rendezvous spot by morning. Abba and I had almost given up on the three of you when you came in. Jotham was the only one conscious and he led you and Gestas to the meeting spot. You should be grateful you were conscious long enough to tell him where to go or you would be lost out in the desert." He motioned his hand at Abba and said, "Abba here patched you up and made a stretcher for us to drag you into town with. It was a tough trip for all of us because we had to get you attention but we needed to stay off of the roads in case the Romans came after us."

Gestas took his turn telling Dismas the rest of the story. "We came north to Nazareth because we were certain that the Romans would have gone to Jerusalem first to at least take their men home for burial and get reinforcements. Besides, it was easier to stay hidden traveling here. Father has a woman friend here that took us in." Tiran gave them a brief smile of acknowledgement, obviously proud of the fact that he had women everywhere.

"How long have I been out?"

"You've been unconscious for four days now. Your fever has been very high and the healer told us that he suspected you might die if it persisted. I told him that he had no idea how tough you were . . . Now look at you!" Jotham was still elated that his brother was alive.

Tiran put his hand up to Jotham's cheek and started patting it "You know Jotham, I just realized something . . . now that you've broken your nose like your brother did a while back, you'll probably start to look just like him again . . . poor boy." Everyone started laughing.

Just then a rather large homely looking woman pulled the veil back from the doorway and said "Alright boys, leave him alone. Give him some space. He doesn't need all of you pawing on him." She shooed the men away from Dismas side and sent them in to the main room away from him. She playfully swatted Tiran on the bottom as he took his turn walking past her. She drew some water into a cup, and then placed a couple of drops of something from a small flask into it. She then handed Dismas the cup and said "Here drink this. You could use it right now."

"What is it?" said Dismas as he took the cup from her chubby calloused hands.

"Well, mainly it's water, which you need, but the drops I put in it will help you a little bit with the pain. Go ahead and drink up, then I'll give you some more water without the drops."

Dismas drank the cup dry and then handed it back to the woman. She refilled it for him. "Are you sure I need the drops? It hurts a little bit, but it doesn't seem like it hurts that badly right now."

The woman chuckled as she handed the cup full of water back to him and said "You'll change your mind when I start changing your bandage young man. Now finish up that cup and I'll go make some meat broth for all of you and see if I can talk one of these strapping men into going to the market and getting some fresh bread."

Dismas downed the rest of the water in the cup and handed it back to her. She turned to leave and Gestas attempted to pass her to come back in. She gave him a stern look and said, "Don't keep him up long now lad. He needs rest." Gestas nodded and eased past her to Dismas' bedside.

Dismas eased himself back on the bed a bit to get comfortable and Gestas stood nearby looking uncomfortable. He could guess that his looking uncomfortable had less to do with the way his collarbone felt and more about what he would say.

"Just spit it out Gestas. I know you want to say something."

Gestas was rehearsing this conversation in his head but now that the moment was here he clearly had not done it enough to make him feel any easier speaking. He knew that he just needed to say and be done with it. "I . . . uh . . . I . . . I just wanted to say thank you for saving us that night. I realize that you may have just wanted to save your brother, but you saved me too and for that I am grateful. If it weren't for you, Jotham and I might be strung up on a cross right now dying a slow death." It was clear to Dismas that Gestas struggled to control his emotions in this moment.

Dismas was the one who felt a little uncomfortable with the conversation now because Gestas was not one to show any kind of appreciation or emotion around anyone, much less Dismas. It always seemed to him that Gestas only tolerated him because he had to. "Don't waste your breath Gestas. I couldn't leave you there to die. You owe me nothing. I'm sure you would have done the same for me."

"That's the problem Dismas. I don't know that I would have. I've always hated you, from the day I first met you. And to be honest, I've always been a little jealous at how my father seems to treat you better than he does me. I guess what I really wanted to say is that I've been pretty cruel to you over the years and I've been thinking a lot since the other night. You've never done anything to deserve it." Gestas paused and then continued. "I feel ashamed."

Dismas was grateful that God had provided him with the opportunity to be given a chance to fix this rift that developed between the two of them since they first met. "Gestas, we have both lived very complicated lives and endured many hardships; I never wanted you to feel that you could not trust me. I have always hoped that someday we could become friends. I hope that today is finally that day."

Gestas let out a rush of breath in relief and put on a very large smile. He was clearly relieved to have said what he needed to say. He was very grateful too that Dismas made it easy for him. He suspected Dismas would, but to show a moment of weakness to someone that was your adversary doesn't always turn out that way. He held out his good hand and grasped Dismas' outstretched arm and said, "Today's the day Dismas. No more distrust and dislike. From now on we are friends for life. I'll look out for you and for Jotham just like you are my own brothers. I swear it."

Dismas was indeed grateful. He recalled the lesson that Joseph taught him many years ago about how God forgives us if we come to him with a penitent heart. He wondered if, in forgiving Gestas, he had done what God would have expected. After all, if he could not forgive Gestas, how could he expect God to forgive him after all he had done? Now the number one thing on his mind was figuring out how to get he and his brother out of this life before they were both killed.

He then felt the first effects of the medicine the woman had given him and he became very drowsy. He laid his head back on the bed feeling that he was losing consciousness. He smiled because the last thing he heard before everything went black was the sound of his brother's laughter in the next room.

CHAPTER 27

A few weeks passed before Dismas was really able to get around and do much. He was going stir crazy stuck in bed for so long. He was grateful that he had enough strength to at least hobble to the courtyard and sit and enjoy the weather on these nice days. It was good for him to sit around and not have to spend all day riding, or all night sleeping on the hard ground or eating poorly cooked food. For now, he had a nice bed, a chance to rest and at least the old woman who took them in was a great cook. He thought he could see why she was so chubby in the first place. Even Tiran, Gestas and Jotham were gaining weight since being here. Abba was staying in another home for the last couple of weeks. It seems he had a cousin that lived nearby and he had decided to go and visit them for a while. Dismas was sure that if he were eating as well as they had been, he would be putting on weight as well.

This particular morning Dismas had decided that he would try to take a short walk. He needed to do so sooner or later so he could build up his strength. The other men had gone off to visit with some of Tiran's business associates and the woman was at the market all day. This left Dismas alone to fend for himself. It was a perfect time for a short walk though. If he got tired, he could just sit down and rest, then continue. He did not plan on going very far just in case he started feeling too ill to continue. At least he would not be stuck out somewhere with no help.

Dismas had no general direction in mind when he set out and just decided he would go where his feet took him. After he had been walking for a few minutes he needed to take a break and he sat in the shade of a small tree close by. He sat there for only a few minutes and was about to get up when he saw a young boy perhaps around ten years of age carrying a bag full of carpenter's tools and following behind a man with what appeared to be a table slung over his shoulders. Obviously it was a carpenter and his son going somewhere to work. As they approached within a few feet he noticed that the boy had the most peculiar blue colored eyes. It was very rare to see someone of this eye color and this boy's eyes were particularly noticeable even from a distance. He could only remember one other time seeing eyes like this and it was many years ago back in Bethlehem before his mother was killed. They were walking at a brisk pace as if they were in a hurry to get somewhere. The boy looked directly at him and it immediately made Dismas feel uncomfortable. It was if the boy knew him but Dismas could not tell why. The boy instantly stopped and set the carpenter's bag down on the ground. Dismas wondered what he was doing. The boy's father continued on unaware that the boy had stopped. The boy immediately unslung the waterskin over his shoulder and approached Dismas in his little perch under the small tree. Now

Dismas really felt uncomfortable and he looked around him as of to see if anyone else noticed this strange incident occurring.

The boy stopped directly in front of Dismas and stood staring at him. "You're injured." he said. He then uncorked the waterskin and handed it to him and said "Drink. You will feel better." Dismas wondered how in the world this boy knew he was injured. He was nowhere near when Dismas got here and he couldn't have observed him doing anything other than just sitting here. It unnerved him. The boy, sensing the hesitation, said to Dismas, "Don't be afraid. Drink. You will feel better."

Dismas saw no reason not to trust the boy and he drank. It was very satisfying and he drank it heartily. He put the cork back in the waterskin and handed it back to the boy. As the boy was about to take it and leave Dismas did not want to let it go until he knew how this boy knew he was injured. "Who are you? How did you know I was hurt?"

Before the boy could answer a man's voice said "Jesus, what are you doing here? Why did you stop like that? I had no idea you weren't behind me. I almost lost you." He looked to Dismas who was still hanging on to the boy's waterskin. "Is this man bothering you?"

"No father. He was thirsty and I gave him a drink." said the boy.

"Well, now that you are done we need to get back to work. Your mother expects us to be home by dinner and we have lots of work to do today. We mustn't upset her." Joseph shepherded the boy back to his tools to fetch them when he looked at Dismas as if he recognized him. "Do I know you from somewhere?" he said.

Dismas instantly knew who he was the moment he heard the name Jesus. This was Joseph. It was doubtful that Joseph would be able to recognize him after all these years but Dismas definitely knew who he was. He was glad that Joseph did not recognize him. He did not think he could bear the shame if he did. He was very glad to see that they were safe though. This much gave Dismas a great deal of pleasure. "No sir, you probably don't. I'm not from this area. I am just here visiting."

"All the same, you look very familiar to me and I can't explain why."

"I get that a lot from people. Maybe I have a twin somewhere." he said with a slight smile.

"Very well . . . I'm sorry if we've troubled you. We'll be on our way." and then turned to leave.

Joseph and Jesus were already starting to depart and Dismas called out to them "He didn't trouble me at all sir! Thank you for the water Jesus! It was just what I needed!" They would never know how much he really meant that. It was good for Dismas to see that they were well. Now it was time for him to get up and head back. He braced himself for the pain in his side as he stood up. He felt none. This was amazing! Maybe that's all he needed was a brief walk to make him feel better. He started suddenly to realize that he should have felt a little something. He was feeling good but a little worried too. Something wasn't right about this. He started to feel his side and did not feel any pain at all when he touched the area of the wound. He was getting a little anxious now and he knew he had to look at the site to see why he wasn't able to feel anything. He started to walk in the direction of the home he stayed in these last few weeks. He felt actually pretty good; uncharacteristically good to be exact. It was as if he had never been wounded. He then quickened his pace and hurried back.

He finally reached the home and ran inside. No one had returned back yet so he was alone. He went to the room and dropped the veil behind him. He shook off his cloak and looked at his side. Nothing. There was nothing there! He couldn't believe it! He examined it more closely and ran his hands over it, all the while thinking that maybe he was hallucinating. But, alas, there was nothing there. It had not only completely healed, but there wasn't even so much as a scar to show that he had ever been injured. He had just seen the ugly red scar earlier this morning and now it was gone! It was a miracle!

His mind was suddenly awash with all the things that his mother had said about the boy Jesus after his birth. She said that the boy would deliver their people. At the time he heard them use the word 'Messiah' but as a boy he never understood what it meant. Later in life he had come to know this word and its meaning and had never given it thought again until now. He now knew in this very moment that this boy Jesus was the prophesied Messiah. His mind raced as he struggled to understand what this all meant. He knew now that he needed to leave this life of being a bandit forever and that he must do everything in his power to protect Jotham. Whatever the cost, he must save his brother. Now at last there was hope!

CHAPTER 28

D ismas did not dare to let anyone know what had happened. He knew these men and he knew they would think he was crazy, or worse yet; think that it was some kind of demon magic. He knew caution would be his best option right now and he decided not to say anything. He had some money saved up and hidden in Jerusalem. The first thing he wanted to do is find an excuse for he and Jotham to get to Jerusalem so he could get his money. After they did this he wanted to take the two of them to Capernaum. Capernaum was a large fishing village on the north banks of the Sea of Galilee and he was sure it was far enough away that they could live there in anonymity, far away from the reach of Tiran or the Romans. Tiran never ventured farther north than Nazareth anymore. It was the perfect place to hide. They could get regular jobs and have regular lives, raise a family. Finally they could live in peace. Now he just needed to figure out how to do it.

A couple of more weeks went by and Tiran decided it was a perfect time for them to make it back to Jerusalem. Abba returned and he had made contact with the men that were left and had arranged for all of them to meet at one of their normal rendezvous points at a well far to the southwest of the city. He had a plan to go raiding along the coastal trade routes. Tiran felt that the Romans would likely be spending most of their time on the trade routes that this band had previously been so successful working all these years; and so it was time to move on. Some of Tiran's men had previously lived out in these areas and had a great network of hiding places, rendezvous points, safe houses and a great knowledge of the roads and byways. It was time for a change anyways. This plan was perfect for Dismas as well because now he and Jotham would be headed far away in the exact opposite direction and had even less chance of Tiran knowing where they would go and this could not have been better news.

The biggest problem facing Dismas right now would be to convince his brother to go with him. Jotham and Gestas had become even closer friends since the Roman ambush and he feared that it would be difficult for him to get him to leave. Gestas was genuinely friendly to Dismas as well since the ambush but he doubted that he could be talked into joining them. He would not leave his father despite the fact that he despised him so much. This is the only life he knew and he loved it. Someday, he feared, Gestas would be just like Tiran. Dismas still hadn't even told Jotham of the incident that day with Jesus. He knew his brother would be equally impacted by this information, but he far too easily showed his emotion and he had never been a good liar on top of that. Dismas genuinely feared that if he told Jotham of his plan too soon, that it would put both of them at risk. He had made up his mind that he would tell him at the last possible moment. This brought the danger of a confrontation with Jotham while he tried to convince him to come with him and that confrontation could invite too many questions. He had to be careful or expose them both to Tiran's harsh justice. He cut poor Thomas and his wife's throats and he had known him for years. He did not doubt that their fate would be equally as harsh.

The men finally arrived at the rendezvous point. It was a small grove far off of any of the main roads and there used to be several homes here many years ago. No one ever knew why but the people that used to live here left many years ago. There were still a couple of low walls here that provided a welcome respite from the night winds, and it was easy enough to find just enough shade from the sun during the day. Another great benefit to this location was the well. It still was able to provide thirsty travelers with much needed fresh water. It probably would be a great place to settle, but it was just too far from anything. Perhaps that's why the original settlers here moved on. No one would ever know. For now, the place was an excellent hideout for this band and it had frequently been used over the years as a rendezvous point for them when they needed it.

Dismas felt surprisingly good after the long journey, but then again, why shouldn't he? His wound was completely gone. He was in good spirits knowing that this bandit life would soon be over for he and Jotham. He dismounted and unloaded his bedroll and found a place comfortable to rest. He was here many times over the years and he soon found his familiar spot and set up. Jotham soon followed suit and unloaded his bedroll and then joined his brother in a spot familiar to him as well. Around them several men had already arrived early and had made a few fires. Some were cooking, some were sleeping, and others were greeting their long lost brothers. For many of them this was the first time they had seen each other since the night of the Roman ambush. They were busy catching each other up on the events of the last couple of months and drinking to their lost brothers that died that night. Dismas and Jotham even laughed at some of the stories they regaled each other with about their fierce battles with the Roman centurions that night.

Abba spoke. Usually when he spoke everyone else knew to shut up and listen. Revelry or not, every man there became silent upon hearing him speak. Tiran was the only other man here that could do that. Abba had grown tired of listening to all the false stories of bravado from men that barely fought before they ran away, some of which never even got off of their mount were telling their false stories of how heroically they fought. It made him sick to hear it. He decided it was time everyone knew the story of Jotham and Gestas' bravery taking on the large centurion and how Dismas bravely risked his life to save them and nearly died in the process when the centurion launched his spear. He held up a cup of wine and saluted their bravery. Every man joined in his salute.

Tiran chimed in at this time and asked Dismas to join him in front of the men. Dismas had no idea what the man had in mind, but he was certain he had done nothing wrong. He had only been thinking it but had told no one of his plans. He nervously stepped up and joined him.

"I want to take a moment in front of you all to tell Dismas how grateful I am that he risked his life to save my son. In saving him he also drove off all of the Roman horses and had he not done that many more of us might be with our lost brothers tonight." The men started cheering. Tiran continued, "Dismas refused to give up when all you other sorry dung sacks turned and ran." Everywhere smiles suddenly disappeared for it was clearly a rebuke to the men here.

Dismas turned a bit red in embarrassment and he looked to Abba who nodded approvingly to what Tiran said. Tiran continued "That's why I am going to say something now that I want all of you to know and understand. This kind of intelligence and bravery is what we need if we are going to survive. The Romans are growing in number and they have shown that they are relentless in trying to stop us. I realize I am getting a little long in the tooth and getting far too old for this life on the road. I want to someday find a nice fat woman who is a great cook and live out my life in luxury." Some of the men chuckled at the comment. "But today isn't that day. When that day does come I want someone like Dismas here to lead you. From this day forward you will follow orders from him as if they come from me. The only man he answers to from now on is me."

That comment drew a fierce reaction from Gestas and he stood up angrily, drawing the attention of all of the men. Tiran looked at him as if he expected the reaction and said "You have nothing to be ashamed of Gestas. You are a brave man and I am proud that you are my son, but you're far too headstrong and wild to be a leader. These men need someone that can keep a cool head and be wise and Dismas is perfect for that. But he'll need you by his side to keep these men together."

Gestas knew better than to challenge his father on this. It did not matter that Gestas was his son. To Tiran justice would be equal to all, even him. He stormed away in anger and Jotham followed after him.

Dismas could not believe this just happened. It was as if the universe had conspired to trap him in this life. The revelation from Tiran had shocked him to the core and he knew now that when he and Jotham left he would be able to count on Tiran hunting them down. He would not stand for this disobedience or the embarrassment he would cause by leaving after this announcement. Still he knew he had to fake it until they were gone. They would just have to be much more careful and give some thought into pushing even further north than Capernaum.

Tiran sensed a little disturbance in Dismas' reaction to this announcement. "What's the matter son? I thought you would be pleased. Don't worry about Gestas. He'll be hurt for a little bit but he will soldier on, he always does."

"It's not that Tiran. It just caught me by surprise. I wasn't expecting that. Are you sure you picked the right person. Abba would be better suited than I would."

"Abba? Are you serious? That rock over there has better people skills than Abba does. How long do you think these men would last with that bloodthirsty killer as the boss? He'd kill every man here one by one because they made him mad or looked at him wrong. Hard to believe he is the son of a Rabbi. You'd think he would have learned to be a little kinder growing up . . . No, you are the right choice Dismas. Every man here knows that you can be trusted and they all know you are smart. You showed us you can be brave against the Romans too and you saw what the rest of these cowards did when they faced them. They need you. I need you."

Dismas nodded and said "I guess. I'm just a little overwhelmed that's all. I need to go sit and soak it in if that's ok?"

"Not a problem son. You probably need to get some rest if you can. We'll head out at first light."

Tiran patted the boy on the shoulder and turned to go bark orders at the men to start wrapping up their celebrations and get ready for the long day ahead.

Dismas walked back to his bedroll and sat for a moment. He sat there for a moment not believing what just happened. It would make their escape even more dangerous now. He knew he had to talk to Jotham now and they had to escape tonight. They would never have another chance as good as this one. If they could make it to Jerusalem by tomorrow, he could gather their stash of money he had put aside and they could be on the way to Capernaum the very next morning. He knew that Tiran would likely not send men out after them right away but they could count on him paying people to find them later. They needed to be extremely careful. He knew that if they kept a low profile and talked to no one they could change their plans later if they needed to. At least they would have a good head start on whatever dangers Tiran would send their way.

CHAPTER 29

Gestas was still fuming when Jotham caught up to him. Gestas turned to Jotham and said, "Why would my father do that? I'm his son. He's supposed to let me take over when he leaves! I've been here. I've done everything he has ever asked of me and I earned it!"

Jotham knew better than to argue with Gestas when he got in this kind of mood. In this way, he was much like his father Tiran. It was best just to let him vent his troubles and get it out of his system. When he was done, he always had a cooler and more rational mind. It's too bad for him that the emotion got between him and that rational side of himself. He was certain that Tiran would have given him the job then. Gestas' problem was that he never took the time to think before he acted. Jotham suspected that he himself was often the same way but Dismas had always there to keep him headed in the right direction. He started to worry that this would put another wedge back between Gestas and Dismas again. He was caught between them for far too long and he was just beginning to really enjoy all three of them being friends. He would be sorry to see it end.

"Surely you can't be mad at Dismas about this. I'm certain he did not know what Tiran was going to say and I am very certain that he did not want to be in charge. I know my brother. He would never do that. You know him too Gestas!"

"I'm not mad at Dismas. He is exactly what my father wanted. I'm furious with my father for not wanting me Jotham! He didn't have to decide anything right now. He could have waited until I had an opportunity to show him my leadership. He definitely had no right to embarrass me in front of everyone the way he did. I should kill him and take what's mine!"

"Gestas, you would never kill your father. I know you. You love him . . . and he loves you. You get mad and you calm down, and then you always regret not taking the time to think when you are mad. That's exactly why he didn't choose you and you know it's the truth." Jotham hoped he got through to him before he acted on his passion.

Gestas was at a point where the anger in him started to subside just a bit and he knew that Jotham made a great point. It was true. He did get mad and threaten to do stupid things. Then he always calmed down. Many times he got to say he was grateful that he didn't act when he was mad . . . and there were a few times he wasn't so lucky . . . but he knew why. "I suppose you're right. So what do I do now?"

"Just do what he said and support Dismas until it's your time. You two will be good together. You both have traits that complement each other well."

Just then they noticed Dismas making his way up the little small hill behind the grove of trees and they immediately knew to discontinue the topic. He looked at them and smiled. Dismas was the one to break the uncomfortable silence. "Gestas, I didn't know . . ."

"I know Dismas. You forget. I was a disappointment to my father long before you came along. I have no right to hold that against you. You've only ever done what you thought was right. I am not mad with you, nor would I ever be. My father is the one I am angered with right now. It's not so much what he did as much as how he did it."

"All the same Gestas . . . I am sorry. I wish it were different. But I wouldn't worry too much. Your father doesn't show any signs of slowing down anytime soon and we both know he has changed his mind many times in the past. Maybe he'll fire me tomorrow for all we know." he chuckled.

Gestas walked directly to Dismas. Normally in this circumstance he would be on guard with Gestas, but this time it was evident from his body language and expression that he had nothing to fear. Gestas embraced him and looked him in the eyes. "I told you that I would look to you and Jotham as brothers and that is exactly what I will do. I will do as my father has asked and be by your side." He smiled a defeated smile.

Dismas embraced him again knowing full well that Gestas would likely be the heir apparent again after the night was over. He just did not know it yet. He wondered . . . would Gestas feel betrayed by their actions tonight? Only time would tell, but he hoped the best for Gestas and hoped that he would be able to get out of this life before it was too late for him too.

"Gestas, may I speak with my brother for a moment?" said Dismas. It was time to fill Jotham in on his escape plan and he prayed that he would be cooperative.

"Sure" said the young man, "I was just heading back any way. Don't take too long. Father wasn't joking; we really do have a long ride tomorrow across some very rough land."

Jotham sensed a bit of worry in Dismas. He did not hold emotions well and you could tell something was really bothering. He knew that Tiran's announcement had come as a surprise to him, but something about this expression made him feel a like it was something different all together. "Dismas, what is bothering you? Is it what Tiran did?"

"No brother, it isn't. It's something else entirely." Dismas squirmed uncomfortably while he tried to think of how to start the conversation.

"It's not Gestas is it? He means it when he says he is fine following you. He's stubborn but he respects you. I think he is just angrier at his father right now. It has nothing to do with you" said Jotham.

"No it's not that Jotham, it's something else. That's why I came to speak to you."

"Well tell me what it is Dismas. You are starting to make me worry. Should I be worried?" said Jotham in utmost sincerity.

Dismas sat on the ground under a tree and motioned for Jotham to have a seat next to him. Jotham made his way to the tree where his brother was and took a seat next to him on the ground. Dismas was so nervous that he trembled. "Bother, I am really worried now. What is it?"

Dismas swallowed hard and then he spoke, "Jotham, I know that what I am about to tell you will make you think I have lost my mind but just be patient and hear me out. Will you promise that?"

Jotham was unsure of what his brother was about to say or why it was such a big thing for him. He nodded and said "Of course. Now tell me what is bothering you."

"You saw my wound and you remember how bad it was. The wound was so large that you know that it would be there for the rest of my life." He loosened his cloak and dropped it to his waist and turned his side to his brother. "What do you see brother?"

Jotham looked at the place where the large ragged red scar had been and saw nothing. He looked at the other side just to be sure he was looking at the correct side, and not finding the scar there either he let out a large gasp. "What magic is this?"

Dismas had a hard time containing his excitement now. He was dying for a chance to tell someone about this and now he was able to finally share it. "It's not magic brother. It's a miracle! Do you remember the boy Jesus from Bethlehem, the day before mother died? It was him. I saw him in Nazareth. He gave me water and told me it would make me better and then the scar was gone! I was completely healed!"

"Why did you wait until now to tell me? We have to tell the others! This is amazing brother!" Jotham started to get excited now too.

"No Jotham. I didn't tell you because these men wouldn't be as open minded as you are right now. Many of them come from families that worship other gods and I have no desire to be put to death because they may think I am some kind of demon. And brother, I did not tell you sooner because you have never been a good liar, nor have you been good at hiding your feelings. You would have given me away without meaning to."

Jotham hung his head in and gave his brother a slightly sheepish look because he knew he was right. "Well this is good news brother, but what do you suggest we do? Can we go see him again? Will he heal other people? Maybe we can become business partners with him and bring sick people to him for a fee. We could be rich!"

Dismas was a little bit disappointed that this was his brother's first thought but he could not blame him, for he had a role in Jotham having to live this life of banditry. Naturally his first thoughts would be in how to profit from this. "No, that's not what we are going to do. I'm sure he heals because he is led by God to do it. I'm sure that God does not intend to give a gift like this so someone could profit from it."

"Then why did he heal you brother? No offense to you Dismas; but you can't say that God means to give him this gift only to have him heal a thief do you? Surely not?" The words clearly stung Dismas because it was a valid point.

"I can't answer that Jotham. Maybe there is another purpose. I believe there is, and that is the other thing I have to discuss with you." He paused for a moment to collect his thoughts and to make sure that his next words were wisely chosen, because it was literally a matter of life or death. "Jotham, I've told you many times over the years that I intended to keep my promise to mother to protect you no matter what the cost . . ." he was interrupted by Jotham.

"You have brother. You almost lost your life to save me from the Romans. You've always looked out for me."

"Jotham, there is much more to protecting you than just saving your life." He paused for a moment and then continued, "I have to try to save your soul if I can. Mine too. You know this is not the right life for us. We aren't thieves. We only do it because we are too afraid to leave this life. I know you feel the same way. Don't you want something different?'"

"Brother, you don't know me as well as you think. I like this life. I like having money and not having to beg. Most of the people we rob have plenty of it. We are just getting what we deserve. Besides they probably stole it from someone else."

Dismas grabbed his bother by both arms and shook him. "Jotham you don't believe that for one moment! I know you! I know you are only saying that because this life is all you've known. You want out, you just won't admit it!"

Jotham was struck by his brother's words. Dismas was right. He did not like taking from other people. He did not like when people were killed, and he especially did not like being afraid all the time that someday they would get caught. The thought of being strung up on the cross the way the Roman centurion described it plagued his nightmares every night since then. He knew he wanted out, but he was too afraid to wind up like Thomas and lying with his throat cut. Escaping was never an option . . . adapting was all he knew to do. He hung his head in shame. Dismas was right . . . again. He sat silent for what seemed like an eternity and then he spoke. "What do you have in mind?"

Dismas smiled. He knew he had been able to make his point with Jotham. He knew his brother was terrified of living this life despite the false bravado he showed to others. Convincing Jotham to leave with him was half of the battle. The rest would be more dangerous though because they had to escape successfully and most of all they had to do it tonight.

"Tonight, after everyone beds down, we will make our escape. We should ride hard to Jerusalem where we can get our money that we were hiding. We can be there by late tomorrow. We will get our money and buy two fresh horses and a few supplies and make our way north to Capernaum. We won't be able to stay there long. I am confident that Tiran won't try to chase us right now, but the first chance he gets he will pay someone to find us and kill us.

"How can we be safe if he will send spies to find us?" Jotham asked. He now became very interested in this plan. Clearly Dismas had thought it through very thoroughly and perhaps they could make it safely after all.

We should plan on trying to find a way to escape further north and out of his reach. All we have to do is lay low and tell no one who we are or where we are going. We will just 'disappear' and never be found again. We can make a new life, get jobs and raise families."

"Dismas, I am afraid. If we are caught trying to escape then today we'll die tonight. I don't want to die." Jotham was now the one trembling. He was really afraid of dying. Dismas knew he had to find a way to calm him.

"Brother I am certain that God did not allow Jesus to heal me only to allow me to be killed tonight. He won't allow it to happen to you either, especially if you stay with me. There is a purpose for both if us and we have to go find it. Let's go make our mother proud, okay?" He then hugged his brother tight.

Dismas loosened his embrace and then looked squarely in Jotham's eye. "We only need enough water and food to last until tomorrow afternoon so take nothing else. We will need to ride as light as possible. Besides, the less we carry the easier it will be when we leave. We need to be especially quiet. When we leave we must walk our mules until we are farther from the camp so we will not be heard when we ride away. Do you understand?"

Jotham was still nervous but he was in control of himself now. "Yes brother, but I'm still scared."

"Me too. Use your fear to keep you sharp. We will make it just fine. Just remember what I told you. Now let's go and get some rest while we can for our long journey and we will leave when everyone is asleep."

"What about the night watch?" Jotham asked? It was an excellent question.

"You will be the one to relieve him and we will leave during your watch. If there is no one to wake the next watch it will buy us even more time to escape. Tiran gave me fairly broad authority. No one will question the watch change if I order it."

"That's very smart brother. We should go before someone comes looking for us now." He smiled a nervous smile at his little attempt at humor.

As the boys helped each other up off the ground they embraced once more. They hugged each other tightly. One way or another this night would change their lives forever and they both knew it. As they turned to walk away they failed to notice that standing only a few feet away behind a tall palm was Gestas . . . and he had heard the entire conversation.

CHAPTER 30

D ismas pulled the men assigned to night watch together to let them know his new instructions. He made a point to let them know that Jotham would now be part of the watch tonight. Dismas knew of the purpose for this order but the men assumed that Dismas would follow in the footsteps of Tiran and make sure that everyone knew he would play no favorites with his own brother. Secretly they thought that was a good sign that Dismas would be fair to all of them and they liked this. While giving the men their orders he overheard shouting over in the direction of where Tiran and Gestas had set up for the night. He thought nothing of it because he assumed it was Gestas confronting his father about the incidents earlier where he had embarrassed him. Then he noticed that they were both looking directly at him. At first he became nervous but then he realized that he was probably just over-reacting. He was certain that they were probably just looking at him because of the role he played in this whole scenario. Dismas had no idea that Gestas informed his father of the conversation he overheard.

A while later in the evening, Dismas was lying awake and noticed that the night watch came to his brother Jotham to wake him for his turn on duty. Jotham was not sleeping either. He rested his body but his mind was racing. He was truly afraid. He got up and started walking the perimeter of the camp until he was sure that the previous watchman had gone to sleep and that no one else was awake to notice their departure. He saw no one stirring. It was time.

Jotham made his way towards Dismas and as he approached close enough he reached down and tapped Dismas on the shoulder. He continued walking towards the tie line where their mules were tied up for the night. Dismas, feeling the tap on his shoulder, immediately rose to his feet and walked directly behind his brother quickly and quietly. They both reached the tie line at the same time. Their mules were tied next to each other. As Dismas turned to untie his mule he felt a firm arm across his forehead and a knife at his throat. He was jerked unceremoniously to his feet where he could see Abba already holding Jotham in a similar manner with a knife also at his throat. They were discovered. How he did not know, but he knew that this meant that they would both die tonight. This was the end. Everything he assumed about being healed by God because he had a purpose to fulfill had only been his wishful dream. Maybe he was a fool to believe it. Dismas was sorry now that he had convinced Jotham to trust him. His intention to save his brother had only gotten them both killed.

Tiran stepped into view and Gestas behind him. "Well well . . . So where is it you think you two are going?"

Jotham nervously thought of an answer that someone might believe and said, "I was going to ride ahead and scout and Dismas wanted to ride along with me for a bit and talk. That's all."

Tiran struck him hard across the cheek. "Wrong answer boy! I already sent a scout out and your brother here knows it. He would never have sent you out and went riding along with you." He was so mad that spittle flew at every word, "Isn't it true that the two of you planned on making an escape tonight and leave us forever? The very people that took you in and gave you a home . . . and a family? How dare you lie to me? I treated you two like my own sons . . . and you betrayed me!"

Tiran menacingly approached Dismas and grabbed him by the cloak, pulling him to his face. "And you . . . you traitor! I gave you everything! I trusted you! You disappoint me more than you will ever know. I gave you a home and I gave you power. You took it all and stabbed me in the heart. So help me, you will both pay for this!" He then threw him to the ground. The man that held him picked him up again and replaced the knife point back at his throat.

Jotham spoke up next. He was still confused about how Tiran knew what he and Dismas were planning. Someone had to have overheard the conversation between them earlier. He searched the faces around him and locked eyes on Gestas. Gestas could not hold his gaze. He looked away in shame and it became clear to Jotham that Gestas had betrayed them both. "Gestas? It was you?" Jotham had said it in a manner that made Gestas shrink from him even further. Gestas began to think back to the conversation that they had had earlier when Jotham reminded him that when he gets angry he sometimes acts before he thinks. This was one of those times. Now his two best friends in the world would be killed and it was all his fault. He would much rather have spent his life knowing that at least the two of them were able to get free of this life. For the first time he imagined that it would have been a smarter choice if he could have just gone with them. For him it was too late. His die had been cast. More so now than ever . . . He may not be the one that would draw the blade that would kill them but he had no illusions . . . their blood was on his hands.

All around them sleepy men were gathering around to see what all the commotion was and soon the word of mouth had gotten around the camp and all of the men were soon present. Tiran had them all dragged down to the main fire of the camp which still burned brightly in the night. At least the previous watch had made sure to stoke it well before he went to wake Jotham . . .

Gestas began pleading "Father, please don't kill them. They didn't mean any harm. Punish them severely but please don't kill them. I beg you!" Gestas was desperate to find a way to atone for what he had just done. He knew he had no chance that Tiran would not harm them, but he felt that he could at least appeal to him not to kill them.

Tiran was still angry, but he too was genuinely hurt by what the two had planned. He was so good to them. Why would they want to leave? What did they think they were going to do? They were thieves like him and they would never be able to do anything but beg. They had no skills for anything honest. Gestas' pleading had gotten to him. He knew exactly how his son felt. He didn't 'want' to harm them but he resolved himself long ago that he could not show favoritism to even his own son. He could certainly not afford to do so now. There would be great dissention among the men. He had to hold them together through fear. No, someone would have to die.

Gestas had still been pleading to his father for mercy and now he began to look weak in front of the men. Tiran did not want to, but for Gestas' sake he needed to stop now. When Gestas opened his mouth to plead again Tiran struck him very hard and silenced him. "You shut up right now with your groveling or so help me you'll be right beside them! You were the one that told me of their plans! Did you forget your role in this? Did you forget how we deal with traitors here? Were you under the assumption that I would give them a big wet kiss and say 'Bye Bye' and then send them on their way?" He looked down at his son and said "Now get on your feet!" Gestas rose to his feet and wiped the rosy stain from his lip. He steeled himself and looked defiantly at his father. More than anything right now Gestas wanted to take his dagger and plunge it right into the man's heart.

Tiran raised his voice for all to hear. "These two men have decided that they don't want to be here with us anymore. I've decided to oblige them with a much quicker journey, albeit not to the destination they had planned. They will certainly be departed from us tonight." Many of the men cheered, but it was mostly those that had not had the chance to be around Jotham and

Dismas all these years. The men who had known them would surely have wanted to show them more mercy and they understood Gestas, however, none of them were brave enough to back him. They did not want to see any harm come to the boys but they understood the need for discipline, especially when everyone you are surrounded by is a bloodthirsty killer or a thief.

Tiran continued, "I have always shown great care to make sure that everyone is treated equally. No matter who you are, you have no special place of honor here. You only get what you earn. Tonight I have decided that only one of these two young men will live. The other will be cast out. I hereby order any of you men that may chance to see him again to kill him on sight. Let the poor bastard live his life running in fear and knowing that he is his brother's killer. I can imagine that death here tonight would be preferable." Tiran turned to the men holding Dismas and Jotham and ordered them to release the boys. They complied and then they shoved them into the center of the gathered men.

Tiran ordered Abba to throw each of them a sword. He complied by throwing his own into the hands of Jotham while the man next to him took his sword and threw it at Dismas. Tiran then raised his voice again for all to hear. "I've just given these young men a means to decide which one of them will live or die tonight." He then addressed Dismas and Jotham directly, "Boys, you are going to fight to the death. Whoever survives can go free. You heard my conditions. A fair agreement I would say given the magnitude of your betrayal. At least one of you has a fighting chance to survive."

Both Dismas and Jotham were terrified by this sudden turn of events. Dismas looked at Jotham and said "I'm so sorry!" He then turned to address Tiran. "Tiran please, I won't raise a hand to my brother. I can't do it! Please I beg your mercy. We meant no harm to anyone. We just wanted a different life! Please have mercy!" Dismas got down on his knees and sobbed in desperation. If there was any idea that he could think of to save them, it had eluded him. All he could do now is beg.

Jotham pled with Tiran as well and said, "Don't do this sir. Just pick one of us and be done with it but don't make us kill the other. Please! We beg you!"

Gestas knew full well that one more word from him would risk bringing his father's full wrath down on him. He knew that to speak to him out loud would risk embarrassing his father and in turn put him in danger of joining Dismas and Jotham in the center of this ring of men. He leaned close to his father's ear and said "Please father, you can cast both of them out and still be thought of as a harsh but fair man. They would still have a death sentence hanging over them for the rest of their lives."

Tiran turned to him and in the same tone of voice said "You think you have any authority to beg me for anything. I'm only surprised you weren't trying to run away with them you coward." Gestas was angered to the point of no return and his father could see it on his face. "What, you want to kill me now? You just slither back to your bedroll Gestas or I'll gut you right here in front of everyone." Gestas looked down to see his father's dagger in hand and pointed directly at his belly. He backed up to give his father room. This conversation would continue, but it would be on Gestas' terms next.

Tiran turned back to the boys again. "You two will fight each other to the death or I will have Abba here insure that both of you get a very slow and painful death. It might take days you know. He is very good at his job. Either way one of you will die. You can fight or one of you can allow the other to strike you dead. I don't care, but make it quick or I will let Abba do his job."

Dismas continued to beg, "Please Tiran, I beg you don't do this to us. You can kill me if you want, just don't make my brother do it. I beg you!" Dismas suddenly felt his head begin to swim and the sounds of the crowd were beginning to pulsate in his ears. He blinked hard as he tried to regain focus.

The men were starting to whip up into a frenzy wanting the fight to get on. Even the men that did care for the boys were shouting. They just wanted it to be over and for the misery to end for them. The frenzied reaction was very distracting to Tiran and he failed to notice that Gestas had drawn his dagger and stepped in close to his father. Even Abba was too busy watching the spectacle in the center to notice what was happening. Abba truly did like both Jotham and Dismas, but he understood Tiran's position. He would miss them both, but he knew his place and would not disobey Tiran no matter how much he may disagree with him. Gestas eased closer, dagger in hand. One more step and he would end Tiran's life and then he hoped he would be able to convince the others to let Dismas and Jotham escape.

Just as he lunged forward with his dagger to plunge it into Tiran's heart, the anxious men in the crowd had decided to shove Jotham and Dismas into each other hoping to quicken their fight to the death. In their haste to begin the fight, one man shoved Jotham far too hard and he fell directly into the sword held by Dismas. The blade went through his chest as he fell into his brother's arms. A few feet away, the blade of Gestas plunged deep into Tiran's heart and he fell into the arms of his son. He was dying. Everywhere around them, the men froze. There was total silence amongst them all. Gestas immediately regretted his action and weeping, he threw his blade away. He fell to his knees and cradled his father's head in his arms and began to plead with him. "I'm so sorry father. I'm so sorry! I didn't mean it! Don't die . . . please forgive me . . . Please!" he cried. Tiran looked back at him with surprise on his face. He could not speak. A stain of blood bubbled from his mouth as he exhaled his last ragged breath. Gestas pulled Tiran's head close to his chest and sobbed while rocking back and forth. Abba never moved. He too was in shock.

All the men stood around them in silence. Dismas' head still pounded hard and he tried hard to regain his focus as he silently cradled Jotham's head in his arms as well, gently rocking him as he wept. Mercifully Jotham had died instantly when the blade ran through his heart. It was an oddly comforting thought to Dismas to imagine that his brother was now that little boy again and he was rocking him to sleep the same way his mother used to rock them. He was in shock. He knew his brother was dead but there was a small part of him that that was grateful that Jotham would be spared the life of misery that Tiran had promised him. He kept gently rocking his brother . . .

Gestas suddenly became aware that he had just killed Tiran in front of all his men. He looked up slowly to see many eyes on him. He let his father's body down easily and stood up. He looked around him and saw that he was surrounded by many angry faces. He was sure that they wanted to take action, but they did not know what to do. These men weren't sure who the leader was now and it gave them pause.

Gestas looked into the center of the ring of men and saw the brothers. His heart sank when he saw that one of them had already been killed. He truly loved them like his own brothers and to see one of them dead at the hands of the other and knowing that it was his fault cut through his soul. He knew that if they were going to escape they need to go now before these men figured out who would be the leader and gave an order to have them killed. He stepped quickly into the center of the group. The men in front of him made a wide path. He grabbed the surviving brother by the cloak and hauled him to his feet. He said "C'mon now. We need to go now or we're dead too." He was still in shock still and said nothing. He had no forces to do anything but step in the direction Gestas shoved him, but he could not take his eyes off of his dead brother. One of the men stepped in and grabbed Gestas by the arm and two other men stepped in and attempted to help stop the men. Abba's booming voice shocked them all into attention. "Let them go!" The men looked at him and he said again "Let them go."

Gestas shoved his friend all the way to the tie line and untied two mules. He helped him onto one and then he jumped on to the other. He was still in shock and could barely hold himself on. He was so weak from shock that he hardly had the strength to even sit up. Gestas swatted his mule to speed up their departure and then kicked his into action to catch them. The two men rode hard into the night. Unknown to them, they were beginning a journey of destiny that would end in both of their deaths.

CHAPTER 31

The years went on for the two young men. After they left that night they never again spoke of what happened. There was a silent understanding between the two of them that to do so would be too painful, and they never said a word. Conversations about their late brother and the father would start as a pleasant memory and always trail off as they realized that they were no longer with them. There was also the sudden realization why.

They finally did make their way to Jerusalem to retrieve the savings that the brothers had hidden and then immediately began their trek to the north. For a while they never settled in one area long for fear that they would be discovered. It wasn't long before the money ran out and they had to resort to doing what they knew best and that was taking other people's money and living off of it. The lifestyle brought with it certain dangers that prevented them from settling for too long in one place. You could only cheat people in gambling or pickpocket in one area for so long before they would be figured out. Then it would be time to move along before they were beaten or killed. They had more than a few new scars to prove how dangerous this type of work could be. After years of this lifestyle both of the men were becoming weary of it. It was too risky to go back to living the life of a highwayman. For one the Romans had only increased in number and now even Herod's men were joining in the hunt for bandits. However, the main reason was that it was simply too easy to run into their former associates, who would clearly have them killed on sight. No, they would not do this. They would have to settle for petty thievery to survive. Times were so bad in Herod's kingdom that even that was now almost impossible. Still, both of them longed for a regular life and they frequently discussed schemes to make it happen. Gestas would always manage to make it worse by gambling away their savings every time they had enough to use it for a fresh start. Dismas knew that he would be better off if he just left him behind and went off on his own, but they were friends for so long that he knew he had to stay. Eventually Gestas would settle down and they would make it. Until then Dismas knew that he was the only thing that often stood between Gestas and death. He had always been a bit on the mean spirited and quick to anger side, but over the years he had become even more so. His love of wine had grown too and it was often hard to ever see him when he was sober. When he was sober, he was often so mean and angry that Dismas sometimes longed for him to get drunk. For him he seemed more manageable that way.

The two men happened to be traveling between towns one afternoon when they came upon a rather large crowd gathering around a stream. It was particularly hot on this day and Dismas and Jotham found themselves heading in that direction to find drink and to rest for a while. Gestas was always intrigued when he saw crowds gathering like this. One because it usually meant that he would be able to pick a few pockets while they had their minds and attention on something else. He was quite good at from years of practice, as was Dismas. They had made their living for many years doing this and there were none better at it than they were.

Dismas was just too thirsty and tired to pick any pockets that day and he only wanted to find water and a nice cool spot of shade to settle down in. He looked behind him to check on Gestas and noticed that Gestas had already set off. He struck up conversations with weary folk and lifted their possessions while he did. This crowd was really large and Dismas had no idea why it had grown so out here in the middle of nowhere. He heard a man's voice shouting over the sounds of the crowd and he started to have an idea that it must be a rabbi to draw a crowd like this, but why would they be all the way out here? From his experience, most rabbis weren't at all that interesting. At least not enough to attract a crowd like this. He wondered to himself what it could be.

He saw a man and his son making their way to the sound of the man shouting and decided to stop them. "What is this? Why is everyone gathering here?"

The old man was clearly put off by the interruption. He was in a hurry to find a place close enough to hear the man that was shouting and Dismas only served to delay him from his task. He couldn't be bothered and pulled away from Dismas and continued his trek. His son stopped and replied. "It's John we are here to see.

He's a prophet come to preach the word of God. Please forgive my father. He saw the Baptist once before and his words changed my father's life. He couldn't wait to come home from his travels to tell us about him. I was intrigued because of the things my father had repeated to me and had to come and see him for myself. My father and I intend to be baptized by him if he will allow it. You must come. I understand that he can be quite mesmerizing." The young man smiled from ear to ear and turned to see if he could still catch up to his father who had not shown any sign of slowing down. "Wait father! I am coming! Please wait for me!"

Dismas was indeed interested now. He thought about his mother a lot these days and he knew that he would never feel the peace he used to feel with her until he put God back in his life. To be honest he longed for that more than anything. He had grown weary of being someone that he despised. Perhaps this man John would be able to help him see a path back to forgiveness. He knew that he had to hear what the man had to say, but first he needed to get a drink. He made his way to water and began to drink until he was fulfilled. He took a moment to splash the dust off of his face and refill his waterskin. He then made his way to the sound of this 'John the Baptist's' voice. He looked around to see if he could spot Gestas, but alas, he was nowhere to be found. He knew without even seeing him what he was up to and it was just as well that he was not with him now, because all Gestas ever did was berate him for his beliefs. Dismas could never speak of God or religion without fear of invoking a long rebuking tirade from his friend.

As he came over the rise of a low hill on the side of the stream, he saw John the Baptist standing there on top of similar hill by the stream. It was a good vantage point for him. Here he could stand on a low rising outcropping of rock where people below him could see him well and hear him. Many other people were gathering in the surrounding slopes that led down to the stream he was preaching at. The place offered an almost perfect amphitheater for the man and all could hear him well even if he weren't shouting his message. As it was, you could hear his message from a wide area around his small perch on top of the rock outcropping.

Dismas was amazed at the amount of energy this wild looking man had. He heard his loud voice for some time and it sounded as if the level of energy he had did not diminish in the slightest. He observed the man preaching to this crowd. He saw a man that seemed rather ordinary except that he looked like he had been living in the wilderness his entire life. He certainly dressed like a poor man. He wore only rags that were practically falling apart. This fact alone struck Dismas as odd because he had expected that a rabbi would have dressed a bit better than he had. He knew of no rabbi that would not at least have taken an offering from his flock. Surely this man had many opportunities to have money if he could draw crowds like this all the time. Why would he live this way? His hair was long and unkempt. It was if he had not a single care in the world about pleasing anyone.

There was something about this man's look and his voice that mesmerized the crowds when he spoke. His words were very eloquent and yet so contrary to his appearance. He spoke loudly for all to hear. Even so, what he said seemed so personal to everyone surrounding him there in this little desert theater that it made no one here feel like he was shouting. Dismas was finally able to hear the man's words for himself and he too had become enraptured by what he heard him saying.

The man they called John the Baptist looked around at the crowds gathering. He raised his staff and said "Brothers and Sisters, why do you allow yourselves to live in bondage every day of your lives? Do you not know that your father commands you to be free? You live your lives in misery wearing the chains of regret for your sins and you look not to the one who holds the keys to loose you from these shackles! God wants you to be free from your sin! Look to him Brothers and Sisters and repent of your sins and he will loose your chains and he will set you free!"

He became much more animated and he moved around through the crowd as he spoke to them. Most of them stayed in place and did not move. They were afraid that they would not hear every word he said to them. The Baptist lowered his voice a bit and his eyes scanned the crowd as if he were speaking to everyone here. "Some of you here have borne chains that are very heavy and you have borne them for a very long time. You have been a slave to sin for so long that you no longer remember what it is like to be free. Like all slaves you want to be free. Like all slaves you feel powerless to your masters." He leapt up on the rock next to Dismas and looked him directly in the eyes. "I say to you, your master is Sin and Sin has no power over God!" He raised his staff high over his head to illustrate the importance of this statement to his followers. Dismas' heart raced. He was certain that this wild eyed desert rabbi spoke directly to him and he knew it.

The Baptist held his gaze on Dismas as he continued speaking to the crowd. "The power of forgiveness is great Brothers and Sisters! If you go to the Father and ask for forgiveness with a truly penitent heart, you will be forgiven!" These words were spoken directly at Dismas and he knew they were meant for him. "Your chains will be shattered, and your false master, Sin, will be cast out! No more will false burdens and false shadows bury you! You will be lifted up! You will be a new creature and washed as clean as snow!" Dismas understood this message was meant for him and he began to sob. The Baptist's words reminded him of the burden he had been carrying all these years. Perhaps he was right. All he had to do was ask for forgiveness and this burden would be gone. Dismas only knew that he no longer wanted to carry his sin.

The Baptist moved down the rock and he lay his staff down next to the water and then he waded in. He raised his hands in prayer and said "Father, witness your children this day that come forth to be washed of their sins! Witness them casting off their false masters and breaking the chains that have bound them! Oh Father, I beg of you to wash them clean and to bless them for their repentance." He scooped up water into his hands and poured it over the head of an old man near him. The old man looked at the Baptist and begged to be forgiven for his sins. The Baptist merely smiled and said to him as the water poured down over his face. "Go forth my Brother and sin no more" he said in the most loving of tones. It was as if he were speaking to his own child. The crowds, upon seeing the baptism, began to move toward him and they practically trampled each other to get to the Baptist. Dismas himself had begun to move toward him. He only knew that he was ready in his heart and soul to beg forgiveness from God. He knew his heart was truly penitent and he knew it was time that he gave up this life of sin.

Suddenly a hand with a hard grip grabbed him by the shoulder of his cloak and dragged him unceremoniously out of the water. He struggled to gain his footing and confront the person controlling him and noticed that it was Gestas. "What are you doing Gestas?" exclaimed a very angry Dismas. "Let me go! Now!" and then he shook off Gestas' grip.

Gestas spoke quickly but he would not look directly at Dismas. His eyes were busy scanning the crowd. He was out of breath and he looked like he had been beaten. "I thought I would never find you. We are in danger and we need to leave now!"

"What for? We haven't done anything!" Dismas said as he managed to jerk himself free of Gestas' grasp.

"Well maybe you haven't but I might have. I tried to lift a man's coin pouch and his companion saw me. He grabbed me and before I knew what was going on they had me on the ground beating me. I barely made it away from them but they are following me." Gestas was still scanning the crowd for the men and Dismas found himself doing the same although he had no idea what they would look like. He supposed that they would be easy to spot because they would probably be the only men not paying attention to the Baptist.

Dismas had a sudden thought cross his mind and then asked the question to confirm it. "Why are they still after you if they already beat you Gestas?" He then spotted two large men scanning the crowd as if they were looking for someone.

Gestas smiled that mischievous smile he was known for and held a pouch up in his fist and said "Because I still have their money!" He then grabbed Dismas again by the collar and started making a dash out of the creek bed as fast as possible. The two men spotted them running away and recognized Gestas. "Thieves! Thieves!" they shouted. Every head turned toward the fleeing pair including that of the Baptist.

The Baptist shouted after the two as they fled. "You cannot run from God! He is everywhere and he sees everything! Repent! Repent!" This was all they heard as they ran away. The men had stopped giving chase and Dismas and Gestas were finally able to stop running. It was well that they did because the day was so hot that they would not be able to run for much longer. They began to walk and act normally so as not to be noticed by the throngs of people making their way from the road to the small stream where the Baptist was preaching. As they walked away, Dismas spotted a tall man in pale robe walking toward the stream with the rest of the crowds. This man stood out from the rest of the people the way he carried himself. As he got closer Dismas noticed that he had the most piercing blue eyes he had ever seen. Only one person Dismas had ever seen had these eyes . . . was it him?

As this man approached he looked directly at Dismas and stopped. He had a waterskin slung over his shoulder and he began to unsling it. He looked at Dismas and said "You are thirsty. You should drink." He then handed the waterskin over to Dismas. Dismas was paralyzed with fear now. What are the chances that he would see Jesus at this time and in this place? He trembled. He wanted to drink it but he could not find the forces to do so.

Jesus could see that Dismas was afraid and he said to him "When what you need is in your hands, why do you not take of it? When what you seek is here, in this place, why do you then wish to leave it?" He paused for a moment and then continued. "You stand in the light and where you go you will only find darkness."

Dismas could not reply but just then Gestas grabbed the waterskin and said "If you aren't going to drink it I will" and then he drank thirstily from it. He finished it off and then tossed it to the ground. Jesus just stood there looking at him.

"Well aren't you going to pick it up?" Gestas taunted.

Jesus calmly replied to him. "It is not necessary when what I thirst for is before me. What you thirst for you will never find."

"Have it your way 'Rabbi'" said Gestas as he wiped his mouth. He then marched back down the road.

"Please forgive him." said Dismas. "My friend is not a polite man."

"You ask forgiveness for him, but not for yourself. If you need forgiveness, you need only to repent your sins to God." Jesus spoke to him in a calm tone and with a familiarity that scared Dismas even more.

"I must go." He paused for just a moment. "I will consider your words." He then turned and ran to catch up with Gestas. He berated himself as he ran away for not having the courage to just stop and go back. Jesus was right. What he sought he would never find until he was able to have the courage to repent himself. Maybe someday he would have the courage to do so . . . but today was not that day.

CHAPTER 32

A little over a year had passed and Dismas and Gestas now found themselves back in Capernaum. Capernaum was their home for a very short period of time years ago when they first ran away after the deaths of Jotham and Tiran. Both of them had loved this place very much back then but they were so fearful of being discovered by Tiran's henchmen that they dared not stay there for too long. Perhaps if they had stayed, they would never have been found and they might have had a chance for a normal life. They both wondered what life would be like if they were able to find some kind of peace back then. They tried to imagine what their lives would have been like if they were able to stay here, find a job, get married and raise big families. Alas, the thoughts were always an exercise in futility because they never imagined they would be free of this overwhelming fear long enough to realize any of their dreams. Now they found themselves back here in Capernaum, this city by the sea, years later to finally try to make it their home. Many years had passed between them now and many miles had passed beneath their feet to reach this point once again.

Things were never the same for Dismas after the fateful encounter with Jesus and the Baptist that day by the stream. Dismas was clearly trying to steer both he and Gestas into an honest life after that. He was quite successful at it more than once, but only for a little while at a time. They would get a good honest job and would do well and manage to save up some money . . . and then invariably Gestas would go and gamble it away or try to throw all of the money into some ill-gotten scheme to turn it into more money. It usually wound up with Gestas going back to his old ways and getting both of them into trouble. They always wound up having to run away and then lapsing back into the life of thievery until they got tired and then tried to go honest again. It was a vicious cycle, but one they felt powerless to get out of. Over the last few months Dismas began to think Gestas was finally starting to feel in his heart that he needed to give up this life of thievery once and for all. Times were hard and it only got harder as they got older. They both longed to be settled before they got too old to enjoy life. Neither of them wanted to spend the rest of their days in search of the next big opportunity or having to watch over your shoulder constantly to make sure someone you lied, cheated or stole from hadn't found you or recognized you. They both wanted to finally feel what it was like to have someone love them and to have a real home and a real bed to sleep in, to have someone call them 'Husband' or 'Father'. Even a boss to complain about became something they longed to experience.

Capernaum was the one place that they felt the most at home in from all of their travels. They had been to a great many places, but to them this was the most beautiful. The Galilee itself was incredibly beautiful to gaze upon, especially when the sun would rise or set upon it. The skies would look like fire burning on the horizon and he often saw colors there that he had never seen before. The fertile green valleys around it were lush with crops and he could always count on getting the best food here. Fish and fruit were plentiful in this place. One of Dismas' favorite places to go when they were here before was up on the mount near the town. He would go there often just to look out over this beautiful place. From his favorite spot on this hill he could see the fishermen on their ships casting nets over the sea and hauling in their catch. He could see the farmers below tend to their fields and shepherds to their sheep. Also down below Dismas could see this bustling city full of life and promise buzzing on indifferently to the world around it. From the hilltop vantage point Dismas could see this entire beautiful valley and it truly calmed his soul. It took him away from the pain he felt from this unfortunate life and he longed to go back there again so he could forget it all once more.

Now they were back. They were older, once again broke and arguably not any wiser than they were when they were here the first time all those years ago. But it seemed like as good a place as any other to begin fresh. They no longer feared the reach of Tiran from beyond his grave for many of those men likely were dead of old age or probably had been killed or captured by the Romans. It was not likely they would be recognized by them anyway after all this time. This was the right place for them. It was where they needed to be. It would be easy to find work here. The city had grown much since they were here years ago. It was still a vibrant place to be but now it was just much larger with even more opportunities. They both suspected that anyone willing to work hard would probably do well for themselves.

Dismas and Gestas made inquiries about work when they reached one of the city's marketplaces. This was a bustling place in Capernaum where people gathered to trade their goods and provide services for both citizens and visitors. All around them the place buzzed with life and activity. People were lined up selling their goods and wares. Customers were lining the streets and practically crawling over the top of each other to get to those selling their goods. Everywhere you looked business was very brisk. Children were playing all around chasing each other to and fro. No doubt many of them were the children of the vendors and customers lining the streets. Elsewhere you could see some children that did not seem so fortunate. These poor children were begging for money or scraps of food to eat. Of course, where people gathered like this one could always find those that preyed on them. Both Dismas and Gestas had spent so much of their lives surviving as gamblers, thieves and con men that it was quite easy to spot their own kind working this crowd. From the looks of it they were glad to be here to become honest men, for it appeared to them that there was probably too much criminal competition for them. It also meant that they may have to watch themselves carefully for fear that they may become the victim themselves. They would not let that happen after all they had been through.

Dismas was the one that did almost all of the talking. It was very difficult to get Gestas to pay attention. Gestas was entirely too drawn to looking at every pretty face he saw or trying to evaluate all the business going on here. He also spent a fair amount of time evaluating the skills of the thieves in this market. He was confident that he would be able to put them all to shame but he had grown too weary of it and, like Dismas, just wanted to settle down and stop wandering. Dismas finally came to a man in front of several racks and bags that were nearly full to bursting with drying fish and told him that they were new to town and looking for work. He asked the man if he knew of anyone that might be looking to hire someone. The particular man he spoke to had obviously worked around fishermen daily in his line of work and might know of someone hiring. He also had a particularly bad habit of talking far too much. He had probably come by this trait honestly by spending every single day standing at this table trying to get customers interested in buying his fish. He was also trying to convince them all why it was better to buy from him than all the other sellers around him. After talking for what seemed like forever, this man forgot what the question even was in the first place. Dismas had to remind him again that his question was whether or not the man knew anyone hiring. The old man finally summed it up by asking them why they didn't just ask that in the first place, to which Dismas and Gestas both had to laugh. He was kind enough to steer them toward a man named Darius just down the road and described to them Darius' home.

It seemed Darius was quite a big man in this town and well respected. He was not a fisherman but he provided a service that all fishermen needed at one point or another, and that business was making and mending nets. The old man was sure he had heard that Darius was looking for men to work for him. He was described as having too much business to keep up with and he was always shorthanded. Most of the men that worked for him usually only did so because they wanted to be around the fishermen and to learn their trade. If they did a good enough job and got noticed they often got recruited by one of the captains to go out and work with them catching fish. It wasn't quite as hard as making and mending nets all day long and they made a lot more money because most captains usually gave them a small share of the haul. As a result men like Darius always had turnover and needed to hire good helpers.

Gestas and Dismas made their way down the lane towards the sea and soon they happened upon the specific pier that the man in the market had described to them. This was where Darius' home was and where he also ran his net making and mending operation from. Dismas was so fascinated watching all the activity going on here that he almost walked right into two young men stretching out a portion of net that they intended to repair. One of the men, clearly annoyed by the visitors, yelled for him to watch where he was going. Gestas was quick to laugh at Dismas' clumsiness. Dismas turned to apologize for his unwitting intrusion into the men's work and asked where they might find Darius. The young men both pointed to a tall man standing directly behind Dismas and Gestas. As they turned to see him the man said "So, you're looking for me, eh? I'm guessing you are looking for work? Am I right?"

Dismas smiled and said "Yes Sir we are. Could you spare some work for two hard working men?"

Darius put his hands on his hips and said, "Not if you are planning on working for me just long enough to get a job on one of these stinking boats. I'm sick of it. If you want to work for me you have to promise you aren't going to leave first chance you get. My business is growing too fast. This work requires a certain amount of skill to do. I don't mind teaching it but it takes time to get it right and I don't need you leaving me soon as you learn the trade. I have a reputation of quality to uphold and I can no longer do that if my help leaves me before I can even get them trained right."

He reached into his cloak and tossed something to Gestas. It was a small flat piece of wood with a point on one end and two small points on the other. In the middle it was slightly narrower and had a center carved out of it with a few feet of thin cord wrapped around it. "You ever used one of these?"

"No sir, I have not." was Gestas' reply.

"I'm going to guess you've probably never even seen one of these either. It's a netting needle. Means I'm going to have to teach you everything from scratch." The man sighed and took the netting needle back from Gestas and put it back into his cloak.

"You two look like you can handle hard work. I'll give you a try and see if you can catch on tomorrow. If you do well I'll hire you; but only under the condition that you stay on with me long term. That sound good to you?"

Dismas smiled and replied eagerly "Yes Sir!"

"Good. Be here at dawn tomorrow and be ready to work harder than you ever have in your life." Darius turned to return to his day's work and then as an afterthought turned back to face Dismas and Gestas. "Oh, and if I were you I would kiss those nice smooth hands of yours goodbye. You'll never see them that way again." He then raised his hands to illustrate what he meant. They were huge and covered with callouses and scars both front and back. Apparently these nets and netting needles were not so easy to handle even by the expert himself.

Dismas and Gestas turned to leave. They looked very stoic as they walked away but the very second they were in the alley and out of sight they both grinned from ear to ear and shouted in excitement. They had jobs now! This was the first step in building a real life. They had no illusions about this work. They knew exactly how hard it could be. They were around men who had been in this trade before. But it was work and they were both grateful. Tomorrow promised to be extremely hard but fulfilling all the same. They had feelings of mingled dread and excitement but they were ready for it. Maybe life was finally going to give them a break at last.

CHAPTER 33

Gestas predictably became restless after a few months and he started his normal decline back into his old life. It started the way it normally had with drinking too much wine. It then led into further decline when he would waste his money while under the influence of the alcohol. It typically would begin with spending it on women, then on bad investments, and when he got desperate he resorted to gambling to make his money back. Gestas had always been a good thief, but he had never really been a good gambler. He only won when he cheated, but cheating was very risky. If he got caught, he risked ruining this new life they had just started here in Capernaum. The end result was that he was broke all the time. Then, as usual, the temptation would strike him to pick a pocket or two just to support his drinking for the next few days. Dismas knew it would soon be the end again and would have to run, but he had made up his mind it would not be his fate this time. He loved Gestas like a brother but he would no longer go down this path with him. All he could do was beg him to stop. He even tried loaning him money from time to time so he could convince him that he did not need to go out gambling again, but Gestas would always waste it. Dismas had saved up a good sum of money for his future and had no desire to dip into it only to allow Gestas to waste it all with his foolish plans for life. Dismas would save his money and one day when he had enough he would start his own business. Maybe he would open his own net repair shop or perhaps buy his own boat and become a fisherman. He had a goodly sum saved already but he knew he had to save for a while longer before he could afford to realize his dreams.

Dismas did quite well at his new line of work and soon became very close to Darius. Darius had become quite proud of him and his handy work. He worked hard and he worked fast. He had a terrific eye for detail and quality. He was excellent with customers and he was a natural with business. They both were very blessed to have crossed paths. Dismas felt that sense of belonging and purpose for the very first time in his life.

Recently a very bad storm came through and struck the Galilee so fiercely and so suddenly many vessels were not able to make it in to shore quickly enough to be safe. As a result of the storm several vessels were lost and many men were drowned. Many more that did make it home came back with harrowing tales of how they had averted their own disasters. One such vessel that did not return was captained by a wonderful old man named Caleb. He was a very close friend of Darius. He saw his friend early that morning when he cast off and by night he was gone along with all of his crew. He was an older man with several sons and two of them, Jacob and Teman, had followed in their father's footsteps and had captained their own boats. They made it back alive and they grieved their father's death deeply for he was a very kind and loving man. He had not been hardened by his daily labors of fishing. He embraced his chances to go to sea and often told everyone that it was when he felt the closest to God. Now he was with him. Although the family grieved his death they knew he had gone to be with the Father and this made them happy. It was as he would have wanted it. He loved God with all of his heart and he also loved the sea. Now he would be with them both forever.

He had many sons but only one daughter. Her name was Adinah. Adinah was the youngest of his many children. She was arguably one of the most beautiful women in Capernaum but she was very ill with fever as a child and it caused her to have a horrible limp. It was for this reason that her father had never had any luck finding a husband for her. She was a kind and loving young lady and everyone adored her, but the men that typically surrounded her brothers and her father in this rough environment would often make fun of her for her limp and it caused her to be very withdrawn. She had two very protective brothers and it often resulted in a lot of fights. Her oldest brother Jacob was a very wise man just like her father, but he had a reputation for getting angry with very little provocation. He was probably the most overly protective of his little sister. Protecting Adinah was very important to her father and thus had become a chief responsibility of Jacob as well. Adinah's next to oldest brother Teman had always been an overly large brute of a man. He was not at all as smart as his other brothers and his sister, but he was by far the kindest and gentlest of them all. His temperament was a blessing given his size. It would have been a deadly combination for Teman to have had the temperament of his brother Jacob. Teman usually fell in line quickly with what Jacob asked of him because he trusted him. Teman was very protective of Adinah as well because she was the kindest person in the world to him.

Because of the brothers' reputation, the men that were around here long enough knew better than to say a word about her or, they had known her well enough to be very uncomfortable saying anything bad about her. Many times they would join in and protect her as well. The problem in Capernaum is that the city had grown so much over the years that there was always a new face . . . and there was always someone needing a lesson in manners; a task the brothers were all too happy to oblige them with.

Adinah would often come round to see her brothers off in the mornings and then again in the late afternoons when they came in. They were often tired and thirsty, and always very hungry. She would bring them food and drink and sit with them enjoying their company. When they finished up, the men would gather up their catch and tote them to a fish market nearby where they would sell their catch to the highest bidder and collect their money. This was usually the extent of the workday for the brothers who were captains. The junior men on the ship were responsible for getting the nets taken care of and repaired if necessary. They would then clean the boat as a final task and then off they went to their own homes and then back again the next day to repeat the same routine over and over again. Sometimes the faces would change but the routine was always the same.

On one of these occasions Dismas had noted that Adinah was struggling to carry the food and drink for her brothers one afternoon and he went to help her carry them to their family's mooring spot near Darius' shop. He had seen her perform this task many times and had even spoken to her a few times over the last several months. She had the most beautiful smile and was extremely pleasant to speak with, and he found himself longing to see her every day even if he didn't get to speak with her. He had no cares at all about her limp. He had seen past that and had truly just been interested in her. This particular day had given him the first of many opportunities to help her carry her goods to her brothers. The brothers had all gotten quite used to seeing Dismas around and they all liked him. He worked very hard and was in favor with Darius whom they had all known to be incredibly tough as a boss. The fact that Darius liked him was enough to satisfy all of them that he was a good man. Before he passed away, even their father Caleb seemed to like him and this meant a lot to them as well. But perhaps the single biggest factor that made Adinah's brothers like him was that he had always been very kind to her and spoke to her like an equal. He did not look down at her like most people did. He never asked for anything in return from her and they felt he genuinely cared for her. He made her smile and he made her happy. Secretly they had hoped that one day they might become more than just friends. Dismas did not have much to offer but they knew she would never find a husband of any means, so what she really needed was a man that would care for her and make her happy. She never cared about riches anyway. In many ways she was the most like her father. She truly loved God as he did and she was often happy with even the smallest and most modest of things. While most people longed for things they could never have, she rejoiced in everything she did have.

Soon Gestas began to spend less time around him. He was always trying to encourage Dismas to join him in his schemes or loan him money from his hidden savings and Dismas would never support him in either wish. It made Gestas very angry to see that his friend had finally seemed to move on without him. Every time Gestas was around him all he would do was talk about work, about his future plans, about Adinah, and it was slowly driving him away. Inside he knew the end would be close and he would have to move on. He was fairly certain that Dismas would not leave with him this time and it filled him with both anger and sadness. Gestas was spending a little time this particular evening with a prostitute he had grown to like lately. Her name was Mary. She was a little older than he normally cared for but she was always good company. Sometimes though, Mary would remind him of Dismas with her dreams of giving up her life of prostitution and just becoming like a normal person. He thought her crazy to think this because no man would ever treat her as a normal person after what she had done. Even if she left this area for good he thought she would never know a normal life. Perhaps in that way she and Gestas were the ones who were more alike. Both of them were marked by a hard life and bad decisions and their sins would never let them go. Gestas was a little drunk and was in the area so he wanted to bring Mary to meet his lifelong friend and perhaps convince him to have a drink with them. Gestas walked in the door to Dismas' small abode and saw him in a corner with his back turned to him. He had not heard them approach and Gestas was curious as to what his friend was doing on the floor in the corner so he shushed Mary so he could observe for a moment unnoticed. Gestas saw Dismas take some money from his cloak and wrap it into a small leather sack and then bury it in the dirt in the corner of his room and then rolled his bedroll back out over it. He turned around and saw Gestas and was startled. He had hoped that Gestas had not seen him but Gestas cleverly made himself look as if he had just walked in the door so Dismas would be more at ease. He did not want to think that his friend would steal from him but he did not want to tempt fate. Gestas had made more than one bad decision in his life and that was enough to make Dismas feel he had to hide his savings in order to protect it from his friend. Gestas had no intention of taking Dismas' money at this time but he filed this secret location away in his memory in the event he may need to 'borrow' some money in the future.

Gestas, slightly drunk, decided to speak first. "Dismas my old friend, it's good to see you again! How is work these days?"

"It's gotten a lot easier since you left" he joked. "I don't have to go back and fix everything you messed up." He grinned and they both felt more at ease.

"Well, as you know my life is not quite as boring as it was fixing nets every single day from sunup to sundown." He looked over his companion from head to toe and said, "I find my new scenery much more appealing than looking at your serious face every day." Gestas seated himself and drew Mary to his side and said, "Meet my friend Mary. Is it okay if she visits with us for a bit? I haven't seen you in so long and I want to catch up with you and we were passing through this area."

Dismas made a slight bow in Mary's direction and said hello to her and went to pour a wine for each of them. He did not intend to allow them to stay long enough to get too drunk, especially since they were close to it already. It would be rude however to not offer at least a drink to them as guests. As he poured the wine Gestas struck up conversation by hitting on the one topic sure to get him talking. "So, I hear you've been seeing a lot of a certain fishermen's daughter lately, you know the girl with the limp. What's her name? Abiba . . . something like that? Are things getting serious now my friend?"

Dismas smiled a bit. Gestas was correct; this was a topic he liked to talk about. "Her name is Adinah, and yes, I guess you could say we have been seeing a lot of each other. I would like to get more serious with her but her brothers terrify me. I think they like me but I have seen them beat more than one man senseless over her and I don't want to be the next one. It creates quite a dilemma for me."

"Nonsense Dismas. They like you. Everyone likes you. Just go and ask the brothers politely if they will allow you to court her.

All they can do is say no . . . and I guess beat you senseless too."
He chuckled a bit, "But at least you will have your answer!" All
three of them laughed.

They spent the next couple of hours speaking about various
topics they were interested in and getting caught up with each
other. It was truly enjoyable to visit with each other like this,
but all evening there seemed to be more of a distance between
the two of them and it was clear to both that the friendship was
slowly becoming more distant. The conversation started getting
quieter as if they were running out of topics and Dismas found
himself absentmindedly humming and tapping to the tune on a
small drum that he had made for himself. Mary noticed it and
said "What is that song you are playing? It's beautiful." Gestas
shuffled in his seat uncomfortably because he knew the tune and
the story of why it was important to his friend.

"It's a lullaby my mother used to sing to my brothers and I
before she died." said a wistful Dismas. Gestas observed Dismas'
face and wondered what was going on in his friend's mind right
now. He suddenly stopped and put the drum away as if the
memory had become too painful for him.

Gestas then stood up and was almost about to leave when
a thought occurred to him about a topic that he knew Dismas
would be interested in. "Say Dismas, do you remember that Jesus
fellow that we met the day we saw the Baptist and I got the mud
beat out of me?"

Dismas felt a chill when he heard the name. He had often
thought of the man. It was well known in Capernaum that

he had been traveling around the countryside preaching and there were rumors that he had performed several miracles. "Yes, I remember. Why do you ask?" As he looked to Mary he saw that the mention of Jesus' name caused her to perk up and listen as well.

"Well I forgot to tell you that he is in town and has been drawing some pretty large crowds of people that have been following him everywhere to hear him speak or to seek his miracle healing. I've never seen anything like it before. I'm surprised you hadn't noticed but since you spend all your day down by the sea maybe you hadn't heard."

Mary spoke next and said, "You knew he was in town and said nothing? How many times have you heard me mention him? I love his messages about getting second chances in life! You knew I would want to know that he was here!"

Gestas looked a bit embarrassed at the reaction. It's true he did know she would be interested but he avoided telling her because he was afraid she would get so caught up in the Rabbi that she would abandon him like his friend did. Perhaps he was too drunk to have considered how she might react to this revelation. "I'm . . . Uh . . . I'm sorry. I forgot." She swatted his arm. "Well you know I drink a lot. I forget things," he said and the she then swatted him again to make her point.

Dismas was more than excited to hear this news. He longed for quite some time now for another encounter with him and maybe tomorrow would be the day. He was more ready now to hear his word than ever before. Perhaps the bad chapters of his life were finally going to close forever. Soon he would see. "Where will he be tomorrow?"

"I don't know my friend but I suspect that by the size of the crowds he will have to move outside the city to speak to all of them. There isn't a place in all of Capernaum where they can gather comfortably. Maybe he will be up on the mount outside the city. Seems like as good a place as any."

Dismas was pleased. "Thank you Gestas. I will speak with Darius tomorrow and ask him to let me go see him. He won't mind. We have a full staff finally."

Gestas finally had the nerve to say why he brought this up in the first place. It seemed he was out of money and he saw these crowds as an opportunity to make some more. "Well, there is one more thing I need to see if you can help me out with. I see a terrific opportunity to make money off of the crowds Jesus is bringing in. They are here for more 'pious' reasons so I'm quite certain I can't sucker any into gambling with me. And you see, well, I have no goods or services I can offer. So . . . I was hoping to make a little extra money so I can get my life straightened back out by working the crowd lifting a wallet here and there. It would be easy money."

Dismas was angry that Gestas even thought to suggest this to him. "No! I will not! I've told you more than once I don't want that life anymore. I've finally started building a good life here and I like it. I don't want to leave. If I help you we'll be caught and everything will be ruined again!" Dismas now knew what Gestas really wanted when he came here. He should have known this would happen.

"Come on! We'll play it safe and cautious. We won't get caught. I just need to get up enough money to get my life on track too just like we planned it when we got here. I like this place too. I don't want to leave it either. Please Dismas, just reconsider it. I promise I'm going to go straight this time. If you'll help me I swear it will be the last time ever." He clasped his hands together and pleaded with his friend in false desperation. Gestas knew he could make a lot of money on his own, but when they worked in pairs they were always more successful and this was truly what he wanted. He had no intention of going straight.

"No. I will not do it. My word is final on this matter. Now leave!" and he tried to usher his friend out the door.

Gestas was angry and he slapped Dismas hard on the face. "You owe me! After everything we've been through and everything we have done. You owe me!" He raised his hand to slap Dismas again and it was Mary that prevented him from doing so this time. She grabbed his hand and caught him off guard.

"Leave him be Gestas!" Mary pleaded with him. "Can't you see that he does not want that life? If he is truly like a brother to you surely you can respect that. Leave him be." Gestas started to calm down and maybe he was beginning to finally realize that she might be right but he did not like it. "Come with me dear, I will calm you down" and then she dragged him from Dismas' doorstep.

As he walked away Gestas turned to Dismas and said "It's not over Dismas. You're a thief. You've always been a thief and you'll always be one. Sooner or later you're going to get desperate enough and you'll do it again, and I hope I'm there to see you fall." Gestas spit on the ground at Dismas' feet and walked away arm in arm with his prostitute friend Mary.

Dismas was stung by those words. Maybe he would be right someday, but right now in his heart he knew he would fight that destiny with all of his strength and all of his heart. He had worked hard to rebuild his life and he would not allow it to be destroyed again, not by Gestas, not by anyone.

CHAPTER 34

Dismas as well as most people here were quite taken aback at the sheer size of the crowds that Jesus attracted. There were hundreds if not thousands of people that descended upon Capernaum to see him. Many were normal people just like everyone else you would see here but they had traveled far. Many of the people that had come here to see him were bringing relatives and friends with them that were in need of healing, for they had all heard that he had the power to heal by miracle and they wanted to see if they could get him to heal their loved ones of their various afflictions. Everywhere there were people with every kind of infirmity you could imagine. The people of Capernaum were also excited to see the Rabbi they knew as Jesus but they also worried about the crowds he brought with him. It was one thing to see so many pious people in one spot but the crowds usually brought with them some unsavory elements that did what they did best and that was to prey on the people here for help. They were the worst kind of human being to prey on those that were poor and infirm. Dismas thought to himself that he used to be just like those people and now it made him sick to think that he ever could have been like that.

Today was different. He had made his way down to his usual place of employment and as he made the turn he saw that also as usual Darius was there to greet him for the day. Dismas helped him get set up for the day's work as all the other men were starting to arrive to begin their duties making and mending nets. He turned and waved to Adinah as she was just finished seeing her brothers off for their day's work. She smiled back at him and made her way up the small hill to join him. They would usually have time for a little conversation while he worked and it was a moment they both enjoyed very much. Though neither one would say so to the other, they were definitely in love.

Dismas thought this was as good a time as any to see if Darius would allow him to go join the crowds and listen to Jesus speak. He was attempting some small talk to work up the nerve to ask when Darius realized he had something to say and just blurted it out. "So, you were about to ask if you could take the rest of the day off and go see this Rabbi and you wanted to know if it was ok. And then you were going to try to convince me by letting me know that everything was caught up and that everyone had shown up for work this morning and that we were not behind on anything. Am I correct?"

Dismas was happy that he didn't have to say it himself but he was still nervous. Darius was kind to him and had done so much to help him rebuild his life. He suspected that at some point in Darius' life he had some of his own misfortunes and someone had given him a fresh start. Perhaps this was what drove him to be so kind to Dismas. Dismas hoped that he would be allowed an opportunity to be the same man himself someday and return the favor in kind to someone else who deserved it. Sheepishly he said "Yes Darius. If it is okay with you I would like to see the Rabbi."

"Dismas, in all my years no one has ever worked for me as long as you have. You do fine work and you have made me more prosperous for it. How could I deny you an opportunity to seek the word of God. I would truly be a poor master if I did not allow you to go. Run along, you have my blessing."

Eagerly, Dismas said "Thank you sir!" and then turned to see that Adinah was standing right there next to him.

"Are you going to see Jesus?" said the beautiful Adinah as she held to his arm.

"Yes, I am now. Would you like to come with me?"

Adinah grabbed her right leg with her hand and said "I could never walk that far on my own and even if I could I would be so slow that he would be gone by the time we made it there. I'm sorry. Go without me. I only wish he were closer. I would love to hear him. My father spoke of meeting him before. He said he was very moved by his words. You probably don't remember him because it was before you were here I think, but there was a tax collector here named Matthew. Everyone disliked him including my father. One day Jesus came here to visit and his words moved him so much that even the tax collector gave up everything he had and became one of his followers. Several other men that my father respected very much also left to follow Jesus. I would love to hear what it is about him that makes people love him so. I think I will have to wait for another time though."

Darius spit on the ground and mumbled the name "Matthew" under his breath as if it brought him a sour memory. Then he raised his back up and faced the pair and said "Nonsense. You're going Adinah. Dismas, throw the nets off that little cart there under the window and use it. I don't have a donkey to spare for you but it's small and easy enough for Dismas to put you in it and pull you out to see this Jesus."

They both grinned at the idea and they both doubly excited about the thought of not only getting to see and hear Jesus but to get to spend the day together. He had so many things he wanted to talk to her about. "Well stop standing there grinning at me. Get that cart cleared off and get out of here. You'll never make it in time if you just stand around. Don't forget to take yourselves some water and if you'll look inside on my table you'll see some bread my wife made. Take some with you in case you get hungry."

Adinah became a little concerned that her brothers might not approve and thinking twice about this plan started to protest. Darius, being a wise old man and reading her thoughts said "Hush Adinah. Your brothers love you and so do I. I've known you since you were born. Dismas is the first man that has ever made you this happy before and I trust him. Your father Caleb was like a brother to me and I am sure he would have agreed. You go and I will take care of them in case you aren't back in time. Besides, what kind of trouble could you possibly get into going to listen to a Rabbi? Go! Run along now. You two have a lot of things to discuss!" He smiled and then suddenly yelled to one of his new helpers that had just overturned an entire cart of supplies.

Dismas couldn't help but smile as he went about his task of clearing the cart for her. It was a bit warm today and he took an extra cloak he had here at Darius' shop and placed it over the cart to give her a more comfortable ride. He then helped her up into the cart. When he did he started to pick up the yoke of the cart and then he realized he had forgotten something. He dropped the cart and absent-mindedly ran into the shop and came back with a waterskin and a sack of the bread Darius had given them. She laughed at his obviously embarrassed face and said "Anything else you've forgotten Dismas?"

"No. I was just too excited" and stood there grinning at her.

"Did you forget what we were doing?" she laughed.

"Oh! "He said and then he turned to pick up the yoke of the cart and turned it around to leave. Adinah laughed even harder now. Darius turned from his duties and saw them leave. He raised his big calloused hand to wave to them. This was truly a great day for him. As long as he'd known Adinah he had never seen her so happy. "Good for you my dear" he said in a voice too low for anyone to hear. "God bless you both."

The throngs of people were so large that it made Dismas' trek very difficult. It probably would be difficult to make his way to where he could hear Jesus speak even if he were on foot and not pulling a cart. But he would never have had the chance to spend so much time with Adinah if he came by himself and worse yet, she would not have had the chance to hear him either. As bad as he wanted to hear him speak he knew in his heart he did the right thing. He really enjoyed all the conversation he had with her on their journey to the mount where Jesus was speaking.

At last they were able to get to a point where they could hear him a little bit but the cart would no longer be of use on this terrain. If only they could get just a little bit closer they would be able to hear him perfectly as he spoke. Dismas saw a nice tree up ahead on a good sized rocky outcropping that would offer up a good view as well. It would also offer a little bit of shade for them but to get to it he would have to abandon the cart. Adinah would never make it. He saw no other choices to get the cart into a better position. The crowds were just too large to get around anywhere else. Dismas stopped the cart and laid down the yoke. He went around to where Adinah sat and he asked her permission to carry her the rest of the way up to the tree. He was nervous about even asking because he knew it would involve more physical contact than he thought she would be comfortable with. He knew it was the only way though, but still he asked her as politely as he could. She blushed at the thought of a man she had grown to love handling her in such a way but it warmed her heart to think of being this close to him. She nervously consented. He made his way gently around to her and with all the grace he could muster he picked her up from the cart and carried her up the hill to the tree on the rocky outcropping. They looked into each other's eyes and this time did not look away. Without exchanging any words they told each other how much they loved one another.

He strained at the effort for the hill was steep and not so easy to climb even without carrying another person. He did so without complaint. She loved him for it. She pressed her head into his shoulder lovingly and it gave him strength. He made it to the top finally and he saw a short, well-dressed man sitting under the tree. The man looked up to him and saw him carrying Adinah and he graciously moved and offered his nice seat to the two of them and then scampered up the tree to a nice comfortable branch where he could still see Jesus and hear him.

The pair did not know that nearby Gestas had begun to start working the crowds his own way. He found that this crowd was quite easy to make his way through pickpocketing from them. It was just the right combination that made it easy for him. Everyone was tired for many of them had traveled a great distance to be here so they were not alert or attentive to their things. They were not focused. Those that had not made their way close enough to hear yet were so busy trying to find a good spot that they too were not alert to their surroundings. Those that were close enough to hear were so enraptured with Jesus that they failed to pay attention to anything else as well. Another factor contributing to his success this day was that there were so many people it made the act of 'bumping' into someone seem even more natural. This crowd was more forgiving of such 'accidents' than most were so it lessened his chances of confrontation. The one thing that was not working in his favor was that most everyone here had very little money. He found himself doing twice as much work for what seemed like only ten percent of his normal yield. Another factor that was not exactly helping Gestas was that he was not the only one working this crowd too. He began to feel a little anxiety about this because it increased the chances that someone would get caught and thus raise the alarm to everyone around that someone was stealing from them. Everyone would then start watching their money so closely that lifting their riches from them would become almost impossible. The young men he had seen stealing in this crowd were amateurs and he felt it was only a matter of time before it would be the end of his day's work. It was now becoming very clear to him that he would not make much of a haul today. It would be nowhere near enough money to get him out of his gambling debts. He owed one particular syndicate in this town so much money that he was certain they would have him killed if he were not incredibly successful this day. If only Dismas had agreed to help him he may have been able to finally get out from in under his debts.

Just then, as he expected, a young man tried to take the money from a man close to him and had clumsily been caught red-handed by him. The man shouted at the top of his lungs "Thief!" and then repeated it over and over again. At first the man was so close to him that Gestas for a moment thought someone was shouting at him and he instantly became alert and ready for action. It was then that he noticed the young boy trying to get away from the man and his friends who had suddenly joined in trying to catch the would-be thief. Dismas, upon hearing the shouts, feared that Gestas was the one that had been caught and he instantly stood upright to scan the crowd in that direction to see what happened. It was then that he saw Gestas standing there near the man shouting looking as if he were frozen in fear. It appeared that his friend was lucky this time and it was probably some young man working with him that was caught. Gestas had still been on alert for any sudden movements and when Dismas stood up on that rocky outcropping by the tree he instantly spotted him and they made eye contact. The look of disgust and judgment Gestas felt from Dismas' gaze only made him more angry at his former friend and it was in that moment right there that he had decided to make his way back to town and take his money. It would serve him right. He could have helped him out today but instead he chose to sit in judgment on his little rocky throne next to his newly found queen and look on his old friend in disgust when he was in all reality no better than he and living in a lie. He had the urge to tumble him from the throne he was on and tell everyone who he really was. His old friend was every bit the thief he was and just as much a killer, for he had taken his own brother's life. Even though he denied it even to himself, it was true. He turned away from Dismas' gaze knowing he would likely never see him again, and if he did . . . it would surely not end well.

As Gestas started down the hill he saw Mary making her way through the crowds to hear Jesus as he predicted she would. She too had heard the commotion and had instantly thought it may have been him and was a little bit relieved that it wasn't. Gestas knew that since the woman was a prostitute she would have never trusted anyone enough to leave her money in her home. He knew that when she left her home she always had her money with her.

He knew from spending time with her that she likely had a good sum of money on her at any time. Since he planned to disappear from Capernaum today he began to think that maybe he could try to lift one last purse. He felt she would be an easy target for him because even though she knew he was a thief she trusted him not to steal from her. He made his way to her and she stopped when she saw him approach. He looked at her only partially feigning being glad to see her. He was glad to see her, just not for the reasons she suspected at the moment. As he approached her he could tell she was not happy to see him here.

"You should not be here Gestas. These people are not rich. You steal from them and you take their lives away from them. Go! Go away!" she said to him. It was in a low tone of voice so no one would hear her speaking to him but it had no less sense of urgency in her tone than if she had shouted it to him. "Go make your money from someone rich and leave these poor people alone!"

"Come now Mary, this is me you are talking to. Do you not think it just as wrong to take money from me when you know I steal it from them to pay you with? Is it really fair to have a prostitute lecture a thief on the moralities in life?"

She slapped him hard on the face which drew the attention of all those around them. He reached out and pulled her to him closely as if he were trying to hug her. He whispered in her ear. "You are angry because I am right." As he held her close with his right arm, the pressure of his embrace was meant to keep her from noticing what his left hand was doing and it had been trying to lift the small satchel of coins she had wrapped to her waist. She was no stranger to this tactic and instantly she knew what he was doing. She pulled away and slapped him hard again. He stood there dazed for a moment and a bit ashamed that he was caught so easily by her. Right now he only wanted to avoid a scene that would attract too much attention to him so he could get away.

"How dare you steal from me! Leave here now, or so help me I will shout at the top of my lungs that you are a thief! Go!" she shouted. To avoid a further scene that might endanger him he turned away embarrassed at what had just played out here and ran down the hill. Next stop for him was Dismas' home where he intended to take his friend's savings. It probably wouldn't be enough to pay off his debts so he wouldn't be killed and it's not likely he would be able to stay here any longer after it was discovered stolen anyway. It looked like he would have to leave Capernaum after all. It was this moment that he felt the most shame he had ever felt in his life. Dismas was not wrong to avoid helping him and Gestas began to realize that now. He only wanted to avoid a moment just like this, when they suddenly realized that everything they dreamed about would crumble again. He admired the fact that Dismas stayed strong this time and did not allow himself to be dragged down with him. He knew that Dismas would be angry and disappointed when he discovered that he had taken his money, but what he feared most is that Dismas would never forgive him for it. Maybe this was the feeling that Dismas had always described to him. He turned one last time to scan the crowd and to see if he could see him. He saw him there in that same place with Adinah. He knew his friend was finally happy. He hoped that he finally found the forgiveness he sought. Then he turned around to head into the city where he intended to take away some of his friend's happiness.

Jesus was speaking for some time now and both Dismas and Adinah were completely enraptured by every word he said just like almost everyone around them had been. It looked to them as if Jesus was becoming tired for he had talked for some time now. The heat of the day took its toll on everyone. His disciples gathered around him now and led him to the shade of a small tree just below where Dismas and Adinah sat. He seated himself where they could almost look directly at him. His disciples and many others gathered around and sat around him wherever they could fit. They had almost forgotten about the little well-dressed man sitting in the tree above them until he shouted to Jesus. "Master, you said that we should not be hypocrites and pray openly only so others could see us praying and think us righteous. How then should we pray to God? We want to know." Many people echoed the man in agreement.

Jesus had taken a short drink from a waterskin handed to him by one of his disciples and he handed it back to him. "My friends, prayer requires no ritual to be heard by God. He knows the desire of your hearts before you can even speak it from you lips. Do you not know as fathers and mothers often what your children want even before they can ask you? Think then how well our Father knows your wishes before you can speak it. Do not feel that he will only hear you if you speak to him in a certain way. If you

wish to know how to pray then pray like this." He then stood up
and stretched out his arms towards heaven and said,

> *"Father in Heaven,*
> *Hallowed be your name.*
> *Your Kingdom come.*
> *Your will be done*
> *On earth as it is in heaven.*
> *Give us this day our daily bread.*
> *And forgive us our debts, as we forgive our debtors.*
> *Do not allow us to be led into temptation,*
> *And help to deliver us from the evil one.*
> *For Yours is the Kingdom and the power and the glory forever.*
> *Amen."*

Another man said "Master, you spoke of forgiving our debts
and debtors. What about those that have sinned against us or
against God. Shall we forgive them too?" The question instantly
got Dismas' attention for it was a question on his mind as well.

"Brother, if you forgive a man of sins he has committed
against you then our Father will also forgive you. If you cannot
forgive a man who has sinned against you, how can you expect
the Father to forgive you of your sins?" He continued. "Do not
seek forgiveness of God or your fellow man without a truly
penitent heart lest you be exactly like the hypocrites who pray
without meaning so that they may be thought of as righteous
by others." The statement made Dismas weep. He knew he was

not the only one the message was meant for but he had certainly heard it enough in his life to know that God intended for him to hear it again here today. He vowed that he would make himself clean for God once and for all and throw off the sins of his past.

Jesus then continued, "If you ask of God he will give it to you. If you seek something you will find it. If you knock on the doors of heaven they will be opened to you. If your faith is even as large as that of a mustard seed you can ask a mountain to move and it will move. Everyone who asks of God with this faith will receive what they seek. Fathers, if your child asks for bread, will you give them a stone? Mothers, if your child asks for a fish, will you give them a serpent? If all of you here, being the sinners that you are, know how to be kind to a child, then imagine how our Father in heaven, who is Father to us all, will give good things to his children who ask?"

Both Dismas and Adinah were weeping now. The pain of his sins weighed heavily on his heart and he sat there with tears welling up in his eyes praying that God would forgive him for all the wrong he had done and to allow him another chance to make his life right so he could become a blessing to others. He was also praying for Adinah to be healed of her affliction because he wanted her to be happy. Beside him Adinah prayed silently and fervently for God to heal her so she could be normal again. She wanted so much to be more help to others but her infirmity became more and more difficult every year and she had been suspecting for some time that soon she would no longer be able to walk and would become a burden to others. It seemed sad for her because she only wanted to serve others so that she would someday become someone that would take more than she was able to give.

Just then a voice brought them both out of prayer. "Adinah. Adinah do you remember me?" She looked up and saw her old friend James standing there before her. He and his brother John had left with Jesus some time ago to follow him. She had seen them in the crowd with him earlier but did not think that they would remember her.

She quickly wiped the tears from her eyes and said "Yes James I do. You and your brother John used to come to our home with your father Zebedee when I was younger. You used to tease me because I could not walk straight." She was angry with him as a girl, but since he was also young himself she had forgiven him long ago for it.

His brow furrowed. "Of that I am truly sorry. I was young and foolish back then and did not realize how hurtful it was for you. I hope you will forgive me."

She laughed and said "Of course I do. I forgave you a long time ago I was just too embarrassed to tell you I did."

James smiled and then his face took a slightly more serious countenance. "We heard about your father's passing. I am truly sorry for your loss. Your father was a great man and I dare say he probably taught us more about fishing than our own father did. May they both rest in peace." Then he put his hands on his hips and said, "My Master sent me to speak with you."

She was in disbelief of the statement and almost could not believe she had heard it, as was Dismas. "James, I don't understand."

"My Master says I'm to tell you to rise and walk home. He also says to tell you that God favors you for you are meek and he wishes you to know that those who are meek will someday inherit the earth. And your friend here I am to tell that those who wish to find mercy shall find it from God."

She wasn't quite sure how to respond to that because she didn't really understand what it meant. She prayed for healing with great faith just now but was shocked when James delivered this message. She peered around him toward where Jesus sat. He was breaking bread with the men around him and he looked up as if to confirm to her what she heard was correct. Jesus smiled at her and then motioned with his hand for her to stand. She looked back up and James stood there with his arm outstretched to her. She reached up and took hold of it. Dismas jumped to his feet to help her if she were to fall. His mind still swam with the message meant for him as well.

"Come on, you'll be fine. I've been around him long enough to know that there is nothing wrong with you now and you won't fall. Your faith, both of you, was strong enough to move him to give you both what you needed. Now get up and go home. Both of you have much to face in your future and now you will be ready for it." He hoisted her to her feet, and just as he predicted she didn't fall. She stood there for a moment, teetered a bit, and then straightened up strong and tall. She had a look of triumph on her face.

Those of this crowd that had known her to be crippled instantly fell to their knees and stretched their arms into the air in praise to God for this miracle. She straightened herself up and for the first time in her life did not feel pain as she took her first step forward. It was a miracle! She felt the urge to jump, so she jumped, and she laughed as she did. Everyone laughed with her including Dismas. Tears were in almost every eye. She felt overwhelming joy. Dismas felt it too but for different reasons. God had seen fit to show him mercy and he would not throw that chance away. He was so glad for Adinah's healing too. How he knew she must be rejoicing right now. He couldn't wait to get her home to her family. They would be thrilled with this news.

James stepped forward and again took her hand. She hugged him tight and looked to Jesus and said "Thank You Jesus!" The Master smiled at her happiness.

James then took Dismas' hand and placed her hand in his and said, "Take her home. I charge you now with caring for her. Go with God." and then he sent them away.

The two ran down the hill as if they were both children again. What a glorious day this was! Suddenly Dismas remembered that he had left the cart behind and suddenly stopped and said "The cart! We forgot the cart!"

She looked back at him and said "Leave it Dismas! It will give us a reason to come back up here again to get it! Unless you want me to haul you home in it!" She giggled at him as he stood there laughing back at her. She turned and playfully shouted back over her shoulder "Catch me if you can!" and started running back down the hill into to town. She found herself enjoying the feeling of wind rushing through her hair as she ran and it made her happy. He ran after her and his heart was full of joy. So this was what forgiveness feels like?

Down the road a lone rider left Capernaum for good, his heart full of shame. He looked back one last time and wished for once that he had listened to his friend and had given up this life. He vowed that he would try to make right the betrayal of his friend as he turned back forward and road into the night.

CHAPTER 35

Soon after, the brothers consented to Adinah's marriage to Dismas and they were married. There was a huge celebration for many people had known them in this community. They were loved and they both were blessed. The healing of Adinah was no small thing for that miracle touched the lives of a great many people. All who had ever known her were moved by it. At first her brothers Jacob and Teman were a little upset with Darius for giving blessing in their stead and allowing Dismas to take Adinah to see Jesus until they saw her running down to their ship to greet them. They knew that if Dismas had not taken her there she would not be so richly blessed with the healing of her legs on that day. They could no longer be angry with anyone then. Dismas had already been favored by them and often wondered why he hadn't asked them permission to court her. It seems another miracle worked that day was that he had the courage finally to ask and soon afterwards they were wed.

Darius had become very ill shortly afterwards and could no longer tend to his business. He had no living children and no one else he trusted to run his business, so the responsibility was given to Dismas. Darius had grown to think of him as a son and had only requested one thing as he bequeathed his business to Dismas to run, and that was to make sure that Dismas took care of his wife after he died, to which Dismas agreed. Weeks later, his dear friend Darius succumbed to his illness and his wife of many years followed soon after him. Many felt that she had died of a broken heart for they were married for many years. Dismas had now become the sole owner of the business and with the exception of losing two very dear friends he could not imagine his life being any better. He often wondered if his mother and brother could see him now and if they would be proud of what he had become. He sometimes found himself wondering what had ever become of Gestas. Dismas was very disappointed that Gestas had stolen his savings, but as Jesus had said earlier, if he could not find room in his heart to forgive Gestas of this theft, how then could he expect God to forgive him of his sins. As it turns out God had richly blessed him anyway and he never really needed the money he had saved up. He hoped in some way that the money would somehow help Gestas find the redemption that he too needed.

Many miles away Gestas had made short work of gambling away everything he had stolen from his friend and once again he was on the run. He found himself on the road to Nazareth to renew some old acquaintances and perhaps make some more money to try once more at getting a fresh start. As he was on the road he had met up with a small caravan traveling in the same direction and decided to travel with them. He had a couple of very good reasons for doing that. He thought that there might be a slight chance he might be able to find a way to make some money off of them and most importantly he was lonely. He knew it would raise his spirits having someone to talk to and it was always safer to travel in groups as he remembered from his own days on the highways. Loners usually got picked off very easily on these roads.

A couple of days of traveling in hot sun had made everyone a bit lethargic and the small caravan decided that they needed to stop for the day in a small grove beside the road that would offer them all a little relief from the heat. There was no water here but they had enough. The shade was the top reason for stopping here. It was late afternoon now and it was time they started searching for a place to make camp anyway and this had always been a popular spot. In fact, Gestas could remember using it many times himself over the years. Once, when he used to roam the road as a highwayman he had even robbed a caravan or two in this very spot. Gestas did not have much so it was fairly easy for him to plop himself down in a choice spot before the rest of his fellow travelers could get settled. He found a particularly large tree to rest under and there was an abundance of cool green grass under it which made it all the more comfortable for him. Within minutes he was sound asleep.

As he slept a number of men armed with swords descended quietly out of the hills behind this idyllic spot and onto the travelers so quickly that no one had time to shout an alarm. They had all been unceremoniously rounded up and the highwaymen that were surrounding them were already starting to go through their things looking for whatever valuables they could find. One of the men noted the sleeping Gestas under his tree and crept up on him quietly and drew his sword and put it to his throat then kicked him awake. Gestas, unaware of his current predicament woke up cursing at the audacity of whoever was foolish enough to kick him. When his eyes and his mind cleared he saw the blade in his face and he swallowed hard in fear. "Bring that one to me." said a familiar voice behind the man with the sword.

The man hauled Gestas roughly up to his feet and led him over to the man that spoke. Before him stood a figure that made him instantly tremble with fear. It was none other than Abba himself. He had aged a bit since the last time he saw him but his face was clearly unmistakable. Abba looked at him for a moment and smiled his most devious smile at Gestas. "Well, well. I've not seen you for a while. I was beginning to wonder whatever happened to you. Did you miss us?"

One of the men turned and asked "Who is this? He looks familiar to me."

"Go ahead and tell them who you are. Tell them why you look familiar" said Abba.

Gestas was afraid to respond. As he looked around he saw several faces he did not recognize but he certainly saw a few he did and suddenly he realized that his life was about to end. He did not reply.

After a moment Abba decided to respond for him. "I am quite surprised that you do not recognize our old friend Gestas, back from the dead." A few men suddenly realized that this was why he looked familiar and they gathered around him. Their swords were all still drawn. Gestas looked and his own sword still lay on the ground under the tree. There were too many men between him and the weapon and he knew that would not be an option for him. There was no way out of this one. His time had finally run out on him. His only hope was to beg for his life.

"What do you think men? Should we take this murderous traitor and stake him out on the desert ground and let him bake in the sun. I'm sure it will take a couple of days for him to die in agony. That is if the wild dogs don't eat him first. Or should we just let each of you take turns exacting vengeance on him for murdering one of his own?" Some of the men were smiling as they saw Gestas trembling even more so now.

"Abba, please don't. Please don't kill me! I don't want to die!" In desperation he flung himself at the feet of his old friend and begged him once more not to kill him. Abba nodded to one of his men and had Gestas hauled back on to his own feet.

"Gestas, relax. We aren't going to kill you. You always were so dramatic." The men who knew him were bursting out in laughter. "Come hug me friend before I change my mind." He then embraced Gestas and Gestas had instantly become ashamed of his cowardly behavior earlier. It was not necessary, for many of these men knew they probably would have done the same . . . and he was unarmed and outnumbered. There really hadn't been another option other than to stand there and allow himself to be slaughtered. His actions did him no harm with these men.

"I thought for sure you planned to kill me to avenge Tiran." said a very relieved Gestas.

"There were those that did want revenge and sought to hunt you down, but their voices all died a couple of days later when the Romans caught up to us. It seemed that they were the unlucky ones. The rest of us couldn't have cared less. Don't misunderstand me Gestas, we all liked Tiran but we also saw the way he treated you all the time and no one blamed you. In fact, I think quite a few of the men wished they had the courage to confront their own fathers in the same way."

"So I didn't have to be on the run all the time wondering if someone were going to find me and kill me? I wish I had known, the fear of it wrecked my life."

"No my friend. No one was hunting you. I am just glad to see you again. I have missed you. I miss Dismas and Jotham as well."

Before he could continue what he was about to say one of the men interrupted and said "Barabbas, forgive me for interrupting, but the men are done and are ready to go. We should leave now before it gets too dark to travel. There is no moon tonight."

"Very well. Find a good mule in the caravan and cull him out for our friend Gestas and help him load his things on it. He will be joining us." He looked back at Gestas as if to confirm and said, "You are joining us again aren't you?"

"I would be happy to my old friend" said Gestas with a wide grin. Maybe this was what he was destined to be after all. At least he did not have to run in fear of these men ever again and that was a positive for him now.

"Don't just stand there, you heard me, go get a mule for my friend." With that, he sent the man away to do his task.

Gestas looked to his friend and said "They called you Barabbas? Why do they call you that?"

"It's a long story. Come let's go and I'll tell you all about it." As they walked over to the mounts being brought to them by one of the men, Abba turned to Gestas and said, "Whatever happened to your partner in crime that night. Did he survive as well?"

Gestas thought for a moment on how to respond to that for it too would be a difficult one for Abba to understand. "Well, while we are discussing name changes . . . let me tell you a long story . . ."

* * *

The men finally arrived at a small farm not far from where they had found Gestas and the caravan he traveled there with. It was tucked away in a well hidden location and it seemed like a perfect place for hiding. It was well off of the road and somewhat up in the hills where you wouldn't find too many normal travelers. There was an abundance of water here and the farm had a vineyard and a small grove of olive and dates on one side. It seemed almost an ideal place were it not for the fact that it was packed with thieves right now. The farmer that lived there likely did not want the men to be here using his home but they paid him well to mind his own business and keep his mouth shut, so he did just that. He knew he would be killed if he didn't comply so why not make a little cash and avoid having his throat slit.

The men had unpacked and started to settle down for the night. A couple of small fires were lit to keep off the night's chill and a few of the men had gathered around them to begin drinking. Inside the farmer's home Gestas and Abba . . . Barabbas, were sitting at the table, having just finished off a nice hot meal prepared by the old farmer's wife and were about to drink a cup of wine she had poured for them.

Barabbas looked wild eyed at Gestas who had just finished telling him his story about the events after their hasty departure that night many years ago. "You don't say? Amazing! I would have never seen that coming. Not from him." was Barabbas' response to the fantastic tale Gestas had just told him.

"Now enough of my story . . . You were going to tell me why they call you Barabbas now. I am curious."

Barabbas pulled his chair a little closer to the table and leaned forward closer to Gestas and began to tell his tale. "Well this is going to make you laugh. Not long back we were laying low avoiding a Roman patrol that was out looking for us. We were pretty successful at it for quite a while and I think the commander of the patrol was a little bit upset about it. He took his men into a small town not far from here and starting roughing up a lot of the local citizens thinking one of them might be in possession of knowledge of our whereabouts." He took a long drink of wine and then continued. "Anyway, during the course of the interrogations some of his men started getting a little fresh with the women in town and the menfolk took offense and several of them got injured pretty badly. The local Rabbi tried to intervene and they beat him so badly it killed him. It took him three days to die though. It was terrible."

"So what does that have to do with the new name?" asked Gestas.

"I'm getting to that. Have some patience. I told you before we started this that it would be a long story. Anyway, the soldiers managed to find us the next day and we had a big fight on our hands. Lucky for us half of them were so drunk from partaking of all the wine they looted from the village that we had the upper hand and we managed to kill the whole lot of them. When the people in the village heard what we had done they sent a messenger to us and told us that we were heroes to the people and asked to have a feast for us. We obliged and when we went to the village they hailed us as heroes for killing their 'Roman oppressors'. They didn't have a clue that that we were a bunch of thieves. They believed God had sent us to them to deliver them from the Romans and then they started calling me 'Barabbas', which means 'from the Father'. The name stuck. You want to know what the ironic part is? The ironic part is that my father was a Rabbi and my given name actually was Barabbas but I never liked it and I always called myself Abba. Now everyone calls me Barabbas. Everyone in the countryside here thinks I am sent by God to fight the Romans. Me? Can you believe that?" he snorted. Barabbas took another long drink of wine and both men started laughing raucously.

Chapter 36

Before anyone realized it, Passover was almost upon them and this year Dismas, Adinah and her brothers Jacob and Teman had decided to make the pilgrimage to Jerusalem to offer sacrifices at the temple and to do a little trade while in town. They had decided to load up several wagons and enlist the help of several men to help them all make the trip. Adinah was extremely excited. Not long ago a trip like this would be impossible for her and now she found herself finally able to go as she had always wished to. She lay awake all night the night before talking to Dismas and asking him questions about what Jerusalem was like. Dismas had not visited there for many years for it was far too close to danger for him to have gone back there for most of his life. He always had that fear in the back of his mind that one of Tiran's men would recognize him and have him killed. He probably didn't need to worry about that anymore, not after all these years have passed. He was sure that no one would remember him after all this time. Her questions were making him a bit uncomfortable because he did not like to talk about his past. Inside he felt a little ashamed of everything that he had done and to this day he had never told his wife of his sordid past. Whenever questions came up about his past he found ways to change the topic or answer so vaguely as not to give away the truth. He felt horrible about not telling her. She probably would forgive him but the secret was so big he wasn't ready to take the risk. So he went on allowing her to think that he was just an orphan roaming the country until he settled here. If she had known that he had made a living as a thief and had also been a murderer he doubted she would be so understanding. That would just have to be a secret between him and God. He did not plan do anything to ruin this second chance he had been given.

Passover had always been a particularly good opportunity for highwaymen to strike it rich. The amount of travelers on the roads increased so much that it made it easy to pick off unsuspecting caravans and to relieve them of their valuables and then blend in to the surroundings as if the men were just part of another caravan going to Jerusalem. There was also the added benefit that in the past the crowds had become so large in Jerusalem that the Romans had generally brought in all of their soldiers to help defend the city. These last few years were particularly disturbing for both King Herod and Pontius Pilate, the current Roman prefect. There was a new Jewish sect forming opposition to Roman rule called the Zealots. They were equally unfriendly to King Herod Antipas, for in their minds, he did nothing to fight or throw off what the people believed as Roman oppression. They saw him as complicit with Rome and therefore he was a target of their hatred as well. It did not help Herod Antipas' reputation with the people when he had John the Baptist beheaded, for the Baptist had been very popular with the people. He had sought during his reign to throw off the horrible reputation that his father Herod Archelaus had acquired when he had ordered the slaughter of Jewish infants in Bethlehem many years ago. The execution of the Baptist only made people feel that it was a family trait and he could never be trusted to represent the Jews against Rome.

One of the Zealot's recent tactics was assassination. Many Roman soldiers as well as the soldiers of Herod were targeted for murder by the sect and they appeared to be so random that almost everyone was in fear for their lives. This terror was part of the Zealot plan. Pilate was moved to add extra defenders to the city of Jerusalem after the deaths of several of his soldiers recently at the hands of what he believed to be a band of Zealots led by a man known to him as Barabbas. He vowed he would not be a target of assassination and he had himself well protected now. He had assigned a large number of centurions to guard the city in case of an uprising during the Passover, but he had sent one of his best men, Longinus, and several of the best men he could spare to find Barabbas and his men and bring him to justice. He did not specify to Longinus whether or not he should bring them in alive.

Barabbas and Gestas, and their band of men were camped in a small area far north of the city overlooking the roads leading alongside the river Jordan. It had always been a well-traveled route for people coming south from the northern cities and in to Jerusalem for the Passover. There were other routes that used to be more prevalent going through Samaria, but it seemed that the relationship between Samaritans and Jews was very poor recently and many chose the route along the Jordan because it was easier to avoid troubles. Even the highwaymen were having difficulties along the Samarian border and had chosen to stick to these roads. It may not have been safer for them with the Roman patrols that frequented the area, but at least the chance for gain would make it more worthwhile for the risks they were taking. What Gestas and Barabbas did not know was that down below them a small caravan made its way from Capernaum to Jerusalem, and in it was a former friend and fellow thief.

Dismas led his mule that pulled a wagon laden down with supplies and goods for trading while in Jerusalem. On top of the wagon was his beloved wife Adinah, looking more radiant than he had ever seen her. She was so thrilled that she was making this trip that she had hardly stopped smiling. To be honest, as nervous as he may be about making this trip, he was thrilled to see her happy and that in itself made it all worthwhile to him. Up ahead leading their own wagons were her brothers Jacob and Teman. Dismas and Adinah were chuckling because Jacob had made the mistake of letting Teman lead the caravan after the last stop. He had a habit of dragging his feet when he walked and he kicked up so much dust that Jacob had started yelling at him and he made him go to the back. Jacob walked past Dismas and Adinah mumbling under his breath that he couldn't see anything in front of them through Teman anyway. Dismas stopped him as he walked past and suggested that they make camp for the night in a small quiet spot on the side of the side of the river that he could see just ahead. He knew that there was particularly rough stretch ahead that would require them to travel uphill and out of the Jordan River valley and it would take a great amount of effort from all of them to make it. It made sense to make sure they were all well-rested before they attempted that leg of the journey. It would not impact their ability to make it into Jerusalem on time, so Jacob, as the leader of the caravan, made the decision to make camp. He trusted the judgment of Dismas on this matter. The four of them, along with about a half dozen others from Capernaum that had joined them started to make camp in the small spot that Dismas recommended. It was an ideal location because they were on the banks of the river and they could all wash up and get water for everyone. The area was flat and it was a big cut into the side of the river with sheer walls on the sides that provided a good wind break. The only disadvantage to the spot was that there was only one way into it and the path was a bit narrow, but it was not so narrow that they could not make it into it easily. They were quite happy with the area.

Up on the hills overlooking this particular spot was a scout employed by Gestas and Barabbas. His job was to look for the best opportunities for the band to take advantage of and to help them to plan the robbery. It was much easier to employ a scout to look for these opportunities because it allowed the rest of the men to stay in a well hidden spot and reduce their movement on the roads as much as possible. By reducing their movement on the roads they would have a better chance of not being noticed by a Roman patrol. The scout saw that this little caravan not only looked like a good prospect given the size of the loads in their wagons, but that they were in an area that could be attacked easily without being seen from the main road in case anyone happened by. If anyone did, the highwaymen would be able to escape easily across the river because at this particular branch of the river was low enough to do so. That was what a good scout would notice. This scout was not very well-seasoned, for he failed to note that on the other side of this particular branch of the river was a small camp being made by several Roman soldiers. It was a mistake that would soon cost him his life.

The scout returned to Gestas and Barabbas and informed them that he had spotted a good target for the men to rob nearby and they immediately began to plan the robbery. They had decided that making an approach into the camp before they bedded down under the guise that they too wanted to camp in this same area, would allow them to get a good number of men in through the narrow pass without raising alarm and giving them a chance to defend themselves. Once inside they would draw swords and take what they wanted and then ride on out. Gestas and Barabbas were in agreement that it was a sound plan and they all mounted up and started riding in that direction.

Dismas had unloaded the food and bedrolls from his wagon and Adinah and another woman in the caravan began to put together the meal while Teman built a large fire. It was a good day of travel and they were all in good spirits because they knew that they would soon be in Jerusalem for the Passover. Jacob and a couple of the other men went down to the river with the livestock to make sure they had plenty of water to drink. One young man in the caravan carried water up from the river. Dismas was alarmed when he first heard the sounds of several hoof beats up on the path above them. The sound would not have normally alarmed the others but he was keenly aware that another caravan would have had the sounds of carts and been slower moving. There were only two groups that would travel with this many men on this many donkeys and mules not leading carts. That would be soldiers or highwaymen, and they were equally as dangerous to a Jewish citizen here. Before he could raise any kind of alarm he saw up ahead riding into this camp area a couple of men. Dismas instantly recognized one of them as his old ally Abba. He became instantly afraid that he would be recognized. As much as he wanted to try to blend into the bunch in order not to be seen, he realized he had no choice but to speak for the group, because every one of the men were down at the river with the exception of he and Teman, and Teman was not bright enough to know what to say or do.

"Greetings my fellow travelers," said Abba. "We noted earlier that this was a beautiful spot to make camp and since there was so much room here, we thought we might ask if we could join you here and make camp ourselves. Would you be troubled if we did so? We promise to be very quiet and we will keep to ourselves." He had gotten down off of his horse already and was walking up to Dismas. Behind him more men were starting to filter in down the path and surrounding the small group.

"We would rather you didn't. Our group is much larger than you see here and there will be no room for you." said Dismas to Abba, who approached almost to the point of being face to face now.

"Well, I don't see anyone else here but you few. Where is the rest of this group you speak of?"

Dismas hoped he would not be recognized but most of all he hoped he could bluff the men into leaving before any harm fell to anyone. "There are a dozen more men by the water and we expect the rest of our caravan to be here very soon with more." Adinah instantly sensed what Dismas tried to do and became afraid. She approached him from behind and held him in fear. The smart thing to have done would be to hide or run, but she would not leave his side. She felt safer with him than without.

The scout that watched their group earlier leaned into Abba's ear and told him that the man was lying to him. "My friend here just told me that you have only half that number of men here. I'm just wondering why you would lie to a fellow traveler such as myself?" He turned to one of his men and snapped his fingers and motioned towards the river, which gave a silent signal to his men to stand watch if the men at the river decided to come back.

Teman sensed the trouble and dropped his load of firewood and reached for his sword. Before he could draw it, Abba said "Easy there my big friend . . . no one here means you any harm as long as you all cooperate." When he saw that men surrounded him with swords already drawn he stood firm. Abba approached Dismas now to the point that they were face to face. He stared at Dismas for a few moments. "You have a familiar face. Do we know each other from somewhere?" Dismas was absolutely paralyzed with fear now. He was sure that Abba would figure out who he was. Not only did he fear that he would be killed, but he now feared that his new family would know his big secret if Abba did recognize him. If that secret were to be revealed he would find himself wishing he had died instead. He swallowed hard and before he could answer, a familiar face came into view of the firelight behind Abba. It was Gestas. Once he saw Gestas, Dismas knew he would not be able to fool everyone into thinking it was a case of mistaken identity because Teman and Adinah knew Gestas and Dismas were friends when they first came to Capernaum.

Gestas smiled. He was genuinely glad to see his old friend. "Barabbas, do you not recognize our old friend?" Dismas would have been grateful to have seen his long lost friend Gestas also had the circumstances been a little different.

Abba . . . Barabbas, looked puzzled at him and said "Jotham, is that you?"

Gestas smacked Barabbas on the back and said, "No, not Jotham . . . it's Dismas my friend!"

Barabbas smiled a huge toothy grin and said "Right! Dismas, yes! That's who you are! I haven't seen you since the night you killed your brother. Why did you run away?" He hugged Dismas like a long lost brother and continued, "Robbing folk got very dangerous for us after you left. Without your brain helping us to plan everything we wound up in a little trouble after you two left."

Dismas felt a flood of shame cascading over him. His wife stood there behind him listening to every word. Gestas himself noticed that it was Adinah standing beside him and suddenly realized from her reaction that Dismas had never told her anything of his former life. Now Gestas himself felt a little ashamed that he ruined his friend's life again. No matter what he said or did at this point he knew Dismas would never be able to go back to his new life. All he could do now was try to minimize the damage by convincing Barabbas to leave them be.

Gestas grabbed Barabbas by the arm and said, "Look Barabbas, why don't we just leave our friend here and be on our way. We owe that to him at least. Let's leave him and his family alone. There are more people out there that deserve this better than they."

Before Barabbas could even reply a loud commotion came up from the side of the river. The highwaymen he had sent to secure the other men had done a poor job. They were spotted in their descent and Jacob and the other men were prepared for them. In short order they were all subdued and Jacob and the other men were hastily charging back up the hill to run off the other robbers. The distraction gave Teman a perfect opportunity to draw his sword and in one swipe he dispatched the man closest to him. Dismas used this same opportunity to draw his own sword. He stood ready to guard Adinah with his life. Teman swung his sword like a madman and none of the highwaymen wanted anywhere near him. Jacob made his way to the center of the clearing and he and his men engaged the highwaymen in combat trying to drive them away. The women began to shriek. The sounds of the screams carried across the river to a small camp of Roman soldiers captained by Longinus himself. Upon hearing the screams they were instantly on alert and they began to make their way across the river, swords drawn.

The highwaymen's scout, who had never known Dismas, began to attack him despite the orders not to from both Gestas and Barabbas. In all of this action, noise, and adrenaline, he could not hear them. Dismas did well holding his own but he struggled to keep Adinah out of reach of the man attacking him and it prevented him from fighting him as hard as he could have. She sensed this and she ran with the other woman behind her to a safe distance. Gestas tried very hard to get to Dismas to aid him when he was suddenly struck by a blow from Teman and it knocked him to the ground. Nearby Jacob was fighting with Barabbas to drive him away. His overprotective temper drove him to fight like a madman himself, and what he lacked in fighting skills he more than made up for in ferocity. Barabbas genuinely felt that he may lose this battle. He had never faced a man that fought this hard before. All Barabbas really wanted to do was to make an escape.

Teman struck a hard blow towards Gestas' head while he was still on the ground and it took all of his might to deflect the blow with his own sword. Teman struck blow after blow at him this way and he showed no signs of growing tired. Gestas was able to fend himself but the blows were so strong and fierce he knew that he would soon lose this fight. Dismas managed to finally knock the scout off his feet and made his way to Gestas and Teman.

Teman swung his large sword over his head and then downward with all of his strength at Gestas. As Gestas swung the blade to deflect it struck so hard that it knocked the blade from his hand. This was the end for him. He could no longer defend himself and there was no way he could scramble to his feet fast enough to avoid the final blow from this huge man. He braced himself for the inevitable blow that would end his life, when suddenly he saw the blade of a sword exit from the man's chest. Teman looked down in surprise as he saw the blade protruding from his chest and just stood there for a moment. A dark stain began to pool from the corner of his mouth and then he dropped his sword and stood for a moment more. He blinked hard and then he fell to his knees. Gestas looked him directly in the eyes now from his seated position, and then the giant of a man fell forward onto the ground before him. Behind where the big Teman had stood was Dismas. Dismas' hand shook for it had been his sword that felled Teman. He stood there with tears welling up in his eyes, frozen, while fighting went on all around them. It was as if the entire world melted away from around Gestas and his old friend.

Adinah, seeing her own brother killed, raced to his side to hold him. Jacob had beaten the bewildered Barabbas to the ground and was holding him at sword point, when he realized that Teman was lying there dead on the ground. He could not believe his eyes. He trusted Dismas. How could he have done this?

Adinah cradled her brother Teman's head in her arms and wailing loudly. Dismas tried to move towards her and she cried loudly at him for all to hear, "How could you kill him? He's your family! How could you choose him over this thief?" she gestured to Gestas, who was just now rising to his feet and still in shock over what just happened. "Who are you?" she shouted again. "What are you?" Dismas could not reply. He just stood there staring in disbelief at what he had just done as the Roman soldiers stormed into the camp and began rounding up the highwaymen that were not able to escape. For Dismas it had merely been instinct for him to try to protect Gestas. He had not even given a moment of thought to whom he protected him from. He only knew that he could not let anyone kill his friend. Now he stood here in shame, speechless, unable to defend his defenseless action. He was a thief, a murderer, and a liar, and now his past had finally caught up to him. Now he knew he would pay the price for them. He only wished that he had not taken so many good people's lives and dreams with him.

The large centurion Longinus strode up to the men who had taken Dismas and Gestas into custody and as he walked by the young man who had been the scout, the young man tried to raise a sword to him and Longinus casually thrust his spear into the man's chest instantly killing him. He withdrew the spear and continued towards the men. One of the men hoisted a struggling Barabbas to his feet and dragged him to the same spot where Dismas and Gestas were being held. The scar faced Longinus looked Barabbas in the eye, and seeing a similar scar across his cheek, soon realized that he looked into the eyes of Barabbas himself. "So, we meet at last, the great Barabbas!" He punched Barabbas hard in the gut and he fell to the ground. He looked down at him in disgust and said "Not so great anymore are you?" Barabbas got to his feet and looked at Longinus with death in his eyes. "So you want to kill me don't you?"

"Just put a sword in my hand and face me like a real man. Of course I understand all Romans are cowards and you probably won't." said the defiant Barabbas, then he spit at Longinus' feet. Longinus punched him hard across the face and again he fell to the ground.

As he struggled to regain his feet the Roman looked intently into the faces of Gestas and Dismas. He squared himself with Gestas and instantly recognized him. "Ahhhh, Gestas, how could I ever be so lucky? The gods must be smiling on me today! Do you know how long I have waited for us to cross paths again? Now here we are. It looks like you get to share a place on the cross here next to your friend Barabbas. I've had to suffer with this scar on my face for years and the least I could do is see you suffer for a few days more yourself. That's the only reason I don't kill you now."

Longinus started looking Dismas in the face and recognized him too now. "Well, well, well . . . so it's you too. I should have known that the two of you would be together. I remember you now. I see that the apple does not fall far from the tree in your family. I shall take pleasure in watching you die slowly as well." He then ordered his men to march them back over to the Roman camp where they would be placed under heavy guard and marched to Jerusalem to meet their fates.

Dismas looked to his wife Adinah, who was still sitting, cradling her brother with tears in her eyes. Her brother Jacob sat next to her and looking at Dismas with revenge in his eyes. He was certain that if the Romans were to let him loose that Jacob would surely kill him. And poor Teman, he never knew what happened to him or who had killed him. How could he ever forgive himself for killing one of the kindest men he knew? Teman was only doing what he thought was right, and that was to defend his family from danger. He did not deserve to die, yet he did, at the hands of someone that he had entrusted his life to. This was a fate that Dismas himself deserved, not Teman. Now he would have his destiny fulfilled. He would finally be put to death for his sins.

CHAPTER 37

T hey were brought unceremoniously into Jerusalem and the three of them thrown into a special cell by themselves. It was a place they normally reserved for certain high profile criminals. Barabbas had become quite a cult hero and keeping him with all of the other men in jail might not be a safe place if they were to keep everything calm. Dismas and Gestas, having been arrested with him, were also imprisoned with him in the same cell. Longinus made sure to report to his superiors a certain "suggestion" that these men be crucified publicly, rather than imprisoned, as an example to all of the Roman justice. He hoped it might also gain the Romans some favor seeing the highwaymen punished. The people were begging them to help solve this problem for years and this particular bunch was the worst of all of the bands roaming the roads. They would be grateful for this. He was not sure how the crowds would react to the crucifixion of Barabbas though. Many of them thought of him now as a big Jewish hero who is a slayer of Romans. The Zealot movement would surely try to revenge his death. They would need to be prepared for anything.

Down in the prison cells for days now, the three men were awaiting Pontius Pilate's return so he could ultimately pass his judgment on them. Which they were all certain would be death. It was agonizing for them to know for so long that they would ultimately be put to the death and then knowing that the death would be a long, slow and painful one. But they had no choice in the matter except to come to terms with it.

They were all three meeting their intended fate differently. Barabbas had become almost defiant and seemed to be the most at peace with everything. Barabbas did not want to die, but he saw it as inevitable and since he had never really feared death he would prefer that the Romans not waste their time. He was just ready to get it over with. The only thing he confessed to being afraid of to his fellow prisoners was how long they would have to endure the cross before they succumbed. Gestas on the other hand was angry and bitter about everything. He had hurled just about every possible insult not only at their captors but to Barabbas and Dismas as well. He was not taking this well. Dismas could tell that it was his fear talking. It was best to completely avoid having conversations with him because you never could tell what would set him off.

Dismas was truly fearful of being crucified, but he too met this fate stoically, however, not in the way that Barabbas was. Dismas had at last come to understand that the life he lived with Adinah was never his own to begin with and that he lived on borrowed time almost his entire life. He came to view his time with Adinah in Capernaum as a gift, but it was one he felt that he never deserved in the first place. He truly did enjoy that time in his life, but now he regretted getting all of them involved in this and he especially regretted killing Teman. He was sure they would never forgive him for this. What he really wanted was God's forgiveness more than anything but now he felt as though his sins were too great and he could never be forgiven. The only anger he felt was towards himself. He was ready to face his fate and only wanted it to be over.

The guards were extremely cruel to all three of the men since they arrived. They had lost many of their own when Barabbas had killed them in the raid that made him famous. At first Longinus had allowed it because he empathized with how his men felt, but soon his sense of duty returned to him and he forbade the behavior. The guards knew better than to challenge Longinus when an order was given. The prisoners were quite sure that he had no love for them at all and they in turn had no love for him, but they were all three silently grateful for his sense of honor about it. Perhaps in another time and another place . . .

Longinus soon found himself in need elsewhere as the crowds grew unexpectedly large when the rumored prophet Jesus arrived in Jerusalem. The man surely brought a lot of worry to everyone in authority here and Longinus could not quite understand why everyone was so worked up about him. Longinus was certain that Jesus was crazy, but he had heard him speak more than once here and he never heard anything violent or threatening from him. He did not see him as a risk to anyone, but as a soldier he would follow orders. If he were asked to bring him into custody he would do so. Right now his biggest fear was that the Zealots would use his appearance here in Jerusalem to start a riot. There were a lot of factions that were maintaining a fine balance until he arrived and upset all of it. He suspected the high priest of the Sanhedrin, Caiaphas, would not be happy that he was back in Jerusalem either. The man got very worked up every time anyone even mentioned his name around him. It did not help matters that the Roman prefect, Pontius Pilate, had not returned from his trip to Rome. He hoped that he would return soon. The man was very level headed and genuinely sought to maintain a peaceful relationship with all the parties here. It was an exceptionally difficult job given the volatility of all the factions here. He knew that Pilate would find a way to regain order. He had a knack for making compromises. Compromise was what they all needed right now. Jerusalem had become a powder keg and it was about to explode soon.

CHAPTER 38

D ismas awoke to the chants of "Barabbas! Barabbas! Barabbas!" coming from the streets outside. Barabbas and Gestas awoke to the sounds as well and Barabbas was the first to say, "What in the world is that all about?"

Gestas sneered back at him, "Well, you have probably robbed a lot of them, maybe they really hate you" and then he laughed.

"In that case they ought to be shouting your name out too" was Barabbas' snarky reply.

They listened intently to the shouts and they heard some saying "Free Barabbas! Free him! Free Barabbas the hero!"

"Hero? Hero? Will you listen to that? The idiots all think I am a hero just because I murdered Romans. If that's all it took to be a hero I would have been murdering more of them long ago!" Barabbas was very proud of himself right now and they could all tell by the smile on his face.

Gestas replied again. "Relax 'hero'. If they really knew you they would be chanting for you to be strung up right now. Be glad they're all too stupid to know what you are." Barabbas stood up as if he meant to menace Gestas, but Dismas stepped over and stopped him.

"Just as well . . . we'll all be dead soon enough. Let's not kill each other." Barabbas put his hand on Dismas' shoulder and nodded in agreement reluctantly and then sat back down.

Now the noise was getting even louder but it wasn't Barabbas name they heard. It was the name of Jesus. The noise was so loud that it was almost deafening to them in their cell. He could make out that they were screaming and wailing for him to be set free. Had he been taken into custody? They had surely not seen him in any of the cells near them, but there were a great many places here they would not have seen nor heard. It sounded as if he had finally upset the high priest enough to get himself arrested. They were hearing the guards speak about the troubles the Sanhedrin were having with him the last few days. They were a bit surprised that someone hadn't had him arrested earlier. They know how these political scenarios worked. If someone in power did not like you, you either disappeared or were arrested, it did not matter whether you were guilty or not.

The big centurion Longinus appeared with keys in his hands. The men all shrunk in fear because they had heard that Pilate had returned and they were sure that their fate was decided already and it was time for them to be taken to the hill on Golgotha and crucified like so many other criminals before them. Longinus opened the door and said "Barabbas. Come with me. You're going to see the prefect Pontius Pilate." Barabbas looked a bit surprised that his name was the only one being called, but he stood up straight and walked to the centurion.

Barabbas turned to Dismas and Gestas and said, "I guess they don't need any challengers to Rome boys and they have a special punishment in mind for me. I'll see you both in the afterlife."

"Wait a minute, what about us?" said Dismas.

"Don't be in such a hurry to die thief. You'll get your turn" said the centurion coldly. He turned and took Barabbas by the arm and led him out the door.

Dismas and Gestas sat back down. These emotional ups and downs were taking a toll on them both. Inside they were ready just to get it all over with. The waiting was just becoming too hard.

Gestas put his hands on his knees and turned his head toward Dismas and said, "You should've come with me that day Dismas. You should have just left that girl to be with her family and let someone honest marry her. It's your fault she has to go through all of this."

"What do you mean it was my fault? Do you know how many times I tried to just live an honest life only to have you screw it up? I finally had a chance this time and you screwed it up again! It's your fault, not mine!"

"Dismas, look at me. Did you ever tell her what you really were or about your true past? I bet you didn't. Do you really blame me because she found out something you should have told her before you even asked her to marry you? Is it more wrong that you lied to her or that we that exposed your lies to her? Think about that!" He lowered his voice and continued. "She probably would have found out anyway. Somehow you would have fallen back on what you really are and you would have eventually hurt her, maybe even worse."

"Gestas, I killed her brother to save your life!" he exclaimed.

"And given how things have turned out for us I wish you had let me die back then. Teman should never have been killed. Face it Dismas, you are a murderer like me." Gestas sat back down and turned away from Dismas.

"I'll never be like you Gestas. I never was!" shouted Dismas.

Gestas faced him again and lowered his voice. "Yes you are. You always were. I murdered my father and you murdered your brother. We are both the same." he said, and then turned back away from Dismas.

"No! I didn't murder my brother! Stop saying that!" Dismas grabbed his head because he felt as if it were about to explode. The world around him started losing focus and he felt a familiar pounding in his ears, and then . . . nothing.

Gestas looked at his unconscious friend and was completely indifferent that he had fallen unconscious. "Tell that to someone that doesn't know you."

CHAPTER 39

The shouting suddenly reached a crescendo and it broke Dismas from his unconscious state. The mention of the name Jesus was enough to capture his attention even from the deepest sleep. Everywhere around their prison they could hear shouts of "Barabbas!" and "Jesus!" They had no idea what it meant, but the name of Barabbas seemed to be getting louder while the name of Jesus was not heard quite so loudly anymore. Maybe everyone was calling for them to be executed now, they could not tell. Then it seemed all at once the crowd erupted in cheers. Obviously something had happened to get them all excited. Dismas and Gestas wondered what had happened. Soon a guard ran down the steps to tell the men that were guarding the prisoners that Pilate had decided to allow the people to decide who should be crucified and who should be set free. Dismas couldn't quite make out what he said next but he thought he said something about Pilate trying to honor some Jewish Passover tradition by letting one go free. The guard that had run down the stairs told them that they couldn't believe it but Pilate had allowed the killer Barabbas to go free. The men were all visibly upset by this. Many of the men that were killed by Barabbas were known to them and they were clearly angry with this decision to support someone that killed Romans. The guards were on the verge of an uprising. Dismas was distraught at the thought that Jesus was to be punished while a killer like Barabbas went free.

The shouting Roman soldiers drew the attention of Longinus. As soon as he entered the cell area they all became quiet. "What's going on down here?"

One of the men decided he would speak for the rest of them, "Sir, Pilate let the killer Barabbas go. He killed our brothers! It is offensive!"

Longinus stepped forward and struck the man so hard he fell to the ground. "Speaking out against Pilate is treason. Do you wish to be crucified yourself or do you want to bide your time until Barabbas makes a mistake that gets himself killed?" The meaning of that was clear. The men would be required to be patient until the time was right for Barabbas to meet his 'accidental' end.

The centurion on the ground stood up and wiped the red stain from his lip and said "I am sorry sir. I meant no disrespect to Pilate. I am only upset about a killer being set free. I know that Pilate is wiser than I. Please forgive my outburst."

Longinus put his huge hand on the man's shoulder and said. "You are forgiven brother. It was only I that heard you. If you had done this anywhere else you would be meeting your fate out there like their false prophet Jesus is about to."

He turned to Gestas and Dismas. "I guess you figured from that exchange that your friend has been set free. The people got to choose who to set free and apparently they must have felt more threatened by Jesus than a murderer, although I don't know why."

Dismas was still trying to understand that himself. Jesus had never done harm to anyone. In fact, he only helped people. He certainly never preached of violence, so why would anyone want to hurt him? He then stood up straight and asked Longinus "What of us?"

"Unfortunately for you two, neither one of you will be given the same opportunity. The prefect is only given the right to commute one sentence under your tradition. He has ordered that both of you be put to death along with Jesus."

"When?" said Gestas. He swallowed hard, not sure if he would like the answer.

"Right now. Both of you come with me." said the centurion with no passion at all in his voice. Longinus reached in and took Dismas by the arm as another one of the centurions took Gestas by his. Dismas was so afraid now that his legs were almost about to buckle. Gestas on the other hand became very violent and started fighting the best he could against the centurion holding him. He cursed at the top of his lungs at them. He managed to get the centurion that held him a little off guard and the guard almost fell. This gave Gestas a moment he was about to take advantage of when Longinus' elbow suddenly struck him on the temple dazing him long enough for the other centurion to get him under control. They led the men down the long corridor and up the steps where they could hear the crack of a whip administering lashes to someone. They could only assume it was to Jesus. Strange, they had witnessed these lashings before and they had never before heard anyone take them without screaming out in pain. Even if the person being lashed were to pass out from the pain, the Romans would often wait until they were conscious again before continuing. They didn't want to be seen as 'unfair' to those that had the ability to remain conscious through it all. Gestas and Dismas both suspected it was because the soldiers here were particularly sadistic though. As they rose up into the light they were almost blinded. They had not seen daylight for some time now and their eyes were not used to it. There they saw Jesus, in the middle of courtyard tied to a post and stripped to the waist. He endured a severe lashing from a huge Roman soldier. This man was even bigger than Teman and the centurion Longinus.

Suddenly they were both grabbed by other soldiers standing near them and they were both stripped to the waist as well. They both trembled in fear. The fear made Dismas quiet but it made Gestas belligerent. He still hurled insults at every single one of the Roman soldiers that made eye contact with him. The soldier behind him drew back to strike him and suddenly found the hand of Longinus around his fist. "Not now boy. You do want him to feel the lashes don't you? You'll get your revenge shortly when you hear him screaming."

The large man delivering the lashing to Jesus had just finished and a couple of men helped to untie him from the post. He was covered in wounds and his skin was shredded from the backs of his legs all the way up to his neck. They were sure the pain had been excruciating to him. Immediately the same two men that so tenderly helped to untie him began beating him.

Dismas turned to Gestas and said "Why are they being so cruel to him? He never hurt anyone."

Gestas replied to him, "The pigs are mad because Barabbas is free and they're taking it out on him. They are going to take it out on us too." He barely finished that sentence when the soldiers holding him and Dismas dragged them to the center of the courtyard and tied one of them to each side of a wagon they rolled in for this purpose. Another really large man stepped up with a whip to join the previous man so they could administer punishment to both men at the same time. Longinus stepped up to him and said "No need. I'll take this one." The man grudgingly let him take over the role. He looked forward to this after hearing about Barabbas' release and was anxious to deal out some punishment to Barabbas' comrades.

Longinus took off his cuirass and then his cloak and handed them to an aide standing nearby and then he too stripped himself to the waist. Longinus had always seemed like an impressively strong man but when he took off his cloak no one had a doubt that this was probably the strongest man that they had ever seen. He had an unusually muscular build and was absolutely covered with scars from battle. This was a man that struck fear in EVERYONE. He was extremely intimidating to everyone who saw him now. He grabbed the whip and walked around to administer lashes to Gestas while the other guard administered the same punishment to Dismas. Nearby, several other Romans were still shoving Jesus back and forth between them and striking him indiscriminately. Everyone stopped however to watch the spectacle of the two thieves and murderers, both friends of the infamous Barabbas, take their punishment. They would all take joy in seeing them beaten. The two men were finally tied up and their guards that tied them to the wagon walked away. As they did one of the Roman soldiers approached Jesus with a bit of thorny vines and wound them into a tight loop and put them tightly down on the head of Jesus. Everyone began to laugh mocking the "King of the Jews" and asked him to give the command to commence the punishment on the two men in the courtyard. Jesus just stood there silently and said nothing. Then the sound of the first lashes and screams filled the air. It was then that Jesus shed his first tear.

As the lashings commenced Pontius Pilate appeared at the mezzanine overlooking the courtyard where the punishment took place. He really did not like seeing to the punishment but he felt it a duty to make sure that when punishment was administered, that his men did so professionally. He was particularly uneasy today because of the events that had just transpired. He was troubled by the Sanhedrin's insistence that Jesus be crucified. For the life of him he could not understand why. From all accounts the man did not seem to have done any harm to anyone, but whatever he had done, the Sanhedrin and Caiaphas must have been very afraid of him. There could be no other good reason why they would choose to let a killer like Barabbas go free while demanding this man's death. They wouldn't even settle for him being scourged and beaten as a punishment. They wanted him dead.

When he saw Jesus standing there obviously beaten as well as lashed and with a crown of thorns on his head he wasn't so sure that his men had been professional this time. He saw the intimidating figure of Longinus furiously lashing one of the men and he looked to his aide and said "Why is Longinus doing this? Isn't this a little beneath him? Shouldn't one of the men be doing this and not him?"

"Sir, that would normally be the case, but I have heard the men saying that the one he is lashing was responsible for the scar on his face." The aide then backed up away from Pilate when not speaking as was customary.

"Gods, I wouldn't want to be him then." he exclaimed. "See to it that he does not kill him before he reaches the cross then."

"Yes sir." said his aide.

"This is a dirty business and I have no desire to visit these men while they are on the cross. I'm tired from my journey and I want to rest. Relay my order to have the men report to me when this business is over and the men are dead."

"Yes sir. I will deliver your command right away." and then he made his exit to deliver Pilate's order.

Before he could reach the door, Pontius turned to him, "Oh, and make sure everyone knows I do not want them killing the Nazarene before he gets to his final destination as well. There will be a heavy price to pay if he dies first."

Soon afterwards the lashes had ended. Both men were in pure agony and bleeding profusely. They were unceremoniously hauled away from the cart where they were previously tied. Both of the men doing the lashings were drenched with sweat. It was obvious they had put much effort into making sure these two were punished severely.

Dismas and Gestas were both barely able to stand. The soldiers dragged them over to a pile of wooden cross beams against the wall of the small courtyard. They had obviously been placed there to be carried by the prisoners to the hill they called Golgotha where all of the crucifixions occurred. The soldiers grabbed a big one out of the pile and placed it on Jesus' shoulders. They then selected two more and the soldiers carried them over to both Gestas and Dismas and placed one of them on each of their shoulders as well. They both screamed in pain when the beams touched them. The pain was searing and made it hard for them to stay conscious. Jesus hardly uttered a single sound during this but yet they were certain he could feel the pain for they all saw it on his face. One of the soldiers told Jesus to follow him and he then led him out of the courtyard and up to Golgotha. The soldiers then took Dismas in behind him and then followed in the rear by Gestas. As they left the courtyard through the gate they finally saw crowds of people that had gathered along the path up the hill. They all wanted to see the men being punished. It was evident that not all of them were happy to see Jesus being punished for there were many people wailing in anguish over his treatment. They did not however care in the slightest for the two men that followed Jesus and there a great many of them that hurled insults as well as other objects at them.

All three of the men were struggling just to stay upright. Jesus was beaten and lashed much more severely and found it almost impossible to stay on his feet. After falling his third time a soldier near him was about to start beating him again when he noticed a man with his wife and two small boys near them. He said "You! What is your name?"

The man straightened up in fear and his wife clutched his arm. His two young sons wrapped themselves around his legs and cried in fear. "Me?"

"Yes you! What is your name?" said the centurion.

"My name is Simon. Ha . . . have I done something wrong?" he said in fear.

"Come here and carry this cross for him! Caesar commands it!"

Simon's boys wailed "Daddy, Daddy, don't go with him Daddy!" They were both crying uncontrollably. His wife was equally disturbed by the centurion's request and begged her husband not to go.

Simon looked at Jesus and Jesus looked back at him, obviously in great pain. He then picked his sons up and pushed them to their mother's arms. He bent to one knee and said "Rufus, Alexander, stay here with your mother. I will return here when I am done. Do not be afraid." He stood up and kissed his wife as she cried and then turned to his task of helping Jesus to his feet so he could help him carry his cross.

He looked back one last time before beginning this journey up the hill with Jesus and he saw the faces of both boys and his wife were wet with tears. They were very afraid.

Dismas followed behind him silently while he could hear Gestas behind him shouting obscenities at everyone. It seemed he was the one that attracted all the attention of all the people that were angry, for most of the objects thrown were directed at him, and not at Dismas. He was grateful for that small respite, although he was saddened that Gestas had to endure it. He knew that it would soon get much worse but he was ready for it to finally be over with.

CHAPTER 40

The road to the hilltop of Golgotha took much longer than Dismas and Gestas had expected. He wasn't sure this would be that easy even if they hadn't all three been beaten before they began the final journey here. Jesus was beaten so severely that making it here even without a cross to carry would have been a near impossible task for him. The irony of their intertwined fates was not lost on him. He felt regret that Jesus would be crucified here with him today. He knew in his heart that he deserved this fate and he was scared, but ready to face it. Jesus did not deserve to die here with thieves and murderers. It was the greatest of injustices and he would have given anything to spare him from it.

They finally arrived at the top of the hill and he knew the end was at last here. He could see that several soldiers were gathered around in various stations on the ground at the top of the hill and they were all carrying out various tasks to prepare for the men's arrival. In front of him he saw three holes in the ground and each of them had a large wooden beam laid out next to them and there were ropes tied to each one. The man named Simon dropped the cross beam he carried for Jesus unceremoniously to the ground. He sweated profusely and was nearly out of breath. The Roman that helped to support Jesus while he made his journey up the hill tossed him to the ground in much the same way Simon had thrown down the cross beam. He landed hard and looked for a moment as if he were unconscious. Simon had felt tremendous sympathy for Jesus. While he had not wanted to be involved earlier, he now felt that he did the right thing. He knew very little about Jesus before this but he had never heard anything bad about him. He was horrified at the fate that he would have to endure. He reached down to help Jesus to his feet again when one of the soldiers grabbed him and threw him to the ground hard. "Get out of here! Your job is done! Leave!" and then he kicked Simon before he could regain his feet. He looked back again at Jesus and he made eye contact with him. Jesus gave him a look of appreciation and understanding that Simon would never again forget as long as he lived. He wiped the tears from his eyes and then he went back down the hill to find his wife and children.

Two of the soldiers grabbed Gestas and tied his arms to the beam he carried here. Gestas cursed them and spit in their faces. The shorter of the two head butted him with his helmet still on and Gestas' knees nearly buckled from under him. "Gestas shut up!" cried Dismas, not wishing to see his friend make things worse for himself than he already had. He was promptly rewarded for his caring with a swift punch in his nose by another soldier.

"You shut up thief! Or I'll knock your teeth out next time." said the soldier to Dismas. The other two soldiers made quick work of finishing their task with Gestas and then turned to do the same to Dismas. They grabbed his arms and pulled them out as far as they could on the cross beam and then tied them so tightly he thought that they had cut them off. Before they even finished his arms had gone numb. When he saw what they did next to Gestas, he was grateful. The men dragged him over to the nearest beam and tied his cross beam to it. There was a notch carved into it that almost made the beam fit into it perfectly. After tying it firmly a big man stepped up with a large nail in his hand and he had the men that dragged him over pull his hand out as far as it would reach. He then placed the sharp end of the nail into Gestas palm and drove it in deeply and swiftly in three short blows. He stood up and then continued over to the other side, where he again repeated this process. Gestas screamed out in pain, but he still managed to throw in a few choice curse words at the man with the nails and his two helpers. The man only smiled and drove the next nail in even slower. It took him several soft blows to make it more excruciating to Gestas before he finally decided to drive the last of the nail in. The same two helpers then took a wedge of wood and the man with the hammer nailed it near Gestas feet. Gestas feet were then tied above it to hold them still while the man drove a larger spike through both of Gestas' feet and into the large wooden wedge. Gestas screamed in agony at this as well, but he was at last in so much pain that he had no forces to curse at the men any longer.

The men were drenched in sweat when they finished but they knew they had more to do so they slowly made their way to

Dismas where they dragged him to the farthest cross and began the same agonizing process with him as well. Dismas said nothing but he screamed out for the pain was almost overwhelming. As they were driving the final nail into his feet he could see that three other men were hoisting the cross of Gestas into the sky using their brute strength, a couple of ropes and a strong mule. The cross finally settled into its hole. The jarring of it made Gestas cry out in pain. The men began to even it up and to throw rocks and soil into the hole to settle the cross in its base. They men finished their task and then began the same process again with Dismas. He too cried out in agony as his cross dropped into its hole. The entire ordeal that both men endured was accompanied by choruses of shouts, insults and curses to them. The noise of the shouts drowned out everything. It seemed to Dismas that none of them were likely to have even heard him scream because they were so loud.

Suddenly it was completely silent with the exception of a few wailing women and the sounds of the Roman soldiers working below. They were about to begin the same agonizing ordeal with Jesus and no one, not even those that were cursing him earlier said a single word. The big man with the hammer drove the nails into Jesus' hands without ceremony. It seemed to Dismas that the man just went through the motions now. Perhaps he was just tired after his tasks with Dismas and Gestas or perhaps he took no pleasure in doing this to Jesus. Many of the soldiers had heard of Jesus and did not think that the Sanhedrin was right to want to punish him so severely but he was never a man to disobey an order, even if he did not agree with it. The two thieves however, he had no pity for. The two younger soldiers helping him prepared the wedge and he quickly nailed it to the cross. He then nailed his feet the wedge quickly. Jesus quietly moaned at each strike but he never said a single word.

Dismas looked over at Gestas now and saw that he had lost consciousness. He was grateful that his friend was spared of the anguish even if it was only for a few minutes. He hoped that the ordeal would be a quick one for both of them but he doubted it would be. He had heard once that some of those that were crucified took even two or three days to die.

His eyes then combed through the crowds that had gathered. He silently hoped that he might have gotten a glimpse of Adinah one last time, but he was certain that she never would have wanted to see this. It was then that he spotted Jacob near the back of the crowd. He suddenly felt an overwhelming shame for the harm that he had brought to their family and especially to Adinah. He looked at Jacob and Jacob stared back. Jacob was crying. When he saw that Dismas was looking at him he wiped his tears with the arm of his cloak and straightened himself upright. He looked one last time at Dismas and then he walked away. Dismas was saddened by the grief he saw in Jacob's eyes. Now he had become even more grateful that he had not seen Adinah in this crowd for he did not think he could bear the shame of it. Dismas felt himself losing consciousness and the world went black around him.

When he finally regained consciousness he heard the shouts of Gestas toward the leering crowd. They hurled rocks and at him and cursed him, and, in return, he screamed fresh insults and obscenities at them. The Romans at first tried to prevent the people from throwing things at him but after a while they got tired of hearing him themselves and stopped trying. The only wish the soldiers had now was that the people had better aim. They only seemed to graze him when the occasional rock did hit its mark and all that did was make him shout more insults.

"Gestas please stop!" shouted Dismas. "Shouting at them won't help you. It won't change your fate. We deserve to be here."

Gestas only sneered at Dismas and then he looked to the crowd for the next person to insult when he spotted Barabbas standing in the back of the crowd with his cloak covering his head. He was there to see his former friends one last time. He felt ashamed that they were up there and he had been set free. Especially since he knew that he was a far more dangerous man than they. He had killed more men than he could count and had never spent a single shekel he had earned from work. He had no regrets over his life and if there was a single man alive that deserved this fate it was him. Only today it was someone else in his stead. He knew very little about this Jesus, but what he did know was that he was a man of peace and he had done a great many good deeds from what he had heard. He definitely did not deserve to die in his place, yet here he was.

"Barabbas! Barabbas my friend! Is that you hiding under your cloak?" said the delirious Gestas. "You should be up here with us! You've killed far more men than I have! Come join us! I'm sure the Romans have a spare cross for the great hero Barabbas!"

Barabbas was horrified at the sudden attention of the crowd around him and he quickly covered his face and made his exit, never to be seen again. Gestas screamed at him as he ran "Coward! All hail to Barabbas the Coward!" The crowds threw rocks at him again, prompting more cursing.

Gestas turned then to Jesus and said "You! You are the Messiah right? Everyone says you are the Messiah! Tell me, is it true?" he shouted.

Dismas cried out for Gestas to leave Jesus alone but Gestas could not hear him. Gestas then shouted again at Jesus, for he became angry at the fact that he could not instigate a response from him. "Messiah! Call your angels down to save us why don't you? Show us your magic and have them fly down here and ease us off our crosses and back to earth unharmed!" He laughed hysterically. He screamed so hard that spittle flew from his mouth at every word. "You are no Messiah! You're a fake like all the prophets before you! You claim to be the Messiah yet you can't get a single angle to even bend a wing to save you! You walk the streets taking money from people that believe in your lies. You are a charlatan and a thief just like us and you deserve to die with us!" He then started laughing again uncontrollably. He started to lose his mind and he was delirious from the pain.

Dismas was very distraught by the insults Gestas hurled at Jesus and he shouted back to his old friend, "Gestas! NO! Do not mock him! He has committed no crime to deserve this fate. You and I are thieves and murderers. We surely deserve our fate many times over, but not him." Dismas sobbed now and his voice trailed off. "Not him . . ."

Gestas was moved by his friend's impassioned plea and he sobbed himself. He looked at Dismas and he cried uncontrollably and said, "I'm so sorry! I'm so sorry! I brought this fate to you. You should never have been here. You were trying to save both of us and I never listened. This is all my fault!" Gestas hung in his head in shame.

Dismas was touched by the sadness he saw in Gestas' eyes for the first time. This time he knew his friend finally grasped the magnitude of his own sin. "I forgive you" he sobbed. "Ask God to forgive you before it is too late."

Gestas swung his head wildly back and forth. He was clearly out of his mind with delirium now. "No! I will not! I seek your forgiveness only! No one else!" He mouth opened wide and he cried aloud and then he mercifully lost consciousness.

CHAPTER 41

Dismas was disheartened because he knew it would do no good to keep pressing Gestas and he knew he could do nothing about it now. Gestas would never ask God to forgive him. He would never become a believer, not even on the cross. Dismas felt his own life ebb from him and he knew it would not be long. This might be his last chance to ask for his own forgiveness. He knew in his heart that this was a fate that he truly did deserve and he was at peace with that at last. He looked at Jesus on the cross beside him and he felt an overwhelming grief wash over him. He knew that Jesus really was the Messiah. He witnessed his miracles personally and he could not understand why he was here. What kind of petty hatred would cause these people to want him dead? He thought to himself how much better this world would be if there were more people like him in it.

He licked his lips and swallowed hard. He was so thirsty now. His voice was weak but he called to Jesus. "Jesus. Can you hear me?"

Jesus turned his head and looked at Dismas. His right eye was swollen shut from the beating he had taken earlier and the crown of rose thorns on his head bit deeply into his scalp and blood ran freely down his face. Still he looked on Dismas' face with recognition and it almost looked as if his lip were curling into a slight smile. "Yes" he said softly. His voice trembled.

"Jesus, I know who you are, and I also know that you know who I am. You must certainly know of all the terrible things I have done in my life. I am not even worthy to be in your presence." he continued "But if I could ask you as humbly as a dying man could ask. Will you please ask God to forgive me for all the terrible things I have done?"

Jesus continued both slowly and deliberately for he knew that what he was about to say would be very difficult for him to grasp. "I do know who you are but you do not . . . Jotham."

The sound of that name sent his head reeling. Why had he said that? Why did he call him by his brother's name? Confused he replied "But I'm not Jotham, I am Dismas."

Jesus looked at him and said a single word which echoed in his head as if it were the loudest thunder . . . "REMEMBER."

"REMEMBER."

That single word echoed around inside his head and suddenly he felt the world was spinning around him. Suddenly in a bright flash of light he saw himself standing there watching two men with swords drawn in the center of a crowd of men whose faces were filled with a thirst for violence that he had seen all too often. He was startled suddenly when he heard a loud clear voice next to him saying "This is where it began." He immediately looked to the sound and he saw the angel Gabriel standing by his side. "Do not be afraid. I am Gabriel. My master has asked me to help you remember what you have lost. Look closely."

Jotham looked around and he saw a younger Gestas standing next to his father Tiran. Suddenly he knew exactly when this event was and he realized that the two men in the middle were he and his brother. This was a thought and a memory that he had blotted from his mind for years and now it was all suddenly coming back to him what transpired that fateful night. He wept. He knew now what he would see.

In the center of the ring Dismas and Jotham stood facing each other with their swords drawn. Tiran shouted to them to begin their fight to the death or he would have both of them killed. Dismas looked at Jotham and said "I'm so sorry!" He then turned to address Tiran. "Tiran please, I won't raise a hand to my brother. I can't do it! Please I beg your mercy. We meant no harm to anyone. We just wanted a different life! Please have mercy!" Dismas got down on his knees and sobbed in desperation.

Jotham stood there, understandably nervous and not sure of what to do. He never really wanted to go with Dismas and he only did so that night out of loyalty, but now that loyalty had proven itself to be dangerous to him. Many of the men liked Jotham and were cheering him on. It made him feel strong and powerful when he heard it. It was intoxicating to him. He looked at his brother now on his knees and for the first time he was disgusted by him. He could not stand to see his weakness on display right here in front of everyone. He had mixed feelings now about what to do. It was clear in his mind that if one of them did not kill the other, that Tiran would indeed have them both killed. If he were to kill Dismas then he would have a chance at life. He even imagined that Tiran might forgive him and allow him to stay here with him and these men and not force him to live a life on the run. He felt conflicted about this and wasn't sure what to do. He knew it did not make sense for both of them to die but he did not want to kill his brother. Just then Tiran shouted his final warning and it spurred all the men to begin cheering his name even louder. Even those that were previously cheering for Dismas had ceased when Dismas would not stop begging on his knees. Everywhere he heard men chanting "Jotham! Kill him! Jotham! Jotham!" Suddenly, and without thought, Jotham lunged forward with his sword and plunged it deep into his brother's chest. Dismas looked at him in surprise. He never expected his brother to have taken action even though he would have preferred this to having both of them killed. He held his gaze as he fell. Jotham instantly regretted his decision. He never wanted this to happen and now he had slain his own brother, the brother who cared for him all these years and took care of him, and a brother that loved him with all of his heart and gave up so much to protect him. He dropped his sword and fell to his knees to hold his brother. The men were all suddenly silent. Jotham pulled his brother's head into his chest and cradled him there, weeping for him. Dismas clutched Jotham's arm tightly holding on to what life he had left. His breathing had become very labored and difficult for him. He pulled his trembling hand up to hold Jotham's face one last time and he looked him in the eye. With his last breath Dismas said "Jotham . . .

forgive me . . ." and then his hand fell limp to his side and his head slumped into his brother's arm. Jotham wept even harder now and rocked his brother back and forth. He moaned a long, loud and low moan that was difficult for the men to stand and witness. They were deep in revelry moments earlier for the fight to commence. Now that it was over and one of their own was dead simply because he wanted a different life, it had begun to unsettle them. Jotham could only wonder why his brother had thought to ask for his own forgiveness when it was he who should have sought forgiveness from Dismas. Just then, the men cleared a path as Gestas, also tainted by murder, came to his side and helped his friend Jotham to his feet.

"REMEMBER."

Suddenly the bright flash of light was there again and Jotham felt himself floating back to another memory he had buried. Beside him stood again the angel Gabriel. He did not want to see what was next. The memory was too painful. "You must bear witness Jotham." said Gabriel as he placed his hand on Jotham's shoulder.

He saw events unfold before him that took place shortly after the events of that tragic night. It was the next afternoon in Jerusalem and Jotham and Gestas retrieved the money that Dismas and Jotham had hidden there. They were in the market to get supplies for their journey north. Jotham was in a complete daze the entire night's journey here and since they left the highwaymen's camp that night he had not uttered one single word. He was clearly in great distress over the murder of his brother. Gestas dragged him to the marketplace and when it was certain that he would not be much help he just left him standing there by a wall while he purchased the things they would need for the journey. Gestas had no sooner started his bargaining with a vendor when he spotted a young prostitute that was one of his favorites and he stopped to chat with her. He figured that it wouldn't hurt to have a little company before such a long journey. He stopped glancing over at Jotham after a bit, thinking he would be alright with just a brief rest.

Jotham stood there staring out at the throngs of people in the market place blankly when suddenly he was grabbed by the cloak and jerked completely off his feet. The big centurion Longinus had seen him and grabbed him. He picked him up and pulled him up to his face to look at him better with his one good eye. Jotham's feet were not even touching the ground. "You! I recognize you! You're the thief who gave me this scar!" He then turned him around and slammed Jotham up against the wall hard. Jotham was bewildered and afraid. This had shaken him from his distant mental state and brought him back to the present. "You're Jotham aren't you?" and then slammed him hard against the wall again and put his large hand across the boy's throat to choke him. There were two other centurions standing behind him and keeping others from intervening. There was no way that anyone would stand between Longinus and his revenge. They doubted that they were doing anything other than keeping him from hurting some poor person innocently trying to help the boy.

Jotham was terrified and said "I don't know what you are talking about! I've never even seen you before!" He was choking now and his face turned red. The commotion by the wall finally caught the attention of Gestas. He was keenly aware that the centurion was the one he disfigured all those years ago. He knew if he saw him too, that he would be able to recognize him as well and they would both soon be dead. He tried to think of how to save Jotham without giving himself away.

Jotham could barely speak and he croaked out "My name is Dismas. You must have me mistaken for my brother Jotham." He suddenly felt as if he were about to blackout. Gestas heard this and he instantly came up with a plan.

"Liar! I know it's you!" said the centurion. "You aren't fooling anyone." He started to loosen his grip a little where he could finally speak, and then set him on the ground. He did not want to let him down but his sense of honor would at least allow the young man to say his peace.

"I'm telling you the truth sir. I have a brother named Jotham and he was killed years ago. He left our family and fell into hard times and became a thief. We never saw him again but we heard Romans had killed him. It is him you seek, but I think you will not be able to avenge your injury against a dead man."

Just then a young woman shouted "Dismas! Dismas! Where are you?" and then she looked over to the small crowd of men surrounding Jotham and said "There you are Dismas. I've been looking all over for you brother. Where did you go?" She stepped bravely into the center of the men and looked fiercely right into Longinus' face. "What has my brother Dismas done to make you so angry? Is it because he is a Jew and you Romans don't like Jews do you? Go away and leave him alone!"

Longinus replied to her "First tell me about Jotham." He knew that if this were a lie he would catch both of them in it. He had not known that she was listening along with Gestas to the entire conversation and she knew just how to answer. Gestas was kind enough to give her a few silver coins to come over here and pretend to be the boy's sister. She was well paid and she intended to earn it by being convincing.

She said "Jotham! Hah!" as if she were disgusted by the name. She then spit on the ground. "That pig brought shame on our family when he turned to thievery. You Romans already gave him his reward? We never did you any harm. Go away and leave us alone."

Longinus paused for a moment of reflection and he let Jotham go. Jotham fell to the ground and he grabbed his throat and rubbed it vigorously. He began to cry and hold his head with his hands. His mouth was open wide but no sound was coming out of it and his eyes were wide open as well. He was shaking and rocking himself back and forth. The prostitute that pretended to be his sister just stood there staring at him. She was fearful that he was injured. She looked and saw the soldiers were walking away and then she scanned the crowd where she last saw Gestas and soon she spotted him heading their direction. He waited until the soldiers were far enough away that they would not have spotted or recognized him. She was glad when he arrived because Jotham's current condition terrified her. Gestas bent down to look his friend in the eye. He was genuinely afraid himself of Jotham's state. He had begun to draw a few spectators and he was a little bit worried that someone would see him like this and think that he was possessed by demons. He tried to get his attention to see if he could get him to snap out of it. He said "Jotham!" but before he could repeat it again, he suddenly realized that there were those around them that had heard him and the girl refer to himself as Dismas. To call him Jotham after what they had seen transpire with the Romans would be dangerous. He liked to think that no one here would turn them in to the Romans but times were hard and people here, from his own experiences, would do just about anything for money, including betraying their own people. He looked him in the eye again and shouted "Dismas!" The mention of the name caught his attention, this much he could tell, but it had not brought him out of this state of confusion he seemed to be in. He said "Dismas!" one more time and then slapped him hard across the cheek. This brought him around finally but his mental state was still very clearly questionable.

"Dismas, do you hear me?" He slapped him gently and repeatedly on the cheek. It was finally starting to rouse him a bit, but not much.

"Who am I? Where are we?" said Jotham weakly.

It wasn't much but at least he was talking again. "Your name is Dismas and I am your friend Gestas. We are in Jerusalem. Do you remember anything else?"

Gestas looked at his prostitute friend who was looking on him still worried for his friend. She said "I have a place near here. We should take him there and let him rest and get him out of this public place. He is attracting too much attention." Gestas agreed and helped him to his feet and slung Jotham's arm over his shoulder and helped him to the woman's place nearby.

"REMEMBER."

Jotham saw everything again dissolve into a blinding flash of light and suddenly he stood alone next to the angel Gabriel and there was nothing but light around them. "You were so overwhelmed with the guilt of murdering your own brother that you kept him alive the only way you could and that was to become him. In turn you destroyed the one that you felt deserved to die and that was your real self, Jotham."

Jotham hung his head now; it was all coming back to him. "I do remember . . ." he whispered

In another blinding flash of light he once again found himself back on the cross looking directly into Jesus' eyes. He did remember now . . .

On the other side of Jesus, Jotham could make out the face of Gestas looking at him as well. He had a knowing smile on his face and it was as if he understood what had at last been revealed to him. He looked as though he were grateful that Jotham finally knew who he really was. He turned and looked forward at the crowd peacefully and instead of shouting more insults at them he hung his head and closed his eyes.

Jotham hung his own head for a moment and wept. He held his head up and looked at Jesus, who had still been holding his gaze on him. "I do remember now. I am so ashamed Master." he sobbed. "I am a thief and a murderer and I deserve to die for my sins." He trembled for a moment and then continued, "My sins are many. I do not deserve mercy." He cried, "But

I wish forgiveness. Could God forgive even me?" He was sobbing now.

"Jotham, you are forgiven. My death will wash away your sins. I promise you that tonight we will rejoice together in my Father's house . . . and you will play your drum." He smiled weakly but his smile filled Jotham with great joy. He continued to weep as Jesus turned his head to look upon the face of his mother. She had finally been allowed to approach the cross. She stood at his feet and wept openly. Jotham looked down and saw here there. He remembered her easily. She had the same raw beauty in her face, but now she just seemed much older and she was clearly distressed that her son was near death. She had heard the conversation and she looked up at Jotham and gave him an understanding smile. Mary was not happy about his or any other man's suffering but she knew her son had just forgiven him of the sins that brought him here to this end. She was grateful that he was forgiven and that Jotham would be joining him in heaven. When she looked at him she could only remember him as one of poor Serah's three sons that were there when Jesus was born. She wondered what ever had become of them. She had not seen them since the night the boys came to them with the highwaymen and had stolen the gifts that the Magi had given them. She remembered with great fondness how little Jotham would play his little homemade drum and how it made Jesus smile for the first time. This was all she could see when she looked on him now. Somehow, Jotham knew from the look in her eyes that she also forgave him. He trembled and the darkness overcame him.

CHAPTER 42

When Jotham came to, he realized that he must have been mercifully unconscious for a long time. He was still in great misery, but his senses were so overloaded with pain since he had been on the cross that he almost felt numb all over. As he surveyed the area around him he saw Gestas and it was clear to him that his friend was now dead. He expected it would be harder for him to know that he had died, but inside he was grateful that he no longer suffered in this life. Jotham was saddened that he never knew true forgiveness before he did and he prayed that God would be merciful when judging him. Jesus was still alive but he labored with every breath as did Jotham himself. It would not be much longer.

As he looked out around the hilltop he saw that many people had begun to make fires as they kept their vigil. The sky had become cloudy and dark and the air became very cold. He saw a fire not far from him where several Roman soldiers were drinking and gambling over a cloak. Jotham saw that it was covered in red stain and he recognized it as the cloak that they had placed on Jesus in the courtyard when they mocked him. All around him he could hear wailing from those followers of Jesus that remained here.

The group of soldiers that were gambling by their fire soon made a lot of noise and it appeared that one of the men had won the cloak finally. He stood up holding his prize up to the sky for all to see when a large soldier that had his back turned to Jotham stood up, apparently angry that he had lost. The soldier was Longinus. He picked up his spear and stood there for a moment staring at Jesus and Jotham. He slowly walked to the base of Jesus' cross. He stood there silently staring at him and Jesus looked intently back into the big centurion's eyes. Longinus seemed to be a little shaken even though no words were exchanged. He muttered something quietly to Jesus. Then without warning, Longinus picked up his spear and thrust it deep into the side of Jesus prompting all who saw this to gasp in surprise. As he drove the spear into his side, slowly the fluid that once sustained Jesus' life ran freely down the length of the spear and onto the centurion's hands. He then withdrew his spear and stood there looking back at Jesus. Jesus muttered something to him quietly where no one could hear and the soldier stiffened up, clearly shaken by what he said. He turned and walked away from the cross. He walked directly through the middle of the soldiers he had been gambling with, treading right through their game. He continued on and disappeared down the hill. They stood there puzzled, unclear what just happened. They knew whatever Jesus had said to Longinus clearly scared him and they had never seen this man afraid.

The throngs of people around the fires gathered around his cross for they knew it was now almost over and Jesus would soon be dead. The clouds rolled in quickly and supernaturally. The thunder rumbled and the winds blew harder and harder. Everyone was afraid but there was no safe place to go so they stood where they were.

Jesus looks to Jotham and he smiled at him one last time and then turned to look on his mother. He gave her his most loving smile and although she still wept, she smiled back to him. She knew . . . He turned his head toward heaven and he took a deep breath and then he slowly let it out. He breathed in deeply one last time and said "Father!" he paused "It is . . . finished . . ." His breath then left his body and he silently hung his head for the last time. All at once the wind blew hard and with it brought a sound that no one had ever heard before. It was as if a thousand angels were wailing in grief. The thunder crashed and the earth shook. Then, with no warning the rain fell and it fell hard. This was no ordinary rain because it was not cold, it was warm. It was as if heaven were crying over the loss of her son. Everyone trembled in fear.

Jotham knew that his life had been spared just this few more moments and that he was granted the gift of witnessing this miracle. He rejoiced because he knew he was forgiven, and now he was washed clean of all of his sins. He looked to the heavens one last time. He closed his eyes to pray, and whispered "Thank you Father . . ." He then took his final breath.

When he opened them again he saw Dismas' smiling face before him with his arms outstretched. "Join me brother . . ."

THE END

ABOUT THE AUTHOR

A Christian foremost, a husband and father of five, Don Willis is a Marine Corps veteran with a Bachelor of Arts in Criminal Justice and has spent a majority of his career in law enforcement and investigations. Don also has a tremendous amount of international experience and has spent several years living in Japan, Russia, and the UK.

It is through these unique experiences and his Christian faith that Don has gained a deeper insight into human nature. In his role, he is often exposed to people going through the worst time in their lives. It has allowed him to have a deeper understanding of the thoughts and motivations that people experience when they make mistakes and they genuinely want to make things right. Through these experiences, Don has also learned to appreciate the value of finding ways to help the youth of today make better decisions to avoid problems later in life. Because of this passion, he has also done a great deal of work volunteering with youth organizations his entire life.

Today Don works and resides with his family in Bentonville, Arkansas.

CPSIA information can be obtained
at www.ICGtesting.com
Printed in the USA
LVHW090213250222
711989LV00014B/52

9 781449 791957